CRAIG HALLORAN

*This new series is for all of the fans and friends that I have made over the past 10 years. Your encouragement and love for my stories has led to over 70 published works, 4 million words, and numerous bestsellers. I want to thank my beta readers, editors, artists, friends and family that have helped me put all of this together. May our journey continue another 10 years and beyond!*

## ABOUT THE AUTHOR

Check me out on Bookbub and follow: Craig Halloran

I'd love it if you would subscribe to my newsletter and download my free books: www.craighalloran.com/email

On Facebook, you can find me at The Darkslayer Report by Craig Halloran.

Twitter, Twitter, Twitter. I am there, too: www.twitter.com/CraigHalloran

And of course, you can always email me anytime at craig@thedarkslayer.com

The King's Henchmen

The Henchmen Chronicles - Book 1

By Craig Halloran



Amazon Edition

TWO-TEN BOOK PRESS

PO Box 4215, Charleston, WV 25364

ISBN eBook: 978-1-946218-44-5

ISBN Paperback: 978-1-793081-06-3

ISBN Hardback: 978-1-946218-59-9

www.craighalloran.com



**Publisher's Note**

This book is a work of fiction. Names, characters, places, and incidents either are the product of the author's imagination or are used fictitiously, and any resemblance to actual persons, living or dead, events, or locales is entirely coincidental.

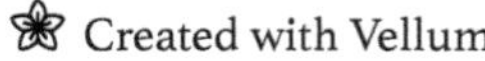

The Lands of Titanuus

Head of Titanuus

Sea of Troubles

Dorcha Territory

The Old Kingdoms

East Arm

The Wound

Black Rock Surge

West Arm

Pirates Penninsula

Eastern Bong

Western Bong

Little Vein

Junction City

Tiotan

Hancha

Giants Vein

South Tiotan

Little Leg

Bay of Elders

Costbeag

Kingsland

Sea of Traversity

Kings Foot

House of Steel

# PROLOGUE

**The Lands of Titanuus - Northern Territories**

---

"Captain." A deep-voiced man spoke softly. "Captain."

Ruger opened his eyes. He lay on a bed of fur blankets inside a large canvas tent. The firm body of a woman lay beside him. She stirred as he sat up. The morning sun shone on the top of the tent, providing natural illumination. Drops of rain softly pelted the tent fabric. He pushed his fingers through his jet-black hair then breathed deeply into his nostrils and rubbed his eyes. He opened them. *Bloody biscuits, I'm still here!*

On the other side of the tent's entrance flap, the person spoke more loudly and urgently. "Captain. Can you hear me?"

"Horace, I can hear you just fine! Hold your bloody horses!" Ruger said in a bitter voice. He shoved the leg of the woman wrapped up in the furs. "Sticks, get your scrawny arse out of my fox furs and go see what the lout wants."

"Did you say something, Captain?" Horace asked. "It's hard to hear through canvas."

"Give me a moment!" he yelled back.

Sticks rose to her feet. She wore a gray nightshirt that hung loose on her firm body. Her chestnut-colored hair was short and tied back in twin ponytails. The slightly fish-eyed woman with a tomboy demeanor bent over, picked up a bandolier of knives, and slung it over her shoulder. Barefoot, she headed toward the flap.

Ruger gave her a smack on the rear end. "Settle Horace down and come right back. No, bring me something to eat." He rubbed the hard ridges on his bare stomach. "I'm hungry."

Sticks gave him an expressionless nod. Quiet as a mouse, she vanished through the flap.

"Where's the Captain?" Horace asked.

"Will you tell me what it is?" Sticks replied in a stern manner. "He's dressing, and I need to fetch his breakfast. Out with it."

"Watch that brassy tone. My message is for his ears, not yours," Horace growled.

Ruger slipped on his trousers. He sat down on a cot, reached underneath for his boots, and stuffed his feet into them. *I hate these things. My feet will burn like fire before I'm half a day in.*

Horace's voice became louder. "You tell the Captain that my words are for his ears and not yours! It's urgent!"

"I don't care. You can tell me. I'm his eyes and ears," Sticks said matter-of-factly. "Spit it out."

"No!" Horace retorted.

Ruger's chin sank into his chest. Finally, he sighed and said, "For the love of money, Horace, just get your bloated belly in here!"

A strong arm with stubby fingers pushed the tent flap open, and Horace marched inside. The big husky warrior was as bald as an eagle but with a nest of beard down his chest. His eyes were as hard as diamonds. He wore a black leather tunic over an elbow-length suit of chain mail. A sword belt complete with long sword and dirk dressed his wide hips. He gave a firm nod. "Captain."

"Yes, I know. I'm the Captain. You don't have to call me that every time. Now, spit it out, *Horace*." Ruger reached behind himself, into the corner of the tent where his own sword belt was propped up. He lay it across his lap and ran his long fingers over the scabbard. "I really hope you didn't waste my precious moments of slumber." His eye slid up toward Sticks. "Not to mention other routines that I enjoy."

Eyeing Ruger's sword and scabbard, Horace swallowed and said, "Never, Captain—er… Never."

"So, what is it?"

"The frights. They escaped."

Ruger stiffened. He cocked his head to one side. His eyes narrowed. "What did you say?"

"The frights are gone," Horace replied. "Red Tunics are dead."

He stood up and buckled on his sword belt then glared down at Horace and sneered. "Show me."

Horace marched outside, followed by Ruger and Sticks. The morning light had come with heavy cloud cover and a steady rain. Surrounded by the tall trees of the forest, the campsite clearing was made up of small pup tents and stone rings around extinguished campfires. A man using a flint stone and hay struggled to light the fire in the rain. Horses nickered. Wagons were being loaded by workers in brick-colored tunics.

Hard-eyed men and women dressed in the same garb as Horace watched Ruger's every step from a distance. Horace led Ruger away from the camp to another clearing, where a nearby stream trickled a few dozen feet away. Three men in red tunics lay dead on the grass in drippings of their own blood. Branches with sharp ends had poked through their bodies with ghastly effect.

Ruger took a knee. He stared at the macabre scene and shook

his head. *I hate this place.* "Who in Hades was on watch last night when this happened?"

"Vern had the last watch," Horace said. "These retainers were from his group."

"And where is Vern?"

"He came to me first, only minutes ago," Horace said as the rain came down harder, heavy drops splattering on his bald head. "He's trying to find the frights' tracks."

"A fat lot of good that is going to do in this rain!"

"We'll find them, Captain," Horace said. "We tracked the witches down once. We can do it again. They couldn't have gotten too far, and they don't move very fast. We have horses."

Ruger rose and kicked his black boots through the grasses. "We just spent the last forty days chasing them over one thousand miles! Now, we get to start all over again. I don't want to spend another hour on this. I want to return to Kingsland!"

"Captain, we'll pursue right away. Rain or no rain, we will find them soon," Horace promised.

"Get Bearclaw on it now. Find Vern and send him to me. He's the one that lost them, and I have no faith that he can find them."

Horace nodded and hustled away.

Ruger stormed over the grasses and stopped where a tree had fallen recently. Sticks shadowed him. He picked up one set of iron shackles with both hands. The frights were an odd group of gangly witches. They'd been tethered to the fallen tree.

"I can't believe this. They aren't supposed to be able to use their powers when iron is locked on them." He held the iron cuffs, bent outward, up to Sticks's face. "Look at this. Magic. Fetch Iris and have her take a look at this. Have the Red Tunics bring the shovels. Bury the dead. But not too deep. There's no time for that."

"The varmints will dig them out and feast on them," Sticks said.

"I don't care about your traditions. We don't have time to dig,

dig, dig. We've dug enough on this journey." He shoved the heavy shackles into her chest. "Don't let Vern elude me either. I'll be in my tent."

---

Ruger paced inside his sixteen-by-sixteen-foot tent, wringing his hands behind his back. He ground his teeth and cursed and muttered, "It's bad enough that I'm trapped in another man's body. Now, I'm going to die in a body that is not my own. In a world that is not my home." He grabbed a cot and tossed it across the tent. "Dammit! I want out of this hellhole!"

Years ago, he'd been transported from America to the world that he now knew as Titanuus. He was changed from Professor Eugene Drisk into a warrior named Ruger Slade, in what he believed was an experiment all gone wrong. Now, he'd been thrust into the service of King Hector and charged with executing the king's business beyond the safety of Kingsland's borders.

Eugene Drisk had his moments as Ruger Slade, but for the most part, he was horrible at it—one mission failed after another. The king's grace was running out. His latest mission was to track down the frights and bring them back to Kingsland alive to be hanged on the gallows. It was a show of the king's strength in a crumbling kingdom, withering from the inside out.

The frights were a nefarious brood of witches who spread poison throughout Kingsland using venomous words and treacherous sorcery. They wrought evil wherever their crooked toes walked. In the city of Burgess, they'd burned down one of the king's cathedrals. Men, women, and children were burned alive within. The frights, five in all, were captured and imprisoned. A day before their execution, they escaped.

Ruger and the Henchmen were sent to hunt them down and bring them back alive. That was the last chance for this motley company of renegade knights and assorted prisoners to redeem themselves. It was their last chance because of all their past failures. The king's grace would end. The existence of Eugene Drisk might end as well if he didn't bring the frights back alive. Most of his Henchmen depended on him. If they failed, their sentences would be executed as well. The rest of the Henchmen would be disbanded or perhaps led by another.

He rubbed the lumpy brand of hardened skin shaped like a crown over his heart. "Cursed mark."

It was a mark of loyalty and faithfulness to the crown that meant "Glory to the king. Honor to the sword." It was given when the Henchmen gave their oath to the king. Breaking one's oath could be fatal. Henchmen who fled their duties were known to die —at the hands of their enemies, by being carted off by sky demons, or just because of sudden death. It was witchery that Eugene still didn't understand. Nor did he care.

"I'm marked like a prize horse. A horse with a time limit."

"Captain," someone with a gravelly voice said outside the tent. "It's Vern."

Ruger dropped his left hand to the pommel of his sword sheathed on his left hip. He faced the flap. "Enter."

Vern pushed the tent flap aside and entered. He was a well-built athlete with a pale complexion and short, kinky blond hair down to his neck. He had puffy lips and carried himself with aloofness. His eyes were sad and heavy. Like Horace, he wore a weathered black tunic over chain mail armor. A finely crafted longsword and dagger dressed his slender hips. "What is it?"

"Don't use that tone with me, Vern. And don't speak as if you don't know what this is all about. I tire of your act." His fingers drummed on his pommel. "You were on last watch last night. Now, the frights are gone. Explain yourself."

With his head leaned over one shoulder and his thumbs

tucked into the front of his sword belt, he shrugged. "I don't know."

"I am going to skewer you if you don't come cleaner than that. Now, tell me what happened."

"What difference does it make now? The frights are gone, and I should be out looking for them." Vern peered up then dropped his eyes back to Ruger. "And not staying dry in a tent like you."

Ruger's blood churned through his veins as his grip tightened on his sword. He stared Vern down. "I'm going to split your face in half if you keep up your obstinance. I have three dead Red Tunics. I can't help but wonder how they're dead and you're still alive."

Vern's eyes fell to Ruger's sword.

"What are you thinking, Vern? Do you think you can take me?"

"If you didn't have Black Bane, I have no doubt that I could. And I certainly wouldn't hide behind the retainers in battle, either. I'd use it."

"Oh, so you think that my sword makes me the better fighter, not the man. That's very interesting." He took his hand away from his hilt. "Have you been concocting these notions all on your own, or have the rest of the Henchmen been entertaining your musings?"

"No one used to concoct anything until you became cowardly and crazy. All you've done is lead us to our doom one mission after the other." Vern sneered at Ruger. "You've lost your edge—either that or your spine."

"Bold words coming from a man who nods off at his post." He patted the hilt of his dagger. "No swords. Just dirks."

"All right." Vern faced off against him. He crossed his left hand over his right hip, where his dagger was sheathed.

Ruger readied himself in a similar stance. "On your word, Vern."

Vern nodded. The moment Vern's lips parted, Ruger snaked out his dirk in a flash and pressed it against Vern's throat. The wide-eyed Henchman gulped. His hand was frozen on his dagger, still in his sheath.

As he pressed his dagger against Vern's neck, Ruger whispered in his ear. "Do you still think that I need Black Bane to kill you?"

With new sweat beading on his brow, Vern said, "No."

"No, what?"

"No, Captain."

Ruger cracked Vern upside the head with the handle of his dagger. The stunning blow knocked the warrior to the ground. He kicked Vern in the ribs. "Don't ever question me again, fool!"

He wanted to lay into Vern with all he had but held back. He needed every Henchman he had. And Vern was a good soldier, just difficult.

"You get your arse out there and find those frights. And you better hope by the Elders that you come through because if you don't, I'll make an example out of you!" He kicked him again. "Go!"

Groaning, Vern slowly crawled out of the tent.

Ruger huffed for breath. He jammed his dagger back in the sheath. Vern had made several pointed statements, and they were accurate.

He shook his head and said, "I didn't ask for this."

Another stern voice came from outside the tent. "Captain."

He rolled his eyes, took a deep breath, and stepped outside. Standing in front of him was a broad-faced bearish Henchman with a head of rain-soaked coal-black hair, a full beard, a hawk nose, and a dark complexion. He carried a twin-bladed Viking-style battle-axe.

"Bearclaw, why aren't you chasing down the frights?" Ruger asked.

"I can only chase one set of tracks at a time. There are five sets, going different directions. I need to split the company into small groups," Bearclaw said. "It will be a challenge to fetch them all, to say the least. We'll need all eyes on the trails. Including yours, Captain."

With a hard rain coming down, Ruger fought the urge to rip his hair out of his head and shouted, "I hate this place!"

---

Riding on horseback, Ruger led a pair of Red Tunics, who traveled on foot through the woodland. He was taking the path Bearclaw had pointed out to him. The rest of the Henchmen split up into small groups while a few Red Tunics remained back at camp. He rode with his keen eyes set for disturbances in the woodland. Even though the rain was coming down, the leaves slowed the hard rainfall on the ground. It took some time to get used to, but Ruger's body had great attributes and instincts. He picked up on things normal people wouldn't. He caught footprints in the soft ground and followed.

He looked behind him. The Red Tunics trudged along in the rear. They were a pair of grubby men, one heavier than the other, with mud-covered boots. They carried spears and had hand axes in their belts. Their tunics were dyed brick red, but they didn't wear chain mail underneath. They kept their eyes to the ground, heads scanning the area side to side.

"Sheesh," he said.

Normally, he'd have taken some of his better men with him, but in this case, he needed every skilled warrior out in the field. The frights had a jump of hours on them. With five of them gone, getting them all back might have been impossible. But he needed at least one—one alive. He was willing to risk all others, save for one. But even with the rain, their chances were good. The Henchmen were trackers, highly skilled woodsmen, and warriors. Some of them were knights, honed by the crown's finest training. They were ready for anything—what was left of them, that is.

He ducked underneath branches and weaved through the trees. They were heading north, above the Old Kingdoms, deeper into the head of Titanuus. The black horse he rode climbed the hilly terrain at a steady gait. Over the course of three hours, he only paused twice, to lock down the fright's trail again. The frights were women, witches to be exact, haggard crones with a stare that could turn a man's blood to ice. They were crafty survivors who had taken months to finally track down less than two days before. But now, the Henchmen had finally caught on to all their tricks.

The rain stopped, and the rustling branches fell silent. Water dripped from the leaves. Ruger tugged gently on the reins. His horse stopped and snorted. The air became still and quiet. Ahead, a steep slope of rocks and boulders made for a perfect den and hiding place. The muddy footprints came to an end. The last one he saw was deep and fresh. He grabbed the crossbow hanging from his saddle. He snatched a bolt from a quiver hanging on the other side and put it in his mouth. Using his strong fingers, he pulled back the crossbow string and locked it into place then loaded the bolt into the slide.

The Red Tunics crept up on his flank with big eyes sliding side to side. They held their spears at the ready.

Ruger didn't even know their names. He tipped his chin toward the rocks and said, "Go take a poke in those rocks."

The retainers exchanged a glance and started up the rocky hill at a slow pace.

"Today!"

The Red Tunics moved at a brisker pace. Up into the rocks they went, splitting up the higher they went. They cast their stares into the gaps in the rocks. They jammed their spears inside the gaps in the holes and hopped from boulder to boulder.

With his crossbow on his shoulder, he eased his horse forward. He only needed one good shot to cripple the fright. The retainers made for perfect bait. Eugene's approach had always been to lead from behind the lines and not in front, like a general commanding the field. Nothing was wrong with that. No doubt his men despised that about him, but he didn't care. It was simple strategy and a matter of survival.

The heavyset retainer traversing the rocks on the right froze in place. He stared down into a gap in the rocks, not moving. His body swayed side to side, and his spear dangled in his grip.

"Hey!" Ruger shouted.

The Red Tunic climbing on the left twisted in his companion's direction.

Without warning, a nest of red-backed and black-legged scorpions, each the size of a hand, scurried out of the gap by the dozens. They crawled up the rigid retainer's legs, over his torso, and over his neck. Scorpion stingers struck into the arms, legs, and neck of the man. His body quaked. Pumped with venom, his body puffed up.

"Get away from there!" Ruger said.

The retainer's face bulged and turned green. The scorpions had covered him up, their tails striking unendingly.

"What do we do?" the other retainer said, keeping his distance from the rocks by his comrade, which were a field of scorpions now. He looked about his feet and made a grim face as his comrade fell over. "He's dead. He's dead!"

"Yes, scorpions will do that to you. Just don't panic," Ruger said, his eyes wary. He didn't see any sign of the fright.

A shrill cackling of a woman carried down from the rocks and echoed all around.

"Show yourself, witch!"

A dozen feet higher in the crags, a gaunt woman in ragged clothing climbed out of a cleft. Kinky hair flowed back behind her head. Her eyes were pinkish red and demonic. The fingernails tipping her bony arms were black talons. She opened her mouth, full of sharp teeth, and said, "What is the matter? Don't you want to partake of my feast?" She held a scorpion in her hand, stuffed it in her mouth, and chewed. "Mmm... that's good."

Without a second thought, Ruger pulled the trigger on his crossbow. The bolt sailed true, impaling the fright through the chest.

Her legs wobbled. She straightened, tossed her head back, and cackled. The fright grabbed the bolt and pulled it out.

"Get up there and finish her!" Ruger ordered the Red Tunic.

The man crept up the rocks at an agonizing pace. The spear he carried shook in his hands.

Ruger fished out another bolt.

The fright leapt down from the rocks, covering over twenty feet in a single bound. She landed right in front of the stunned Red Tunic. With a swipe of her hand, she tore his throat out. He crumpled at her feet, clutching at his bleeding neck.

Ruger locked the bolt into place and aimed. He locked his eyes on the burning red eyes of the fright and fired. She vanished. The bolt clacked off the rocks and skipped out of sight.

"Sonuvabitch!"

The fright's wicked cajoling carried down the rocky slope.

He spurred his horse forward. This wasn't the first time he'd seen a fright's disappearing act. He led his horse up the rocks, away from the scorpions and past the dying Red Tunic, where he spotted new blood on the ground. The frights might not fall to wounds easily, but they still bled, though they used their magic to hold themselves together. A bad feeling crawled down his spine. This fright was probably the leader, the strongest of them all. He moved forward at a trot. He had her on the run and wounded. She'd be desperate and more dangerous. But so was he.

For a leathery witch who could have passed for a mummy, she covered ground as quickly as a rattlesnake. Her staggered trail climbed higher up the forest slope. Ruger fully expected a wild beast she'd summoned to burst out of the brush at any moment.

That didn't happen. He climbed higher and higher, tracking her almost an hour. Clearing a tree line, he caught a glimpse of her less than fifty yards away. She looked back over her shoulder and hissed.

"Now I have you!" Ruger snapped the reins. "Eeyah!"

The fright fled on bony legs with the speed of a wildcat. Her eyes were fixed on a large cave mouth that opened up in the mountain.

"No!" Ruger roared.

He needed to cut her off. Inside the cave, he might lose her once and for all. He'd seen his share of caves filled with twisting caverns and jagged corridors. And he had no light to find the way.

"Go, horse, go!"

The horse thundered onward at a full gallop, making a straight line after the fright. She moved quickly on her sprinting legs, and with one last final cackle, she vanished into the dark mouth of the cave.

Ruger pulled his horse to a halt a dozen feet from the mouth of the cave and squinted. A strange sound caught his ears. A quavering light caught his eye. His heart raced. Bravery was not usually Eugene Drisk's cup of tea, but today it was.

"Fools rush in where angels fear to tread. Humph. What choice do I have? I'm going in."

# 1

**Virginia, 2018**

Abraham Jenkins took a yellow-and-black bandana out of the back pocket of his jeans. With the hot summer wind in his face, he mopped the sweat from his brow. It was the hottest time of the day, with the sun dropping above the Appalachian Mountains. The heat index was over one hundred five degrees. The back of his shirt was soaked with sweat. He'd just finished delivering several cases of beer at the Superfood Center in Wytheville, Virginia. He stuffed the damp bandana back into his pocket then loaded his dolly into the beer truck. He closed the side-panel slat doors. Clasping his hands on his hips, he arched his back and groaned.

He'd packed over thirty pounds onto his rangy frame over the past ten years. Sitting in the truck made his back as tight as a banjo string during a long ride. He was too young for that.

Twisting at the hips side to side a few times, he moved around the truck, checking that all the rolling slat doors were closed. His coal-black truck shone in the sunlight. The old gold lettering, hand-painted, was like new.

The truck was a Chevy Kodiak crew-cab turbo diesel, the bed converted into a beverage hauler. It was a stout truck, unlike the others Abraham had worked with. This truck was his. It had three storage panels on each side. The middle panel had the beer-brand logo of a wooden keg with a steel helmet resting on the top and two battle-axes crossed over the front.

Abraham took his bandana back out and wiped off a smudge covering the helmet. "That's better."

From the passenger side, he made his way around the front of the truck, past the chrome headlamps, and climbed into the front seat. He slammed the door shut then turned the key in the ignition. As the air conditioning blasted out ice-cold air, he eased back in the seat. "That's way better."

The truck cabin, with a gray interior, had all the bells and whistles available for the 2009 model. That had been ten years before. It was relatively clean, with a small black wastebasket stuck in front of the passenger seat. It was full of crushed energy drink cans and fast food wrappers, some of which had spilled out on the seat. The only other thing in the passenger seat was a kid's Pittsburgh Pirates backpack. Abraham reached over and patted it. He shuttered a sigh.

He reached up and touched the truck's sun visor, feeling the edge of a photograph pinned to the visor. It was a family picture of him, his wife, and his son, the last photograph they'd taken together before they had died. He swallowed a lump in his throat, dropped his fingers from the visor, put the truck in gear, and headed for the interstate.

As soon as he hit the highway, he put on his sunglasses and

ball cap. He turned on the radio, and the sad whine of a saxophone filled the truck cabin. "You've got to be kidding me," Abraham mumbled. "Nothing against you, Bob, but your timing couldn't have been more perfect. But lonesome highways aren't so bad. Just the people that ride them." He changed the radio channel.

He had one more stop left on his route before he could head back home. But he wasn't in any hurry, with no family to go back to. On the long open roads he tried to pull his life back together. Abraham had been driving the beer truck for two years. The eight years before that, he'd done next to nothing as he wallowed in sorrow over the loss of his wife and son. He'd been an ace pitcher for the Pirates and made a crap load of money, but after he lost his family, it wasn't long before he lost it all.

With nothing but endless green mountains to his left and right, he cruised north toward the Big Walker Tunnel. About two miles away, traffic backed up and slowed to a twenty-mile-an-hour crawl. Traffic was being merged into one lane.

"Ah, crap."

Abraham didn't mind being on the road, but he hated moving slowly. His beer truck wasn't a speedster, but at least he could get it to seventy-five miles per hour and keep with the flow. He reached back to the seats behind him and flipped open the white lid of a cherry-red Igloo cooler. He grabbed a Mountain Dew out of the ice just as Metal Maiden came on the radio playing "Head to the Hills."

He cracked open the can's tab and said, "Maiden, I've already arrived. Now it's Zombie Dew time."

With gray clouds filling the sky, a spitting rain came down. Traffic in the southbound lanes was moving fine. Thirty minutes passed before he entered the mouth of the one-way tunnel. The eerie yellow glow of the tunnel shone on the pasty tiles making up the walls of the tunnel. Travelers were honking their horns. The tunnel was long. He and his son, Jake, used to try to hold their breaths from one side of the tunnel to the other. It was a fun game they played when they traveled south from Pittsburgh on vacation.

"I won't be able to hold my breath long enough this time, Jake."

A quarter of the way into the tunnel, he saw military vehicles lined up in the left-hand lane. Soldiers in camouflage gear, with flak vests, helmets, and M-16 assault rifles, were waving traffic through. Humvees with M-60 guns mounted in their turrets were there, as well as the big trucks called Deuces and several other armored vehicles that Abraham wasn't as familiar with. As he passed the first soldier, the young man with bright blue eyes and a friendly smile gave him a thumbs-up. The soldier's partner pushed his hand down.

Fighting the urge to slow down and ask them a nosy question, Abraham gave them a little salute when he passed. He got a thumbs-up from time to time in the beer truck. It was different and a hit at beer festivals. People liked to get their pictures with it.

About midway in the tunnel, a huge tarp was covering up the left side of the road, big enough to hide an eighteen-wheeler.

"Whew!" he said, pinching his nose.

He smelled something foul, like a car that had been set on fire and put out, but it wasn't that. It was something else, foreign and rank. Creeping by the odd military quarantine scene, he rolled down his window and stuck his head out like some of the other drivers. With his head out the window, he scanned the canopy's edges. Dark char marks were on the yellow-tiled walls. New cracks had started in the ceiling, and tiles had fallen onto the road.

A big soldier came right at him and stuck a meaty finger in Abraham's face. "Roll up that window, rubberneck! Certainly you've seen stranger things before!"

Abraham jerked his head inside, bumping his head as he did so. The gruff soldier looked as if he could chew lead and spit bullets. Abraham waved gently as he rolled up the window. Then all the overhead lights in the tunnel flickered and went black.

# 2

Tire rubber squawked over the road. The cars in front of Abraham rocked forward and back, and the line of traffic came to a dead stop.

Abraham laid on the horn. "Come on, you idgits. Your headlights still work."

Even though the roof of the tunnel had become a strange canopy of blackness, the head- and taillights from most of the cars were giving off plenty of illumination. Suddenly, a beam of light struck Abraham's cabin, washing him in bright light. He shielded his eyes with his forearms.

"Gah!" He hit his horn again. "Turn that thing away!"

The white spotlight turned away from his cabin, toward the interior of military activity.

Abraham lifted his glasses off the bridge of his nose and rubbed his eyes. "Thanks for the new migraine, fellas. I was starting to miss the last one." He pulled the glasses down over his eyes and tried to blink away a few spots though they didn't go. "Jingle bells and shotgun shells. Misery loves company."

In 2009, Abraham had been in an accident that killed his wife

Jenny and son Jake. Abraham didn't come out unscathed, either. He had a cracked skull and three brain surgeries that came with it, not to mention the other parts of his body that were busted up. As a result, he inherited the pain and discomfort that came with it. He inherited a drug addiction too: pain killers and antidepressants. It wasn't a lifestyle. It was survival that became a lifestyle.

With the help of energetic hardcase soldiers waving their black Maglites, traffic started moving again. A few minutes later, Abraham drove his truck out of the Big Walker Tunnel. For some reason, he let out an audible exhalation. The sky was cloud covered, and the rain was still spitting. The radio came back on, and some easy-riding classic rock came back on. Abraham was relieved by the cloud cover. Road glare from the sun might trigger his migraine, and he didn't want that. He just wanted to make his final stop, gas up, and go home.

Miles up the road, he took the interstate exit ramp into Rocky Gap. It was a very small town, and he wasn't even sure why it was on his route. The old man—his boss, Luther—had some connections there. He pulled underneath the gas canopy at Woody's Grill and Gas Up. He shut off the engine and got out. Then he opened the slat doors, fetched the dolly out, and loaded it up with cases of bottled beer. He pushed it toward the double glass doors leading into Woody's Grill. The grill had cedar wood siding, giving it a county-general-store look. Two soda machines were on the right side of the door and a sitting bench on the left side. He stopped.

*Oh no.*

Inside the doors, an attractive brunette woman was working behind the register. She wore a tight plum-colored V-neck T-shirt. Her name was Mandi. She'd been flirting with him ever since he started making deliveries to the store. Now, she was checking out an older man wearing a green John Deere ball cap. The older man made a toothless smile at her when she handed him his change.

He ambled through the double doors. That was when she caught Abraham's eye, and a playful smile formed on her lips.

*I was really hoping she wouldn't be working today.*

The old man held the door open for Abraham and asked, "What are you waiting for, sonny? An invitation?" He waved his hand inside. "Get moving. Every minute is precious to an old goat like me."

Abraham pushed the dolly through the doors. "Thank you, sir."

The old man teetered off toward an old army-green Dodge pickup that had seen its best days thirty years before.

He walked up by the counter and said, "Hi, Mandi."

Twirling her finger in her ponytail, she popped a gum bubble and said, "Running a little late, Abraham?"

"I'm never late. I arrive at the exact time I'm supposed to be here."

She stood on tiptoe and leaned over the counter in a showy fashion. "Ha ha. Did you hear that one in a movie?"

"Sort of. I'll just put these back in the cooler." He patted the top case. "This is six."

"I can count just fine," she said as she popped another bubble. "And take your time. Now that you are here, we have some catching up to do."

He tipped his chin and headed away.

Woody's Grill was divided up into two sections. On the right was the convenience store. It was typical in fashion, mostly modern but with a decorative charm to it. On the left was the grill, which had a completely different look. The same checkered tiles were on the floor, but rose-red booths and shiny round bar stools were posted in front of the grill's service counter. The smell of hot delicious greasy American food lingered in the air. Several LCD screens were hanging high on the walls. A small mixed crowd of patrons watched sports while they chatted and ate. He slipped into the freezer section, pushed the cases off the dolly, and slid them back into the corner.

Then he turned around and froze.

Mandi was standing right in front of him with her hands stuffed into her back pockets. With a coy smile on her face, she slid her hands free of the denim, jumped into his arms, and kissed him.

# 3

Mandi wasn't an ordinary kisser—she was an extraordinary one. Her soft lips drew Abraham deep into the moment. Standing a head taller than the shapely woman, he abruptly broke off the kiss and gently pushed her shoulders away. "What are you doing?"

"It's called kissing, Abraham. Did you forget what a kiss was?"

"No, it's just… inappropriate." He rubbed the back of his neck. "Awkward."

"Don't act like you haven't been kissed by a beautiful woman before. You might be kinda scruffy now, but you still have it." She took some lip balm out of her jeans and put it on. "I've been wanting to do that for over a year. I shouldn't have waited so long. You liked it, didn't you?"

"Look, I have work to do."

He tried to pass her, but like a playful teenager, she remained in his path. He liked Mandi. For a woman living out in the middle of nowhere, she had it all in the looks department. Abraham had gotten to know the family well. They owned most of the property in the area, from generations back. The grill was their business where they liked to play around and have some fun. "Besides, you're married."

She lifted her hand and wiggled the fingers. "Separated. So you can have me now," she said with frosty breath.

"I can see the tan line where your ring probably was a few minutes ago."

Mandi toyed with his beard and said, "I know you want to put those Johnny Bench hands on my tiny waist. Quick holding back, Abraham. I'm all yours. And just so you know, I am legally separated. You can ask Mom." She draped her arms around his neck. "Come on, stay with me over the weekend. You'll regret leaving on that long ride back home. You know it."

Abraham and Mandi had done this dance before. As reserved as he'd become, he still liked the attention. She was captivating. But there would be baggage, he was sure of that. She had a husband and kids. He could never tell whether she was being fully forthcoming or not. He liked her, but not enough to take the risk. He'd had all the heartache he could stand in this world. Now, he was just passing through, waiting for a fresh start in another. He picked her up.

She let out a delightful squeal.

Then he set her down behind him, grabbed his dolly, and hustled out the freezer door, where he ran right into Mandi's mother, Martha. The matronly woman had her arms crossed over her chest as her foot tapped on the floor. Thirty years before, she could have been Mandi. Now, she was a pleasantly plump, gray-haired version of her daughter, with a warm sparkle in her eyes.

"Hello, ma'am."

"'Ma'am?' *Please* call me Martha, Abraham. You know better." She hooked his arm in his and said, "I came to rescue you... again. I'd apologize for Mandi, but I think we both know that it wouldn't change a thing. Once she sets her sights on something she wants, it's hard to pull her claws off of it."

"I know." He glanced back at the cooler.

With her eyes averted, Mandi started stocking the shelves.

"Is she really getting a divorce?"

"Who knows? I can't keep up with what she does. She does have a lawyer, though. It's a shame that Alex ended up being such a putz." Martha led them toward the restaurant section of the store. "Come on, now. I started them fixing you something to eat the moment you pulled up. And Herb is excited to see you."

"Just let me finish up my delivery, and I need to wash up."

"Oh, don't be silly. That can wait. Mandi will fetch the beer."

"But…"

Martha hustled him onto a bar stool. It was one of the round stainless-steel ones, like those in old soda shops, that spun around. She moved behind the counter and put on a black apron that said in white lettering, "God's in charge, but I'm the manager."

"I'm really not very hungry," Abraham said.

She gave him a warm smile and said, "I'll fetch Herb. He's so excited you are here." She scurried back into the kitchen.

Abraham set his ball cap down on the bar. He liked Woody's Grill but could never relax with Mandi prowling around. In his broken heart, he was still married to Jenny. They had been friends, boyfriend and girlfriend, on and off, since middle school. They married two years after he turned pro when he was twenty. Women had come before her, but none like Jenny. She was sweet and beautiful. She was his rock even when he thought the world revolved around him. He loved her but took her for granted. His wandering eye landed him in trouble more than once. The "all the babes love Abe" reputation didn't help much either. It made the road trips difficult.

Martha ushered Herb into the diner. If she was sixty, Herb was eighty and moved as if he was ninety. He had half a head of cotton-candy hair crumpled up on one side of his head that looked like it could blow away in a stiff breeze. His wore a long-sleeved knit shirt and checkered golf pants.

He pumped his shaky fist at Abraham and said, "If it isn't the Jenkins Jet."

"Stop saying that, Herb," Martha warned.

"Oh, he's fine," Herb said with youthful cheeriness. "No one around here knows him. Go fix him something to eat, will you, darling?"

She shook her head at Abraham. Herb was legally blind but refused to wear his glasses. On his own, Herb ambled around the bar and sat down by Abraham.

Herb grabbed his shoulder. "So, did you see any UFOs in Wytheville?"

# 4

OLD MAN HERB CHUCKLED. HIS BIG EARS WIGGLED A LITTLE AS HE did so, scratching his bushy sideburns. Then he said, "They think they are so important down in Wytheville... ever since they made up that bull-crap story about seeing a UFO and all of the national media came in."

"Herb, watch your language," Martha said.

"What? Crap isn't a curse word," Herb said.

"Yes it is." She set down a red plastic basket full of home-cut french fries covered in melted cheese and jalapeños. "There you go, Abraham. Eat up." She gave Herb a dirty look. "You watch your mouth."

"Ah," Herb said with disdain. "That's not a bad word. It's a little bad, but not that bad." He grabbed a napkin and rubbed an eye. "Anyway, they are full of bull crap down in Wytheville. I think they made it all up just so that they could get on television because no one wanted to stop in their crummy town."

Abraham tucked his napkin into the unbuttoned collar of his black polo shirt and started eating. He didn't understand what Herb's beef was with Wytheville, but Herb never failed to mention it. For some reason, the elder had a problem with that city. He was jealous, perhaps. Still, Abraham couldn't resist goading the man a little.

"I saw some signs in the Super Center down there about a UFO festival they were going to be having this year."

"What?" Herb flung his arms so hard he almost slipped out of his seat and would have if Abraham didn't catch him by an arm. Fastening both hands on the counter, Herb continued his tirade. "There ain't no such thing as UFOs in Wytheville! They say anything to draw attention to themselves. What's next? They gonna report a herd of unicorns prancing through their overrated city?"

"There was some military activity down in the tunnel. It seemed like something strange might be going on again."

"Pah!" Herb flapped his hands outward, and his lips twisted back and forth. "Ain't no such thing as UFOs. It's the biggest lie that was ever told." He looked at Abraham with his smoky bug eyes and made an impish smile. He gently punched Abraham in the shoulder. "At least in Wytheville!"

Abraham nodded as he pulled out a tangle of fries covered in cheese and jalapeños. The combination was a specialty at Woody's Grill. The secret was the home-cut fries with melted longhorn cheese and canned jalapeños out of Herb's garden. It was a local delicacy at $9.99 a basket. It was a little something Abraham got hooked on the first time he came through. A burning sensation started in his mouth, and he lifted a hand.

Herb cackled. "Sneaks up on you, don't it?"

Wringing her hands on a dish towel, Martha hustled over to Abraham. "Oh dear, I'm sorry. I didn't bring you anything to drink. What do you want?"

"Beer. It's always best with beer. Especially that ale he's hauling," Herb said. "That stuff keeps us in business. The locals love it."

After he swallowed his fries, he said, "Milk and an ice water." He tapped his chest. His eyes were watering. The first bit was always the strongest of the batch, and he needed the milk to break down the heat from the jalapeños caught in his throat.

Speaking with a spacey look that seemed to pass right through Abraham, Herb said, "The secret is chewing it up all together. You have to mix it. You didn't chew enough. So how's old man Luther? Is he still as cranky as ever?"

Martha set down tall glasses of ice water and milk filled to the brim. "Here you go, hon."

Abraham sucked down half the glass of milk. "Ah. Thanks, Martha. That hit the spot. I think I can handle it now."

"Well, your burger will be out in a few." She patted his arm. "Take your time, and chew at least twelve times before you swallow."

"Thanks." Abraham took a sip of water, turned his attention back to Herb, and said, "Luther's doing fine—a cranky curmudgeon twenty-four seven, waiting for the world to end. He sends his regards, as always."

"He's a good man. Rigid, but good. You'd think a man that ran a brewery would be more cheerful." Herb cackled. "Say, I could use one of those beers. We ran out two days ago, and people have been asking."

"They're in the cooler," Abraham said.

"Heck, it doesn't have to be cold. It's just as good warm, you know, like they serve in England."

As Abraham turned in his stool, his eyes drifted toward the diner window over an empty booth. Outside, Mandi was loading cases of beer onto the dolly. He could see the almost feline muscles in her arms as she stacked one box on top of the other. It was one of the sexiest things he'd ever seen. *Now that's a woman. Why don't I just give in?*

"She's something, isn't she?" Herb said.

"Huh?"

"Mandi really likes you. She wouldn't do that for anyone." Herb wasn't even looking outside. He was looking right at Abraham. "She wouldn't pour water on a burning man if she didn't like him. I think you'd make a good couple."

"I don't think I'm suited for marriage anymore."

"You just can't move on in this world, can you?"

"No, I think I'd be better off in another."

"That's a strange thing to say. Hey, maybe you could catch a UFO in Wytheville." Herb cackled loudly. "So, what's Luther into? Is he ever going to expand?"

"There are plenty of companies that want to buy him out. He won't budge." He started back in on his fries.

Martha reappeared and set down a huge hamburger that filled half the plate. Three pickle spears sat on the side.

"He says they'd just ruin it. As long as he lives, he'll keep it as is. He's content."

"Content is the best way to be," Martha commented. "Not wanting for anything. It brings a lot of peace. So many people running around like chickens with their heads chopped of, trying to find happiness... They need to find contentment in the surroundings they've been blessed with. People look too hard for happiness, not realizing it's on the inside."

"He doesn't need a sermon, Martha. Let the man eat," Herb said.

"You hush," she said. "Did you bless your meal, Abraham?"

"Uh, no, I just figured it was blessed since you made it."

Martha showed a serious look, letting him know that she wasn't buying it.

He closed his eyes and said the inward prayer he'd learned at the table when he was rehabbing in The Mission. The Mission had helped him crawl out of the well of despair and get him back on his feet again. He opened his eyes and said, "It's done."

"I always keep you in my prayers," Martha said.

"I appreciate it," he said.

Mandi pushed her way through the double doors. Hauling the cases of beer by the counter, she didn't even glance Abraham's way. He got the feeling that he'd hurt her, having brushed her off one too many times, perhaps. Perhaps today was the day that caught up with him.

"Hey, Mandi, bring me one of those beers," Herb hollered.

Outside, military vehicles pulled into the station, a Deuce and three Humvees. Their diesel engines rumbled loudly. Everyone in the diner stared out the window at them.

Scratching his nose, Herb said, "Humph. That's odd. We never get those convoys stopping here. They always stop in Wytheville."

# 5

WITHIN SEVERAL MINUTES, THE ARMY MEN FILTERED INTO THE GRILL. Uniform caps and helmets removed, they filled almost every table and bar stool in the diner. Martha hollered for Mandi. The daughter quickly made her way behind the bar, donned an apron, grabbed an order pad, and hustled over to the tables. With a welcoming smile on her face, she started taking orders from the uniformed men and women.

Martha's face was flushed when she said, "This is odd. We never get a rush like this. I'd better call in Maggie. Gonna need some help behind the counter and in the kitchen."

Facing Abraham to his left, Herb addressed a soldier on Abraham's left. "Hey, are there any UFOs in Wytheville?"

The soldier on the stool had the eagle rank insignia of a colonel embroidered on his camouflaged collar. In his thirties like Abraham, he had a high-and-tight haircut and a thick, neatly trimmed moustache. He smiled at Herb and said, "You know it."

Herb shook his head, harrumphed, and looked away.

Abraham chuckled. He nodded at the officer and started eating his burger. The officer gave a nod and peered deeply at his face. Abraham turned back toward Herb, who resumed their previous conversation.

"You know, I think Luther should sell out and make a pile of money off those big breweries." Herb licked his lips. "That's what I'd do. I'd just let them have it. Spread your brand all over the world. That's all it's about these days: the branding."

"I know," Abraham agreed.

He knew all about branding. He had been his own brand for a time, with T-shirts and hoagies named in his honor. The Jenkins Fastball. One Hundred Three Degrees Jenkins's Flame Thrower Hot Sauce, which was actually kinda mild. The Jenkins Jet Sandwich.

"But if the brand gets too big," he said, "they forget about little places like this. I think Luther likes it the way it is."

"Pfft. I can go buy it at the wholesale market. Plus, it'd probably be cheaper, too." Herb made a good, out-loud giggle. "I like to save a buck."

The diner became noisier as the new crowd settled in. Most of the soldiers had hard looks on their faces, but Mandi brought the smile out of all of them. She worked the room and must have sold everything on the menu. She giggled playfully at all the soldiers' flirtations and jokes. Never once did she glance back at Abraham as he sought her eyes out from time to time. He had been able to brush her off before, but this time, it was more difficult. That made him feel guilty too, as though he was cheating on Jenny and his son. His friends and family told him he needed to move on, but he kept telling himself he wasn't ready yet.

"So have you listened to any good books lately?" Herb asked. His heavy-lidded eyes followed Martha slipping back and forth behind the bar and kitchen as she took the orders and ran them straight back. "Hey, where's my beer?"

"Get your own beer. We are busy, hon," she said just before she vanished behind the kitchen's swinging door.

"I'll grab you one," Abraham said.

He moved out of his stool, slipped over to the store side and back into the freezer, and cracked open a case. He pulled out a dark bottle wrapped in the keg-barrel label. The logo read The Beer for What Ales You.

"That's a new one."

Luther alternated slogans back and forth. Some weren't bad, but others were just horrible. His favorite was Beer Happens. He made his way back to the diner.

Mandi was sitting in his stool, fully engaged in a friendly chat with the officer whom he'd been sitting next to. As she took his order, she would touch the man's shoulder and laugh at his comments. Abraham felt ashamed. At the moment, he looked like a slob compared to the neatly dressed man in uniform. He was out of shape and probably couldn't run a quarter mile to save his life. He remembered when he'd been fit as a fiddle and sharp as a tack in his dress. Now, he felt more out of place. He set the beer down hard on the counter.

"Oh, there it is," Herb said.

Mandi turned, gave Abraham an uninterested glance, and hopped out of his seat. As she continued her conversation with the officer, he eased back into his stool, huddled over his food, and slowly started eating.

Herb nudged him with his fist full of beer. "I need a little help. Will you do it?"

Absentmindedly, he said, "Huh? Oh."

He took the bottle in his hand. The beer bottle wasn't a twist-off. It required a bottle opener.

"Don't you have any paint-can openers? They work great, you know," Abraham said, thinking of the trick Luther had taught him.

The old man gave out cheap paint-can keys because they were perfect bottle openers and super cheap to buy in bulk.

"I got to see you do it," Herb said with a grin.

"Okay."

Abraham had hands like a gorilla's. They were strong as a vise, too—the one gift he had that he'd never had to work at. Using the power of his thumb, he pushed the cap right off the top of the bottle. The black cap, with its war-helm insignia, fell onto the bar.

Herb clapped his hands and cackled gleefully. He took the bottle from Abraham and took a long drink. "Ah, man, that's good. So tell me—have you listened to any good books lately?"

"Some." He had plenty of time to listen to lots of things in the truck. He tried to mix it up between audiobooks, radio, and satellite. But he preferred the quiet most of all. "You?"

"I like that *Game of Thrones*. I can't see it so well on the TV, but we listen on the road to Richmond. Man, that's good."

"It's awful," Martha said as she passed by with a coffee pot in hand. "They do the most horrible things to each other in those stories."

Herb grinned. "That's the fun part."

Martha rolled her eyes as she filled up a soldier's coffee.

"I still listen to a little bit of everything, that included," Abraham said. "I just have trouble sticking with the same story, so I jump around a lot. I like biographies about real people because you get a finished story. Some stories I don't like starting if there isn't a finish. But I figure I'll get around to finishing all of them one day. I've got nothing else going on."

"Huh. Well, what about sports? Do you listen to any games?"

"No."

# 6

This was the part of the conversation where Abraham would squirm. Herb tended to rehash the same topics, and baseball always came up. The elder wasn't preoccupied with the past. He was mostly only concerned about what he was interested in at the moment, which tended to be the same topics: money, beer, books, and sports.

Since the accident, Abraham had walked away from the game of baseball completely. Agents, managers, and reporters hounded him after the accident. He had a contract, a big one, that wouldn't be fulfilled. Maybe he could have played again, but he didn't care, and when the baseball business didn't leave him alone, he became bitter toward it. It amplified his sorrow. His life spiraled down further from there.

He was an ace pitcher, a strike-out king. When he was on the mound, he felt like a demigod. He'd struck out every batter he ever faced. He held that white leather ball in his hand like a lethal weapon. He humiliated batters time and time again. He would wind up that lanky arm of his and unleash the baseball off the tip of his finger as if it were shot out of a pistol. Batters went down, one after the other, pounding their bats on the ground to the roar of the crowd.

But the away teams hated him. They hated him with a passion. The signs in the stands read Jenkins the Jerk and Abraham Stinkin. He laughed at all of them. He didn't laugh after the accident. Plenty of flowers and fan mail came, even from the folks who despised him. But after that day, he realized life wasn't the mound, and some things in life, no matter how good you were, you just couldn't control.

He finished up his meal while Herb rambled on. He wiped his fingers on his napkin and pushed back the empty plate and the basket of fries. The sky outside was darkening.

"I need to get going. Let me go grab my delivery ticket and gas up."

"Sure, sure. I'll sign off on it. Looks like the girls are pretty busy," Herb said. "It's good seeing you."

Outside, under the gas station's canopy, he grabbed the gas-pump nozzle and fed it into the beer truck's tank. The digital meter converting gallons to dollars moved slowly. It was always slow at Woody's Grill but slower now as a few soldiers were also filling up their vehicles. His truck had a forty-gallon tank, so it would take a while.

Halfway through pumping, a man in a deep authoritative voice said, "Nice truck."

He turned to see the officer he'd sat beside in the grill. The man stood almost as tall as him.

"How are you doing, Colonel?"

The polished officer made an easy smile. "You know your insignias."

"I'm a military brat. My dad was an Air Force pilot in 'Nam. I wasn't born then, but he flew F-4 Phantoms during the war."

"I see. A napalm warrior, huh?"

"He used to say he set the world on fire. I was pretty young, and he was pretty old by the time I came around. I never knew what that meant until I saw *Platoon*."

The colonel chuckled. He brushed his finger across his moustache and said, "Look, I'm a big baseball fan. A big Buckos fan, as a matter of fact. I thought it was you back when I first locked eyes on you but wasn't sure until you peeled that cap off that beer bottle like it was the skin of a banana. Man, that was something."

"Oh."

"I don't mean to bother you, but I'm really a big fan. I don't want an autograph or anything. I just wanted to shake your hand and express my regards."

"Well sure, Colonel"—he looked at the man's name tag —"Dexter." He offered his hand. "And, I'd be happy to give an autograph, anything for you and your men."

"That's a mighty generous offer." The colonel shook with a strong grip. "It's Colonel Drew Dexter. But a handshake will do just fine."

"You mean you don't want a selfie with me?" he joked.

He dug in his pocket. "I'm not big on social media, but what the heck? How about one for me to show my family. My wife will get a kick out of it. Private Griffith, get your tail over here."

A young woman in uniform wearing a soft cap ran over to the colonel and saluted.

He returned the salute and handed her his phone. "Take a few good ones of me and my friend here."

"Yes, sir," she said.

The men stood shoulder to shoulder and smiled.

She silently snapped the photos. "It's done, Colonel."

"Thank you." Colonel Dexter took back his camera and said, "Dismissed, Private Griffith." He turned to Abraham. "Technology is something, isn't it? It's 2019, and our precious worlds live under our fingertips." He slid the phone into his shirt pocket. "I appreciate it."

"No problem. So are you part of that group that was working in the Big Walker Tunnel?"

"I can't say whether we are or aren't."

"No problem. I understand. I just hope the East River Mountain Tunnel is free of interruptions." Abraham checked the darkening sky. "Looks like it's going to be rain all the way either way."

"We came from the north. The East River Tunnel is smooth sailing. Anyway, my best to you, Mr. Jenkins. It's been a pleasure chatting with you."

"You too, Colonel. Say, would you like a couple of cases to share with your troops?"

The colonel's eyes got big. "We don't say no to beer." He patted the doors on the truck. "Especially this brew. You sure it's no trouble?"

"I get a few liberties on the job. Plus, the owner's a vet too. He'll understand." He unloaded two cases of the bottles and handed them over to the colonel. "Enjoy."

Taking the beer to his Humvee, the colonel said, "Will do."

The gas nozzle clicked. He racked the hose and finished paying with his gas card. The pump spat out a receipt. He took it and put it inside the truck. He made his rounds at the truck, checking the tires and making sure the slat doors were all closed except one left open for the dolly. He reached back in the truck, grabbed his clipboard, and headed inside.

Mandi was still working the tables. A skinny young man wearing a Woody's Grill T-shirt stood behind the register. He had jet-black hair that hung in his eyes. Abraham wondered if he was one of Mandi's kids.

He moved over to Herb, who was staring up at the television over the bar. "Time to hit the road. See you next week."

"You leaving already? It's gonna rain. A lot. I can feel it in my joints. The more rain, the more it hurts. I think it's the Indian in me," Herb said. "I'm one quarter Chippewa. One of a kind. Heh

heh." With his tongue stuck out of his mouth, he signed the delivery receipt. "I can't read it, but I trust you."

Abraham gave Herb his copy then flagged down Martha, delivering orders behind the counter, and waved goodbye.

She caught his eye and waved. "See you next month. Be careful out there. Storm's coming."

He fetched his dolly, which Mandi had left in the cooler, and headed out. He glanced inside the diner. Mandi was on the far side of the room with her back to him, serving drinks to the soldiers. She never turned his way. *I guess I'll see her next month.*

Back at the beer truck, he loaded up his dolly and secured it inside the compartment. He closed the door and made one last walk around his vehicle. Coming around the front from the passenger side, he almost ran right into Mandi. Her arms were crossed over her chest. She tapped one foot, a storm brewing in her eyes.

"You're an idiot," she said.

"What did I do?"

"You could have at least walked up and said goodbye. Would that have killed you?"

"I think you were doing just fine entertaining the troops. Don't act like you were missing me." He tried to walk around her, but she stepped in his way.

She pointed in his face. "Ah ha! You do like me. I made you jealous, didn't I?"

Looking away from her penetrating stare, he said, "No."

"You're lying. You can't even look me in the eye. Just admit it—you like me. I know it because you never leave without two slices of Mom's homemade pecan pie."

He decided to flip the tables on her. "So you're an actress now. How can I trust someone that puts on a show like that? Look, I don't have time for games, Mandi. I've got to go. I've got work to do." He tried to move by her, but she shuffled in front of him. He rolled his eyes and sighed. “Will you get out of my way?”

“No. Not until you admit the truth. You like me.”

“Don’t make me do this.”

“Do what, admit the truth? I know you are hurting, but let me help you unhurt,” she said as she grabbed his waist and hooked her fingers in his belt loops. “I can help you move on.”

“Mandi, you don’t know me that well.” He put his hands on her waist, lifted her up again, and set her aside.

“Hey!” she yelled, furious. Her cheeks turned as red as roses. Her stare filled with daggers that could kill him. Her fists balled up at her sides. She started to shake her head. Her hands opened up. Then the flames went out in her eyes, and tears started to form. “You know, Abraham, go ahead, let the road be your mistress.” Her shoulders sagged as she walked away. “See you next month… or not. I don’t care.”

# 7

ABRAHAM HIT THE ROAD FEELING AS EMPTY AS HE'D FELT IN MONTHS. Mandi liked to dig her nails into him, and he would usually shrug it off, but this time, somehow, she got them in deep. He felt as though he didn't want to feel at all. As he was driving in the steady traffic north on I-77, he looked over at his son's backpack. It gave him comfort, as if his son were still sitting in the seat.

"I think I might have blown it this time."

Overhead, heavy clouds had built up, which came in from the ocean, to the east. The rain was barely spitting. No doubt a storm was coming. He didn't like driving in the rain. A single headlight in his sideview mirror caught his eye. Two seconds later, a babe on a jet bike zoomed by him, wearing only a red-white-and-blue helmet, cowboy boots, and a bikini. Her auburn hair was flowing out from underneath her helmet.

Abraham would have chuckled. He'd seen plenty of wild things on the road, but this view was a first. He figured she was leaving the lake and trying to beat the rain, not that it was any of his business. Three seconds later, another rider on a crotch rocket soared by. The man, with more muscle than motorcycle, must have been moving over one hundred miles per hour. The fool didn't even have a shirt on, just biker boots, jeans, and a black helmet.

"Idiot."

The last thing Abraham wanted was to have to pull over to scrape the two fools up off the road. It had happened before, and it was an ugly scene—wreckage and broken bodies all over the highway. It brought back memories that haunted him day in and day out. Now, his belly started to sour, and his head ached. The aggravation was probably activating his ulcer. With the combination of too many jalapeños and cheese and a juicy hamburger with almost as much grease as meat, things weren't gonna go well. His tummy gurgled in a loud, bad way.

"Oh no. Here we go."

His forehead broke out in a cold sweat. He fanned himself with his cap and turned the air conditioner up another level. The spitting rain came down harder on the windshield. He turned on the truck's wipers.

"I really need to cut back on the jalapeños."

For some reason, he reached up and pulled his sun visor down. While driving on a brief straight stretch of road, he took a long glance at the picture of his family, Jenny and Jake. Jenny was a tall athlete of a woman with pretty eyes and short sandy-blond hair that covered her ears. She always had a warm smile on her face. Jake, at eight years old, had more of his mother in him than his father. He was a handsome kid, lean as a string bean, but with big hands and feet like his dad. Both of them had ball caps on that day in the picture. It was the day he'd signed a huge contract with the Pirates. Not long after that, all their lives had turned inside out.

"I miss you, baby," he said as he kissed his two fingers and touched the picture. "Both of you, more than you'll ever know." His eyes watered. "I'm sorry."

His belly moaned. He reached over into Jake's backpack and fetched a bottle of Pepto-Bismol. He shook up the milky pink elixir, twisted off the cap, and drank. It was one of the few drugs he took, now that he'd cleaned himself up, and he felt guilty even for taking that. He'd lost faith in a lot of medicines that took hold of him. They were as bad as the depression itself. But with help from his friends at the mission, like Mike, Dave, and Luther, he was able to live with the pain and loss on his own. His heart ached because he missed his wife and son so much.

He put the bottle back in the backpack. "Thanks, son." He looked closely at the picture of his wife. "I love you, love. Sorry about Mandi. I hope you'll forgive me."

He knew in his heart that Jenny would understand. She had patience and a strong temperament and was as understanding as they came. But if he stepped too far from the line, she would let him know it. His head got swollen often, but she kept him grounded. She was the best thing that had ever happened to him: his best friend. No person could replace her.

A possum crept onto the highway and darted out from the berm on the right. Abraham jerked the wheel hard left. The truck wheels screeched and bumped over something.

"Geez! Stupid varmint!"

He pulled the truck back into the right lane and checked his mirrors. No other cars were around, coming or going. That was odd because this stretch of interstate stayed continuously busy, especially during vacation season.

With his belly gurgling like the crashing waters of a waterfall, now bloated and gassy, he unbuckled his belt. "Good Lord, this feels awful. No more jalapeños. I swear it. I swear that milk is curdling in my stomach. Go, Pepto, go. Work that magic."

He was about two miles away from the East River Mountain Tunnel. The storm clouds shaded the mountainous hills to black.

Sheets of rain were coming down from the sky, and lightning streaked and flashed in the purple sky above the tunnel.

With almost two hours of driving left, Abraham said to himself, "Looks like it's going to be a long drive."

He rounded the last upward twist of the interstate that led him right to the tunnel. The subtle yellow glow of the tunnel mouth waited to swallow him whole. The rain came down harder, splattering loudly on his rooftop. A bolt of lightning that looked like it had been cast from heaven itself lit up the dark sky with white fire, striking the mountaintop. A thunderous boom followed, shaking the truck cabin.

"Whoa!" he cried out.

The beer truck engine sputtered. The dashboard lights flickered on and off. Still, the truck chugged along with the diesel turbo engine, renewing its laborious fury. With sheets of rain coming down, he plowed his way through into the tunnel, where he was alone—no head- or taillights in front of him or behind. It wasn't the oddest thing in the world to see, but normally, unless in the wee hours after midnight, plenty of company would be ripping through the tunnel. At 1,650 meters, the tunnel was just over a mile long, taking about one minute to pass through. The tires hummed through the tunnel, making a unique sound all their own. The lights inside the tunnel flickered on and off like the wink of fireflies.

"Not again."

Abraham liked the road, but tonight, he was ready to get back to the security of his cabin back home. Things just didn't feel right. The tips of his fingers tingled, his stomach ached, and his head pounded. Halfway into the tunnel, he saw a quavering light ahead. It made a sun ring inside the tunnel.

Squinting, he said, "What the heck?"

Suddenly, the eerie quavering pool of light shot right at him and his truck. It passed right through him, bathing his truck in strange light. An instant later, the truck started jumping up and down on its tires. The engine bucked and rattled. A sea of flying bats, in the hundreds, bounced off his windshield. He slammed on his brakes and screamed.

# 8

DRENCHED IN SWEAT, ABRAHAM SAT IN THE TRUCK SEAT WITH HIS eyes wide open. The bats had cleared out. The truck lights shone on the dusty debris in the tunnel. It was a tunnel that wasn't the same one from moments ago. It was now nothing but black rock and clay.

"What on earth?"

He blinked hard several times as he caught his breath. His heart thundered inside his chest. Far ahead, at least over a quarter mile that he could tell, was an opening of daylight.

Rubbing his temples, he said, "No more jalapeño cheese fries for me."

The truck headlights and dashboard lights flickered. The diesel engine knocked hard and died. The cabin went black.

He smacked the wheel with the butt of his hand. "Ah, come on."

The tunnel was pitch black, but in his side-view mirror, he caught the quavering light hovering far behind him. "Lord, tell me this is just some episode, because things are getting creepy."

Abraham popped his door open a crack. It groaned as he

pushed it wide-open. Slowly, he stepped outside. The ground beneath him was solid dirt. The tunnel walls around him were those of a cave just as big as the tunnel he'd been driving through. He peered at the quavering light. It was too blurry to see right through, where the rest of the real tunnel would be. All he could think of was his encounter in the Big Walker Tunnel. Perhaps this was a bizarre part of a military operation he'd gotten caught in.

He shouted, "Hello?" He did it again, but even louder. "Hello!"

He heard no response. The cave tunnel was as quiet as sleeping field mice. He looked in the direction the truck was facing. The daylight was natural, not alien like the strange pool of illumination behind him.

"I don't know what's going on, but I'm going to play right through it. I have to wake up sometime, dead or alive."

He got inside the truck's cab and cranked the key. The engine battery was stone cold. Shaking his head, he grabbed Jake's backpack. It had some of his son's personal items as well as a few of his own.

"Let's go on a little hike, son."

On foot, with an unsettled glance behind himself, he moved forward in the direction the truck was pointed. From Jake's pack, he grabbed a flashlight then flipped the switch. The light came on.

"Whew. At least something's working."

He lit up the field of dirt and rock at his feet with the welcome beam of illumination. It was as if nothing had ever passed through the cave before. It smelled like damp rocks and dirt, nothing out of the ordinary. He made it about fifty yards when the flashlight died. He slapped it on the side a few times. No light came.

"Great." He placed it back in his pack and shouldered it.

Trudging through the uncertain footing, he headed straight toward the tunnel's end light. He'd made it another hundred yards or so when he saw a figure darting into the tunnel.

"Hey," he said, waving his hands.

The figure sprinted toward him. Judging by her build, he guessed she was a bony woman. She moved quickly and looked desperate, taking glances over her shoulder as she ran. She had nothing on but a slip of ragged clothing. She didn't even look at Abraham the deeper she penetrated the cave. Twenty paces away, he got a closer look at her face as her demonic eyes locked on his.

Abraham's blood froze. "Sweet mother of mercy."

The pasty-skinned red-eyed woman looked like something spawned out of hell. She had a bushel of wiry brown hair that writhed like living wormlike snakes. Her eyes were red-pink angled slits, her leathery skin tight over her bony features. She showed a large mouthful of teeth as sharp as razors. She locked eyes on Abraham and changed direction, angling toward him.

Frightened out of his boots, he turned and ran away, yelling, "Lady, stay the hell away from me!"

He made three long strides before his toe clipped a hunk of sunken rock. He fell hard and sprawled onto the ground. He rolled onto his back just as the woman pounced on top of him. He screamed his own bloodcurdling scream.

# 9

Terror. It suddenly had a new meaning in Abraham's life. Now it took on the form of a bony witch who looked like an evil schoolteacher who had tormented him in second grade. Somehow, he fought the fierce little monster woman off as they rolled over the ground. She hissed awful sounds at him. Her teeth bit at his neck. He pushed her face away with his big hands. He set a boot in her gut and sent her flying.

She hit the ground hard, screeching like a wild banshee. Once she came to her feet, she eyed him and clacked her sharp teeth. Her talonlike fingernails clutched in and out at her sides.

Abraham sucked for his breath. His lungs burned, and his limbs were exhausted. The wiry witch woman had already taken the fight out of him. He was out of shape but managed to get back up on one knee. Before he made it to both feet, the witch of a woman was rushing him.

"No," he huffed. "No, get away!"

The whinny of a horse and clomp of horse hooves stopped the pink-eyed witch in her tracks. Her head lifted upward. Her slanted eyes turned big. The ugly scowl on her face turned to wroth anger. She shuffled side to side as if uncertain where to go.

With a concerted effort, Abraham made a backward glance. The last thing he wanted was for the wiry woman to pounce on his back. What he saw startled him. A man riding a black horse rode into the tunnel's entrance. He was some sort of medieval knight or warrior, just like he'd seen on television or heard about in stories. Abraham rubbed his eyes. *This can't be real.*

The horse trotted deeper into the tunnel. The rider's eyes were locked on the witch woman. His face was obscured in the darkness, and he held a crossbow in one hand.

The witch woman let out a screech, her gnarled hands and bony fingers massaging the air. The loose dirt on the ground shivered as her eyes rolled up in her head and turned black as pitch.

Abraham's heartbeat pounded in his ears. He couldn't catch his breath as the air turned icy and shimmered around him. The witch's breath turned frosty. Bugs and insects and worms popped up out of the ground. Centipedes crawled over his fingers.

He jerked away. "Gah!"

The witch spoke in strange words that twisted with arcane energy.

*Clatch-zip!*

A crossbow bolt struck the witch woman right between the eyes and stuck out from one end of the skull to the other. Her widened jaw hung open as her lanky, bare arms shook. She pointed a crooked finger at the rider and let out a deafening shriek.

Abraham couldn't believe his eyes as he plugged his ears with his fingers. The witch woman lived. She commanded bizarre power. Her crooked fingers needled the air. The icy wind in the caves howled, gaining strength and stirring his hair.

The rider and horse reared up. The warrior tossed his crossbow to the ground and slid a shimmering sword out of its scabbard. "Yah!" the man said. The horse lunged forward. The beast bore down on the screaming witch, who ran at the rider with fingers poised like daggers. The horse veered left. The shining sword sang. The witch's head leapt from her narrow shoulders, bounced off the ground, and rolled to a stop. Her black eyes turned pinkish red, flared once, and dimmed.

The tunnel fell silent. The crawling insects slipped back into the cave dirt. The icy chill in the air lifted away. Abraham clutched his chest, panting. He could feel his heart beating in his head. He swallowed the lump in his throat and slowly turned toward the man on horseback.

A few dozen feet away, the knightlike warrior sat coolly in the saddle. Eyeing the witch, he dismounted with casual ease. With long strides, he made his way through the cave toward the witch. Without giving Abraham a glance, he stood over the witch, pointed the sword at her chest, and stabbed her in the heart.

Abraham sat on the ground, sweating like a lumberjack and gasping. He knew what was happening wasn't real, but it felt real. *Wake up, Abraham, wake up! This isn't even entertaining.* He stared at the warrior. He was a tall athletic man, black haired with a neatly trimmed beard. His facial features were strong and angular, like many action heroes' he'd seen in the movies. The warrior wore a finely crafted metal breastplate that had seen action. He was dark, imposing and formidable.

Abraham lifted a hand and, not sure what to say, said, "Uh, hello?"

The warrior gave Abraham a sideways glance. His eyes hung on him long enough to soak him in. Then, the man's head snapped around and looked at the quavering body of light that hung deeper in the tunnel behind the truck. His glance slid over to the truck, and he shook his head. He did a double take between Abraham and the vehicle. He looked at Abraham and started talking in strong words.

Abraham couldn't understand what the man was saying. The warrior's words were a strange language, but he babbled on intently. He dropped his crossbow and drew his sword. It was a fine length of steel with a keen edge that shone in the dimness. He pointed the blade at the truck and started shouting.

Waving his hands in front of him, Abraham said, "I don't know what you are saying."

The man's dark eyes seemed to catch fire. His harsh words became stronger. The man's chest heaved, and his nostrils flared. He spoke in rough, broken-up English that Abraham began to understand. "What year is it?"

Finding his breath, Abraham managed to say, "Twenty eighteen."

"No!" The warrior hustled toward the truck and ran his hands over the hood. "I can't believe it. I thought I'd never see the day."

"What day?" Abraham asked.

"Your time has come. My time is done!" the warrior shouted at him. He stripped off his armor and slung aside his sword belt. Bare-chested, he was nothing but muscle and built like a linebacker. He looked at Abraham and in the same broken speech said, "Take off your clothing."

"What? No."

The warrior looked back into the tunnel. The quavering portal was shrinking. He turned on Abraham and, gripping his sword tightly, shook it at Abraham and said, "Do it now!"

"I'm not doing that! Who are you? Where am I?"

In two strides, the warrior crossed the distance between him, grabbed Abraham by the hair, and lifted him up to his toes. They were about the same size, but the man had the strength of a grizzly. The warrior then choked Abraham with his free hand while looking him right in the eye. "I am Eugene Drisk. This is Titanuus. It's a long story, and I don't have time to talk. Just give me your clothing!"

Abraham shook his head. "No."

The warrior looked back at the shrinking portal of light in the tunnel. Angrily, he shook his head then punched Abraham in his soft belly.

Abraham doubled over and let out a loud "oof" as he dropped to his knees.

The warrior ripped off Abraham's shirt and took his hat and glasses. He took his pants and shoes. He pulled Abraham's head back by the hair. He stuck the blade in Abraham's face and said, "Take my sword if you want to live."

"I don't want your sword."

"Take it!" The man tried to stuff the sword into Abraham's hand.

He clenched his fists and crawled away. "Leave me alone, you freak. I don't want your sword!"

The man pushed him to the ground. He pinned Abraham down with his foot on his chest. He lifted the sword high overhead. "Take the sword or die!" He stabbed downward.

Abraham flinched. He eyed the sword, stuck in the ground by his face. The witch's fresh blood ran down the blade.

The warrior kicked him in the ribs. "Take it. Take it, armor belt and all, or I'll kick the life out of you!" He drew back his foot again. "You must do as I say!"

"Fine!" Abraham fought his way up to a sitting position. "I'll take it! Just quick kicking me, you deranged Renaissance reenactor!" He reached for the pommel. "I'll take your bloody sword, seeing how none of this is really happening anyway! Then I'm going to beat you with it." He grabbed the sword and locked his fingers on it tightly. A charge of energy like a thunderbolt from heaven went right though him. He shook all over like a flag beating in the wind.

Energy exchanged between him and the warrior. An out-of-body experience occurred. Muscle and sinew popped. His entire body flexed and bulged, and he let out an agonizing scream. As quickly as the pain came, it was gone, and he was on his knees, chest heaving. The sword was clutched in his hand. The witch's blood ran back down over his fingers. He looked up and cast his eyes on a shabby-looking man holding a rock in one hand and his clothing in another. He was a balding, portly, scholarly-looking fellow, naked from the waist up. The man studied his own puffy fingers. He gave Abraham an incredulous stare and said, "Perhaps you'll be a better servant than me. But you're the king's fool now."

"Huh?" Abraham said. He took his eyes off the man for an instant.

The man walloped him upside the head with the rock.

By the time Abraham shook off the blow, the man was dashing away as quickly as his chubby legs would carry him toward the dying portal. He jumped through the ring of light just as it closed. The tunnel went black.

Abraham blinked his eyes. "What just happened?"

As he started to stand, the ground quaked, and debris rained down about him. The tunnel started to collapse.

# 10

With hunks of dirt dropping down on his head, he yelled, "No! This isn't happening. No!" But it wasn't his voice that was speaking. It was the voice of the warrior who'd forced the sword upon him. With the weapon in hand and ground shaking beneath his feet, he started to run. On his way out of the tunnel, he snatched up his son's backpack and ran as if his feet were on fire. The tremendous sound of earth collapsing on itself followed after him. He dashed out of the tunnel into the shrubbery of the woodland. A blast of smoke and debris caught up with him, covering him in smoke and black soot.

Abraham coughed and stumbled around until he was free of the dusty smoke. Looking back at the tunnel entrance, he clutched his head and said, "No, no, no."

He sat in the daylight, staring at the collapsed cave. Huge hunks of rock had come down. He wandered back inside the entrance. Seeing only darkness, he came back out. He brushed the debris out of his hair, wondering what had just happened. *This doesn't make any sense.*

Abraham sat on the damp ground, staring at the cave listlessly for what could have been hours, trying to make sense of what had happened. His stomach's chronic gurgling finally came to a stop. He heard a horse nickering and followed the sound. Before long, he came upon the black horse the warrior had been riding. He'd never ridden a horse before but had been to races and knew this stallion was one of the big ones. It stood in a clearing, head down, chewing on the tall grasses.

Coughing a few more times, he said to the horse, "If this is a dream, then I want you to be a unicorn."

The horse's ears flapped.

Rubbing the back of his neck, he said, "Great."

He looked about. His surroundings weren't any different from the Appalachian Mountains he was used to driving through. The trees were tall and green. Pines, maples, birches, and oaks grew in any direction he looked. The odd thing was that it was daytime, not night, as it had been when he entered the tunnel.

He pinched a big hunk of skin on his forearm. "Ow!"

The effort didn't wake him.

"I suppose I'm going to have to ride this nightmare out." He rubbed his face. His thick brown beard had been replaced with one that was neatly trimmed. The hair on his arms was black. The muscles in his forearms twitched noticeably when he moved his fingers. Without being able to see himself, he surmised he was in the body of the man who had accosted him. A strange transformation had taken place. He looked at his hands. They weren't the same fleshy spades he had been born with, but big strong hands with hard calluses on his palms. "I guess it could have been worse. I could have been turned into that witch." He shivered and grimaced. "And my belly's no longer rumbling like an angry river." He made a slow pass through the clearing. "So where in the world am I?"

He took the horse by the reins. "I don't know how this is going to work out, but let's start moving."

He headed down the slope and walked aimlessly for miles. Riders on horseback crashed through the trees and into the clearing. It was a hard-eyed bunch of men and women, much like the warrior he'd crossed in the tunnel. Wary-eyed men and women brandished swords and spears. They all cast dangerous looks right at him as the group encircled Abraham.

He said, "I want to wake up now."

# 11

Abraham didn't wake up where he hoped. Instead, he remained fully alert in his new surroundings. He could feel the heat of the sun, the breeze blowing through the branches, and the sweat running down his face. He scanned the company of coarse faces trapping him. A husky warrior spat brown juice on the ground. His head was bald, but his beard was full. He wiped his sleeve across his mouth.

The brooding men wore worn black tunics over shirts of chain mail. Two women were there, appearing just as rugged in their garb. They all looked Abraham up and down with their heavy eyes. That's when he realized that he was half naked, though he didn't feel as though he had anything to be ashamed about. He held his sword in a defensive manner. Making a slow turn, he eyed the rest of the group. Each of them seemed sullen eyed or carried a deadpan stare.

One woman spoke to him in foreign words. Her chestnut-brown hair was pulled back in twin ponytails. She had charm in a tomboyish sort of way. Her leather tunic was worn. She didn't carry a big sword, but a bandolier of knives crossed over one side of her chest. A sword belt carrying daggers rested on her curvy hips.

"What?" Abraham said.

The woman looked at the faces of the others in the company. A couple of men shrugged. The other warriors started looking concerned. The husky bald man in the saddle and carrying a spear started to speak. He was huge and heavy shouldered. He spoke to the woman. He pointed in the direction of the tunnel from where Abraham had come.

She nodded at the big warrior, and he, along with two others, rode for the tunnel and vanished out of sight. Then she dismounted. With her hands on the pommels of the daggers dressing her hips, she approached Abraham.

He stuck his sword out. She froze in place. With wary eyes, she lifted her hands up to shoulder height. Judging by the looks of the group he couldn't tell if they were some sort of fallen knights or misbegotten brigands he'd seen in fantasy movies.

Not knowing what else to say, he said what someone would typically say: "Who are you? What do you want?"

The half-decent-looking rogue warrior of a woman spoke at length. Years back, he'd had a friend that helped out with the baseball team. The man, Dougy, was deaf and always read lips. For some reason, Abraham picked up on it. He tilted his head and studied the woman's thin lips. Once she stopped, he shrugged.

He tapped himself on the chest and said, "Abraham. Abraham."

The rugged company exchanged concerned glances. Their hands and fingers toyed with their weapons.

He was making them nervous, but as far as he could tell, they knew him. He stuck his sword tip into the ground. "Abraham. Abraham Jenkins."

"Who is Abraham Jenkins?" the woman who had been speaking asked, clear as a bell.

Abraham gaped. He didn't think she was speaking in English, but he did think that it was a language that he could understand. The wheels in his new mind started to turn. A vague familiarity came over him. "Say that again?"

She looked at him and said slowly, "Who is Abraham Jenkins, Captain?"

"Captain?" He laughed. "You think I'm your captain? That's funny." He looked around. "So if I'm the Captain, then who are you? My first mate?"

The woman's eyes narrowed. Her slender hands deftly fell back to the weapons on her hips. "Sticks," she said.

A funny feeling came over him as the name did seem to ring a bell. He wondered whether she was an imaginary version of Mandi or someone else. In case he was the company's captain, in this imaginary world, he decided to play along. He rubbed the side of his head. Blood was caked on it where the strange man in the tunnel had clocked him upside the head with a rock. "The witch woman clubbed me."

"The witch woman?" Sticks said. "You mean the fright we are chasing down? She got to you, didn't she? Iris, get down here and check the Captain out." She scanned his body. "What happened to your belt and armor? Is the fright dead, or did she slip your fingers, Captain?"

"She's dead. Or it's dead, rather." He couldn't get the terrifying image of the fiendish-eyed witchy woman out of his head.

Looking at his blood-crusted sword, she asked, "Did you chop her head off with Black Bane?"

"Oh, the sword, eh? No, well, yes," he said, recalling the event in the tunnel. "I shot her then stabbed her." He looked at the sword and twisted it left to right. "With Black Bane."

The husky woman, Iris, ambled over in well-worn forest-green robes. Her auburn hair was tied up in a bun on her head. Unlike the others, she didn't carry armor or weapons but walked with a canelike cudgel. She had a leather satchel hanging on her shoulder. "Can I check that blow to your head, Captain? We want to make sure the hag didn't leave any lingering trouble."

"Sure," Abraham said in a language that he'd only moments ago somehow mastered. His memory was still in a fog.

Iris ran her soft, pudgy fingers over his face. She smelled like wildflowers, and cheap wine was on her breath. She moved all around him, brushing her curvy body against his. Her fingers probed the hard muscles of his body. She got in front of him and rose on tiptoe. She peeled his eyes open with her fingers and looked deep into them. "The Captain is fine. I think he might need some salve for his noggin for the swelling, but I can apply it back at camp. The bump on his head must have rattled his gray matter. It will come back with some rest."

"Thanks, Iris," Sticks said.

"Always an honor to care for the Captain."

Abraham wanted to ask, "Captain who?" but decided going along with it would be best. After all, he might not have more of a name than that. Whatever imaginary world he'd fallen into, maybe that was just who he was. *The Captain. Might as well stick with it. Perhaps I'll dream myself up a better name later. Though I wish I'd wake up first.*

The three warriors returned. The big bald rider had the breastplate armor, crossbow, and sword belt over his lap. Frowning, he looked down at Sticks.

"The Captain is coming around, Horace," she said.

"Aye." He dropped the gear down on the ground. "The cave collapsed in the middle, but the fright is dead." He frowned. "I thought you wanted her alive."

"Er... Why would I—" Abraham cut himself off, realizing the story clearly had more to it. "It didn't work out that way."

Horace grunted. "Are we returning to camp, Captain?"

Abraham felt all eyes on him. He was clearly in charge. All he could think to say was, "Aye."

# 12

After a couple embarrassing attempts to get into his horse's saddle, Abraham finally got on top. He'd never ridden a horse before but told himself that since it wasn't real, he should just imagine he'd been doing it all his life. In moments, he had control of the black beauty and rode with ease in the saddle. Playing the role of the Captain while at the same time not having any idea where he was going, he ordered Horace to lead them back to camp. He rode back beside Sticks, stating that he still was under the weather. In truth, he felt better than he'd felt in years.

The horse ride was long. The dreary party traversed the forest without any incident. Two hours into the journey, his backside started to burn, but his new body was made for it. Instead, he took advantage of soaking up his new surroundings. His heart pounded in his ears. His mind raced to find a shred of reality he could relate to. The grim forest fed his despair. His face brushed against the branches of the pines.

*No dream can be this real.*

Abraham's mind backtracked through all the events that had

happened over the last several hours. He was in his truck, feeling sick. Storms filled the skies. His head hurt as he drove into the tunnel. He saw a bright flash of light. That was when everything changed.

He ran through every possible scenario he could think of to explain the madness he was in. Perhaps the light was another vehicle that had hit him head-on. He recalled the floodlight in the Big Walker Tunnel, which the army had used. Maybe he'd had an aneurysm. Possibly, he'd had an allergic reaction to the food he was served at Woody's Grill and passed out from it.

*For all I know, I probably crash-landed the beer truck in a creek bed and have been left for dead.*

The longer the journey went on, the more real it became, beginning the moment a white mosquito the size of a slice of bread landed on his face.

He smashed it with his hand and wiped it on his legs. "Yecht."

The other odd thing was his backpack. He figured it would be a conversation piece, but no one had said a word to him about it. They didn't even look at it. One thing was for sure—he wasn't about to part with it. He was Abraham Jenkins, and it was keeping him attached to his world and not the fantasy one he'd somehow landed in.

Finally, at dusk, the company made it to a clearing down by a wide creek. At least a score of men wearing brick-red tunics were milling about the camp. Small pup tents were set up, a campfire burned, and meat cooked on a spit. Men carried sticks and chopped wood and branches. Others fished in the waters. They moved with a military purpose but, for the most part, were very haggard looking.

"Who are they?" he absentmindedly asked Sticks.

"What do you mean? The Red Tunics are our retainers. You handpicked them all, the same as us. Perhaps you need more time with Iris tonight."

He looked back at Iris, who rode in the middle of the ranks. The husky woman had a welcoming look in her eye. She lifted her eyebrows at him.

"Uh, I think I'll be fine after some rest."

"I was only jesting, Captain," Sticks said. "I hope you are feeling better tomorrow. You'll need your wits about you for the return journey."

Without having any idea where he was, he fought down the urge to ask, "What journey?" or "Journey where?" even though not doing so was killing him.

The company dismounted, and the Red Tunics took the horses away. As they did so, Abraham caught a glimpse of a group of two frights staring right at him.

"Holy sheetrock!" he said. "What are they doing here?"

Sticks looked at him as though he'd gone crazy. "They are our prisoners. We caught two but lost the other three, yours included. We are taking them back to the king to be executed. That's why we are here. To take these infidels to Kingsland and make an example of their troubles."

Eyeing the frights, Abraham arched a brow. The witches' hands and feet were bound with irons. That didn't stop them from hissing at him.

"How far is Kingsland?"

Sticks grabbed him by the elbow and pulled him away from the Henchmen working nearby giving him strange looks. She found seclusion near the creek, more than an earshot from all the others. "Captain, respectfully, please be mindful of what you are saying and who you say it in front of." She crouched back and winced slightly as though he was going to strike her. "You are not yourself. On a journey like this, they can't witness any weakness."

"Just refresh my memory. How long is this journey back to Kingsland?"

"Roughly a thousand miles."

He spoke so loudly the entire camp could hear. "On horseback?"

# 13

One tent in the Henchmen encampment was bigger than the others. It wasn't huge by any means but was the size of a family camping tent, more or less, big enough for about four to six people. It was made of heavy tan canvas with a flap for a door. Inside were fox-fur blankets stretched over cots. A woven carpet covered most of the floor, giving it a cozy homelike effect. A small table had a top made of wooden slats. Oil lanterns sat on each corner of the table. Some other supplies and dried food were neatly stacked in the corners.

Abraham sat on the wooden folding chair with his elbows on the table. It seemed odd to him that the chair was collapsible, given his medieval-seeming situation. But he noticed the entire chair was intricately crafted with wooden parts, without metal pins or screws. He yawned. All that had happened in the past several hours had finally caught up with him. The rush was over.

*Once I sleep, I'd better wake back up in my reality.*

Sticks entered the room, still wearing her armor and weapons. Even though she was much smaller than Abraham, the bandolier of knives made her look as formidable as any man. The expressionless woman eased deeper inside with feline grace, sat down on one of the cots, undid her ponytails, and began stripping her gear off.

They hadn't spoken since Abraham's outburst over the length of the journey. Sticks managed to respectfully guide him into the tent, and he'd been waiting for her inside ever since. Now, he watched her with a drying throat.

The more Sticks took off, the more woman she became. She tugged her boots off and removed her bandolier and dagger belt. Gracefully, she wiggled out of her leather tunic and slid off her buckskin trousers. She was stripped down to a close-fitting white cotton jerkin that revealed she had a lot more to offer than her armor was hiding.

Abraham swallowed. Sticks's bare arms were taut with muscle. Her body was like a well-honed dancer's. Her dark eyes locked on his. She walked over to him and ran her gentle fingers through his hair. He looked up with his face at her chest level, and his blood churned through his body.

"We need to get you settled, Captain," she said.

"I, uh, what do you mean?"

She hauled him up to his feet, turned to grab the fox and mink blankets, and tossed them onto the ground. With ginger fingers, the inviting chestnut-haired woman started undressing him.

He stepped back.

She grabbed him by the waist of his pants and reeled him in. Sticks was all woman, a woman who wouldn't be denied. Thoughts about his wife, Jenny, and visions of Mandi raced through his mind. Absentmindedly, he shook his head.

*Okay, Abraham, this has to be a dream. You know every time a dream starts like this, you wake up. So what the heck? Go with it. It's not real anyway.*

Abraham grabbed her by the shoulders, pulled her up into his arms, and kissed her. Sticks didn't engage at first, but as their bodies came together, their lips caught fire. Moments later, they were on the ground, unleashed in the throes of passion, which went on deeper into the night.

---

Abraham was awoken by the sound of a wild rooster crowing. He rubbed his eyes and sat up on his elbows. Darkness surrounded him, so dark he could barely make out his surroundings. As his eyes focused, he began recollecting the intimate details of his dream. He rubbed his head. *I've never dreamed anything so vivid before.* He was ashamed to think it, but he thought it anyway: *That was awesome. Now that I'm awake, let's figure out where in the heck I am.*

A warm figure stirred beside him. A hand grazed his chest, and he felt a scar over the heart.

He jumped up with a shout. Backing up, he bumped into a cot and fell over. His eyes finally adjusted to the darkness, and he quickly realized he was in the same tent where he'd been. Sticks scurried to one of the corners. An oil lantern's flame created a soft glow inside the tent.

She peered at Abraham and said, "Settle yourself. You are among friends."

Pulling on his trousers, he said, "You're a friend, all right. Oh my, what have I done? What is going on?"

Wearing only her open-necked cotton shirt, she approached him. "Keep your voice down. The Henchmen don't want to hear weakness."

He tipped up the cot and sat down. Nodding his head vigorously, he said, "Oh, I'm sure they heard plenty of things last night. This is embarrassing."

"You are the Captain. Nothing embarrasses you." She kneeled

before him and put a hand on his thigh. "You are the leader of the King's Henchmen, the boldest one of all."

He looked down her shirt. A king's crown was branded over her heart. He noticed it last night. He rubbed his fingers on his mark. *Why do we both have one of these?* He looked her dead in the eye and said, "Lady, I am not the Captain, I am Abraham Jenkins."

Sticks looked deep into his eyes. "I know that you are different, Captain. A woman knows these things. I... believe you."

Taken aback, he said, "How come?"

"Because... you've never kissed me before. Normally, you treat me like a tavern whore, but last night was... very different." She gripped his hand in hers. "You were... gentle, at times. Inexperienced at others."

"Inexperienced?" *Well, a long time has passed since I've been with anybody.* "Listen to me, Sticks. I am not from this world. The man, the Captain... Well, I took over his body."

She slapped her hand over his mouth. "Shush, you cannot say such things!" she said in a whisper. "You can be killed for it. If you want to live, you must be the Captain."

# 14

THE COMPANY BROKE CAMP WITHOUT ABRAHAM LIFTING A FINGER. The Red Tunics continued to move about their business in a very military fashion. None of the other Henchmen lifted a finger. Abraham, with Sticks's help, got all his gear on, including a new pair of trousers and a shirt under his breastplate armor. He looked like a warrior and felt like one too. Subtly following Sticks's lead, he got on his horse and followed after Horace, who led the company into the woodland.

Oddly enough, the terrain seemed familiar to him, as though he'd been there before. The woodland was much the same as it was surrounding his small farm tucked away in the West Virginia hills. He'd used it as a hideaway after the accident with his family. They'd died in a place like this. He started to wonder if he'd died again and didn't know it yet.

In the meantime, he tried to get familiar with what was going on. Sticks had really freaked out when he mentioned he was someone other than the Captain. Her eyes grew to the size of plates, making him think of the Salem witch hunts, where women were burned at the stake because of their abnormal behavior. He read similar stories in medieval history books when he was in high school. The priests and royalty of those days didn't tolerate the occult. He had a feeling he was in a place very much like that. The last thing he wanted was to wind up with his neck in a noose or exposed beneath a guillotine.

*Just play along. It has to end sometime. I can't sleep forever.*

He started sorting through what had been revealed to him. According to Sticks, he was the leader of the King's Henchmen. Very clearly, they served the king. In what capacity, he wasn't certain. The group was anything but a bunch of knights in shining armor. They were more or less a group of durable adventurers or a host of brigands if one judged by first appearances. But it was a large group, like a caravan, with the Red Tunics serving the others, making for a basic pecking order. Horace led the way on horseback, but two other Henchmen rode out ahead, scouting. All of them were well equipped.

Abraham peered about. *Let me see, I think I have this figured out. I have the Red Tunics, who don't have horses but drive the wagons. And the Henchmen all ride on horseback. I'm the Captain. The Red Tunics guard the frights. The Henchmen guard the group.* To him, they seemed like knights and squires but without all the cumbersome and gaudy armor. The arrangement seemed strange for "henchmen," which he normally would have considered to be a bunch of labor for hire. This group, however, was different. They were stalwart and stern looking, veteran soldiers who had seen a thing or two.

Shifting in his saddle, Abraham glanced backward at a pair of Henchmen riding behind himself and Sticks. One had jet-black tangled hair with coarse hairs on his forearms. He was broad faced and tan and had a dark scowl on his face. He carried a double-bladed battle-axe, fashioned in a Viking style with smaller axe heads, unlike the big, broad blades on his beer truck. "Bearclaw," he muttered.

Sticks leaned toward him and said, "What, Captain?"

"That's Bearclaw," he said.

"Yes," she said quietly.

Abraham didn't have any idea how he knew that, unless he'd picked up someone else saying it, but somehow he knew. He seemed to have gained not only a new body but also some of the knowledge that came with it. The other rider behind him was another man, thirtyish, tawny headed, with an aloofness about him.

"And that's Vern?"

"Yes."

An unsettling feeling turned his stomach. The last thing he wanted was to lose his own identity. *I am Abraham Jenkins.* He reached down and touched Jake's backpack, hanging from the saddle. *Don't forget it.*

As far as he could tell, the Henchmen were a mature bunch, war-torn and gritty. The Red Tunics were younger, hardworking, but not a smile among them. That was the group he was riding with now. They were soldiers, a team, on a mission for the king. The question was: who was the king? He didn't even know that man's name or his own, for that matter. *What the heck is my name? It can't be the Captain.* His back straightened.

*Slade Ruger! That's my name. No, Captain Ruger Slade. At least I think it is.*

Abraham didn't pick up any more bits and pieces that day. Instead, he rode, and the best he could tell, they were moving southwest. At least, based on the sun's position, that was the case. But he had no idea how that would actually work in another world. The times and the distances would change. Finally, the group broke out of the woodland into flatter prairies. Seagull-like birds were flying in the sky. A stiff, salty breeze rustled Abraham's hair. They rode on, over the rolling plains. A few hours later, they crested a hilltop. Abraham pulled his horse to a stop. Miles of shoreline stretched out along a seashore as far as the eye could see. The ocean, green and turbulent, crashed into rocky ledges. It wasn't possible for him to be in such a place so far from what he knew. It didn't make sense.

A flock of birds in a *V* pattern flew toward them. They were tiny at first but getting bigger. Every man in the group drew some sort of weapon. Even Sticks pulled her daggers. The closer the birds came, the bigger they grew. They weren't birds. Birds had beaks and feathers. These things had scales like lizards and were bigger than horses. They were dragons.

Abraham swallowed. His hand fell to his sword, and he said, "I'm not in Kansas anymore."

# 15

One hundred feet above, the dragons passed over the campaign without even giving the company a glance. The dragons had dark natural-colored scales and hard ridges on their bodies like desert lizards. They were ugly. Saliva dripped from slavering jaws in globs of rain that sizzled on the grasses. In seconds, the tight formation was gone out of sight.

The tension in the group deflated as they secured their weapons back inside their sheaths. Horace hefted his spear and said, "The dragons fear us. Ha ha!"

The Henchmen let out a cheer of relief.

"Either that, or fortune favors the foolish," Abraham said.

Sticks jammed her daggers into the sheaths on her hips. "It's about time we had some good fortune. We've lost enough men already."

"We have?" Abraham asked.

Taking a quick look about, she got close to him and said, "We've lost over a dozen men since we left the House of Steel. Fine men and women among them. I consider us lucky that we have this many left."

"It seems like a large group for such an adventure," he said.

"It was your decision."

Abraham didn't have any idea what she was talking about. And it seemed silly to send so many after the frights. The ugly crones were bound up and sitting in one of the wagons. They never said a word. He got the chills just looking at them. Goose bumps rose on his arms when—as one—their fiendish stares landed on him. He looked away.

He kicked his horse, and it lurched forward. They were heading downward toward the beach. "It just seems like a lot of trouble to round up a bunch of witches. If you don't mind, Sticks, would you fill me in?"

"Later, Captain. Everyone's ears are too big. We'll do it in privacy."

"If you say so."

"No, it's if you say so. I'll do it. You're the Captain." She rode farther away.

Abraham got the feeling she didn't want him to say too much. He needed to keep his mouth shut and start thinking. He'd just seen dragons. That wasn't a concept he was unfamiliar with. Plenty of dragons were in fantasy works he'd watched and read, but those he'd just seen were plain ugly. When he was younger, in middle school, before he blossomed, he played Dungeons & Dragons with his friends on the Air Force base. His dad used to tease him by saying he flew a real dragon, back in his days. Now, those imaginary fantasies had somehow become real.

*I must have hit my head and engaged an overactive imagination. This isn't real. And I didn't have this big of an imagination to begin with!*

The company hit the beach about two hours later. Of course, Abraham could only guess at the time, based on how quickly they moved. For all he knew, it could have been ten hours. But, to his relief, the sun was about to set in the west. It did appear bigger than what he was used to seeing. He couldn't glance at it long, but it had a purple glare around it. As they moved down the white sands of the beach, he couldn't help but think that would be a great spot to vacation. A big part of him wanted to jump in the foamy salt water. Instead, he drifted toward the back of the company.

No one said a word to him. They kept their eyes averted even when he looked right at them. The Red Tunics distanced themselves. One of them, carrying a pack as big as himself, waddled away in the other direction. That was when he decided to test the waters and ride up alongside Horace.

"Captain," Horace said with a stiff nod. The beefy man clawed at his beard.

"Are you sure you know where you're going?"

Horace's mouth clamped open and shut like a fish. "Er... Captain, the beach is the safest route until we get to the West Arm of Titanuus. From there, we'll take the land and navigate the mountain passes. There's no other way I know of, but if you have new orders, I'll follow them to the letter."

"No, Horace, that will do."

"Aye, Captain. Any other concerns?"

"It's a long way. At this rate, how long do you think it will take?"

"If we don't stop, twenty days, but I can only suspect as much trouble coming up as going down. With fortune on the king's side, I'd say thirty days but hope to make it in twenty-five."

"I see. Carry on, then."

He kept riding beside Horace. The man cast a nervous look at him from time to time. Behind him, Bearclaw and Vern were leaning forward in their saddles. Farther back, Iris eyeballed his back and looked away when he turned.

The company rode along the coastal waters until the sun dropped from the sky and the stars and moon hovered in the night. Standing far away from the others, Abraham studied the sky. The face of the moon was different. The constellations he knew were gone too.

*This can't be possible. Tell me... please tell me I didn't drive through a portal to another universe. I might have wanted to leave home, but I didn't want to go this far.*

# 16

Abraham sat facing the ocean. Sticks joined him, her hair down. She carried a blanket.

"Your tent is ready," she said, "but it is probably safe for us to talk here. The breath from the Sea of Troubles will drown our conversation. Captain, speak freely now. My ears are yours."

Abraham had a thousand questions. Not sure where to start, he bluntly asked, "If I'm Ruger Slade, then why is it such a secret?"

Sticks spread out the blanket and sat down. He joined her. Together, they both stared out at the turbulent sea waters crashing in the distance.

Without looking at him, she said, "It's your order. Everyone calls you the Captain to keep your identity secret. That's what you say. Your name is renowned in Kingsland." She twisted her head left and right. "You are Ruger Slade, considered to be the greatest sword master in all of Titanuus. Now, you are secretly the sworn sword of the king."

"I have a sword, but I didn't think there was anything extraordinary about it." He rubbed his neck. "I mean, it's a nice sword, but I don't feel like a master of it."

He removed the sword from the sheath and thumbed the razor-sharp edge. The blade was a hard, dark steel with a dull shine in the metal. The broken runes carved above the cross guard were intricate.

He flipped it over with a twist of his wrist. "Have I killed many with my blade?"

She gave him a bewildered look. "You've killed every man or beast you've ever fought. Your skill is extraordinary. That's why you lead this group. They wouldn't follow just anyone. Well"—she shrugged her shoulders—"aside from the king that they've sworn their lives to. But leading this group... no easy task unless they respect or fear you. But many have been with you a long time. Don't you remember that?"

Abraham shrugged. He rubbed the hard calluses on his right hand with his left thumb. They were as thick as a bricklayer's. He had an uncle who did masonry work, Uncle Robert. He had big strong hands that were heavy and thick. A slap on your back from Uncle Robert's hands would knock the wind out of you. Abraham switched and started rubbing his left hand. The calluses were the same.

"I can use either hand, can't I?"

"You have no weakness. One is as good as the other."

He closed his eyes and tried to envision himself fighting with a sword. Bits and pieces of Ruger Slade's memories had come to him, but they were vague. At the same time, he couldn't imagine himself killing anything. He wasn't scared of doing so, but he'd never really hurt anyone with anything other than a fastball pitch. He knocked a baseball player out cold once. Now, to believe he was an incredible fencer seemed a stretch. No way could he be a master of something he'd never done before.

*Well, at least I have a badass name. Maybe that will win some fights before a sword is even drawn.*

He pulled his knees up to his chest and said, "You said we lost a lot of men coming up? North? How so? And give me the Cliff Notes version. Maybe it will jar my memory."

"What are Cliff Notes?"

"Never mind the Cliffs—just the short version," he said.

"There are the elements. Skirmishes with brigands and raiders. The battle with the hill folk in Bog was the worst. I think that is why Horace is wanting us to hug the coastline." The brisk sea winds stirred her ponytail from one shoulder to the other. "You bring plenty of Henchmen on every journey, but most of them don't make it back. The king's missions are dangerous, to say the least."

Abraham wished he knew the king's name, but he didn't want to ask her. For some reason, that seemed embarrassing, so he put his inquiry another way. "So we don't mention the king's name either, I take it?"

"No. We keep our mission very discreet. Only the ranking members of the Henchmen know what is going on. The Red Tunics don't. We pose as traders and well-armed merchants. If the others knew that we served"—she lowered her voice—"King Hector, the king's enemies would be upon us. We'll die before we reveal the purpose of our mission."

"But taking the frights to the, er..." he gave her a questioning look, "the House of Steel... Won't that expose us?"

"They are criminals, mostly. If anyone asks, we are swords for hire or slavers. Our business can easily be explained that we are dealing with someone else other than the king. In Kingsland, there are plenty that don't care for the king. And we, well, we aren't the type of group that fits in with the king's lofty standards."

"You make it sound like the king is not someone that you like. So why do you serve him?"

"No, we revere the king. It's an honor for miscreants to serve the crown. Whether for good or for bad, the king gave us purpose."

"Are there other kings or kingdoms?"

"Many. And they all want King Hector's head on a platter. That's where we come in."

# 17

THE KING'S HENCHMEN RODE ALONG THE SHORELINE THE FOLLOWING day. Abraham stayed close to Sticks and Horace. The husky warrior said little but commented from time to time about the weather and expressed his concerns about the route they traveled. The man was clearly looking for approval. Abraham told him to stay the course. Sticks kept quiet and more or less shadowed him, riding at the back of his horse's right flank.

Abraham didn't want to say much either. He wasn't sure how Ruger Slade would have spoken. Who was the man at the tunnel, Eugene Drisk, who moved out of Ruger Slade's body? How did he act? Were they the same person, or were they two different personalities? He wanted to play the part. The last thing he needed was for someone to think he was possessed, like Sticks had warned him about, and to end up dead.

The two frights let out a unified bone-chilling shriek.

Many of the horses whinnied. Others stomped their hooves hard into the sand. Bearclaw turned his horse and led it toward the back, where the witches rode in the wagon. He untied a lash from his saddle and turned it loose on the wicked frights. With the sharp crack of leather on skin he beat the tar out of them. They grimaced and winced, but their leathery lips stayed clamped shut as they huddled over. Bearclaw handed the lash to one of the Red Tunics.

"Whip the wicked worse than I did if they do that again," the bearish warrior said. He shoved one of the frights in the back, knocking her to the floor. "Save your screaming for when you burn at the stake."

Abraham wasn't certain what to make of that. One thing was certain, though: the Henchmen were all business. But even after Bearclaw's theatrics, the frights kept their leathery scowls fixed on him. They flicked their tongues like a venomous snake. Their slitted pink-red eyes were narrowed as if they were creatures ready to strike at any moment.

"They were a lot of trouble to catch, weren't they?" he quietly asked Sticks.

"Tougher than a den of eight-legged wolverines," she replied.

He nodded. An eight-legged wolverine was something he could picture. In an odd way, that gave him some comfort.

Hours later, Horace slowed his horse until Abraham came along his side. "Captain, we are approaching Hamm's Inlet. It won't be so easy to slip along the coast without being noticed. The sea folk and pirates are territorial folk. They'll pry like a miner picking for gold."

Abraham narrowed his eyes at Horace. He slid his hand down onto the pommel of his blade. It was mostly an act, but something about it felt natural. "Don't you think I know that?"

Horace's eyebrows rose. "Aye, Captain. I'm just talking. No disrespect intentioned."

"Then don't state the obvious unless I ask for it."

New sweat trickled down Horace's bald head and ran past his ears. "Aye, sir, aye."

An emboldened part of Abraham wanted to laugh. In the real

world, he'd never cross a man like Horace. The balding and bearded warrior was built like a defensive tackle or one of the massive overweight pro wrestlers who would squash men on the mat. Abraham wasn't any slouch for a pitcher, but he didn't have the look of a natural-born brawler either. Horace did. He looked like that kind of man who would run over kittens with a motorbike, and he'd just backed the man down.

"We should get some supplies in Hamm's Inlet," he said to Horace. "Some fresh food and drink is in order, too."

"Aye, Captain. Hamm's Inlet it is." Horace turned his back and trotted ahead.

Abraham straightened up in the saddle. He felt a degree of confidence that he knew what he was doing. He gave Sticks a sideways glance. She wasn't looking his way. He did have her to thank for much of his decision, though. In his tent the previous night, they'd looked at a map of Titanuus. She showed him the course they were taking and explained what lay ahead, like Hamm's Inlet, for instance. The coastline territory located above the West Arm of Titanuus was more or less hamlets and large villages filled with seafaring people. He didn't connect with the map at first, but the more he rode, the more familiar his surroundings became. At least he had some idea of where he was. He was in a world made just like other continents he'd seen.

He pulled his horse toward Sticks. "Why don't you make the rounds? Figure out what supplies we need. We'll take a small group into Hamm's Inlet, get what we need, and go. The rest can camp and keep moving. We'll catch up with them."

She nodded. "Aye, Captain. Is there anyone in particular you want to take?"

"You, Horace, Bearclaw, Vern, Iris, and two pack bearers. Just do the inventory and let me know if you think we need more."

Sticks's brow rose.

"Is there a problem?" he asked.

"No, Captain, it's a sound decision. I'll take care of it." She led her horse away.

Taking command felt good. He wasn't one hundred percent sure about his decision-making process, but he thought it might have something to do with the body he was in. His mind was still his own, but traces of memories of another consciousness seemed to be guiding him. Either that, or he was just doing what he did as a kid when they played Dungeons & Dragons. He just went where the adventure was. Perhaps that was the only way to find answers. If he was trapped in an imaginary world, he'd just have to play it out until it ended.

Horace led the small group of Henchmen, following the coastline to the top of Hamm's Inlet. They rode several miles before encountering the first city—out of dozens that ran along Hamm's Inlet—called Seaport. Wooden and stone buildings were built along the seashore, which ran from the water's edge into the gentle hills. Long docks stretched out to the sea, accompanied by fishermen's wharfs. The ships ranged from small skiffs and fishing rigs to mighty brigantines and galleons, without the portals for cannons.

They reminded Abraham of movies he'd seen about sailors or pirates from an early colonial period, or perhaps the Dark Ages. He didn't know which, but he did have some understanding of it. With the salty wind in his face, his thirst grew, and his stomach rumbled. He hadn't eaten much of anything recently, aside from dried strips of beef and some sort of hard fruit that tasted like chewy bark.

"Iris," he said to the husky woman, who had her hair in a bun and wore loose-fitting robes. "Take the reds and get our supplies. I think we'll eat. I'm starving. Once you've finished, join us." He sniffed in the smell of baking fish.

Iris gave him a pleasant smile and said, "As you wish, Captain."

In a rugged voice, she said to the pair of Red Tunics, "Come on, boys, we have some dealing to do."

"Horace, find us a quiet spot to eat."

They stabled the horses in some barns just inside the edge of the fishing town. From the barns they followed stone walkways that led into the town. Many people were out along the dock, men wearing long-sleeved cotton shirts and the women just the same, but with skirts. Sailors were there too, walking arm in arm, with squarish caps on their heads and tassels on top. They swayed as they walked and sang while drinking from jugs of wine or rum hooked in their fingers.

Horace pushed his way through the double door of a white-washed stone building with red clay tile roofing. The tavern was poorly lit by candlelight and small windows on the front of the building. The smell of fish and smoke was like a slap in the face. Not many people were inside, but the ones who were there shrank behind their tables with wary eyes. Horace found a table big enough to seat them all. He pulled out a chair at the head of the table.

Abraham took his seat at the head of the table. Sticks sat to his left and Horace to his right. Bearclaw and Vern followed suit. They sat like statues with tight expressions on their faces.

Abraham didn't care. He was starving. "Sit. Let's eat. Let's drink."

One of the other patrons with shifty eyes scurried through the tavern and out through the front door.

# 18

THE HENCHMEN QUIETLY DUG THEIR SPOONS INTO THE BOWLS OF fish stew they'd been served. All of them huddled over their bowls like children who were being punished. Abraham wasn't certain what to make of it, but he was famished and ate. The fish stew, a gumbo-like mix, was loaded with savory hunks of seafood. He tasted lobster, crab, and scallops, along with some strong spices mixed in with broth and rice. It was good, far better than what he'd expected in a crappy run-down tavern where the floor creaked with every step. A spicy hunk of fish meat caught in his throat. He coughed and tapped his chest.

"Are you all right, Captain?" Sticks asked.

"Sometimes I forget to chew before I swallow." He grabbed a metal goblet. "Just have to wash the bait down." He drank. The strong spiced rum burned all the way down his throat. It did him little good, and he coughed more.

Out of the corner of his eye, the men at the other table gave him a funny look. He lifted his head, and they looked away.

Abraham would have killed for a glass of water. Asking for

water instead of rum wasn't the best idea either. That would only make him a bigger fish out of water. So rum it was. He nursed it. The last thing he wanted to do was get drunk or even tipsy. After the accident, he'd used a lot of pills and alcohol to numb his pain, inside and out. He took years to regain control. He didn't want to lose that again, no matter what world he was in. He sipped more rum.

Looking at Vern, he asked, "How's your stew?"

"Er... fine, Captain." The aloof warrior pushed the wavy locks of blond hair out of his eyes. He drank from his goblet and resumed eating.

Those were the first words Abraham had spoken to the man. He wanted to see what sort of reaction he'd get. He hoped to trigger a memory, but the answer garnered him nothing. He sipped more rum. The liquid tasted sweeter after several sips.

Sitting straight up, Sticks said, "Iris should be along soon. If you like, I can check for her."

"I'm sure she'll find us."

Back in the corner opposite their table, two surly men were puffing on pipes. They would look at him and snigger. He could smell the bittersweet aroma of the burning leaves. It made him think of his father, who smoked cigars until the day he died.

"Did anyone bring any tobacco?"

Horace's eyebrows clenched.

"I guess not." He took another drink of rum. He finished his bowl of stew and ordered another one from the serving wench. She was attractive, wearing a loose blouse bound tight around her waist and very revealing. He gave her a big smile when she bent over to serve him a new bowl.

Sticks showed a Mona Lisa frown.

Abraham drank more rum and dug into his stew. Every spoonful tasted better and better. Halfway into the bowl, he stopped eating as every head at his table turned toward the front entrance. Loud and bawdy, a gang of greasy pirates entered the tavern, filling the tables and crowding the bar.

Abraham chuckled.

*Pirates. Hah. I used to be a Pirate. No doubt this is a figment of my imagination. And if it's not real, then I might as well get drunk.* He swallowed more rum.

Even though Abraham had pledged to himself not to indulge in the rum, its intoxicating effect blinded his reason. He sat in his chair, staring at the pirates. They were all Jack Sparrow types, a variety of shapes and sizes, but without the mascara. He burst out in loud laugher.

That drew the attention of every pirate in the room.

The tavern fell quiet, except for Abraham, who couldn't stop laughing.

Several feet away, sitting at the corner of the bar, a pirate slung a mug at him.

Without even thinking, Abraham plucked the speeding goblet out of the air.

*Holy* Big Trouble in Little China. *I have lightning-quick reflexes.*

"Did you see that?" he said to the Henchmen. He spun the mug on the tip of his finger. "Did you see that?"

"Aye, that was fast, Captain," Horace said.

A grizzly-sized pirate entered the tavern. The pirate stood tall and broad shouldered. He had a head full of red hair and a beard just the same. His overcoat was as red as blood with tarnished brass buttons running from top to bottom. His sword belt was black leather, and he carried a heavy cutlass on his hips. The pirates, one and all, stood at attention and saluted him.

One of them shouted, "Boyjas! Flamebeard! Boyjas!"

The excited cheers drowned out every sound in the room. Flamebeard lifted an oversized hand, and the pirates quieted. A parrot, which had escaped Abraham's notice, was perched on Flamebeard's shoulder. It let out a loud squawk.

Abraham erupted in uncontrollable laughter, and with his fist, he pounded the table. His wide-eyed Henchmen stiffened.

The pirates snaked out their blades and closed in.

# 19

In a gravelly voice that carried through the tavern, Flamebeard looked at Abraham and asked, "Do we amuse you, stranger?"

Abraham took a breath and regained his composure. He studied the pirate, who had a countenance as fierce as any. He was a big man too, bigger than any other in the room. His red beard and hair came together around his face like a lion's mane. Abraham wagged a finger at the parrot, which, upon closer inspection, didn't have the feathers of a bird but leathery skin that resembled feathers. It made for a hideous bird, with solid yellow eyes and a thick black tongue that licked its beak.

Abraham cleared his throat. "Sorry, Flamebeard. But your ridiculous appearance and ghastly bird took me by surprise."

"Is that so?" Flamebeard's bushy eyebrows came together until they kissed. "I don't believe we've had a proper introduction. You are?"

"The Captain," Abraham said.

"That's it. The Captain." Flamebeard showed a sinister smile. "Certainly, you have a fuller name than that?"

"No, that's the name that I go by. I keep it simple for my friends and simpletons like you." Abraham's words flowed out with no thought behind them. To him, everything that was happening reminded him of a really well-done reenactment at a pirate restaurant, as a family might go to when vacationing at the beach. It was all make-believe. "Say, is that beard real, or is it a fake one like the mall Santas wear?"

Flamebeard stroked his bushy facial hair with his sausagelike fingers. "Keep up the insults, and you'll soon be the new anchor of my ship."

The pirates chuckled. One of them said, "Just kill him, Captain. He's earned a quick death."

Tilting onto the back legs of his chair, Abraham said, "I'm getting the feeling that this tavern is not big enough for two Captains. I tell you what. Walk out now, and you and all of your men will live to see another day at sea." He winked at Sticks, whose frozen look didn't change. "Fair enough, Flamebeard?"

"That's enough!" Flamebeard ripped his cutlass out of his belt. "Clear the floor, men. I'm going to teach the land hound a lesson that he'll never forget. On your feet, dust-eating coward. Let's see what you have to say with a belly full of dorcha steel."

The pirates pushed all the tables and chairs out of the way. They formed a ring around their captain, who unbuttoned his long red coat. The lizard-skinned parrot flew up into the rafters and let out a vicious squawk.

Every eye from Abraham's company was fixed on him. He put all four chair legs back on the floor. His chest tightened, and his nostrils flared. Back in his baseball-playing days, he'd talked a lot of smack. He'd let his emotions run high to pump him up for a game. Now, that spark of testosterone was running a new course through him. He couldn't turn it off. Without even thinking, he came out of his chair and crossed to the manmade arena.

The Henchmen rose from their benches and followed him.

Abraham was a well-built, long-armed athlete and one of the biggest men in the room, but the moment he stood across from Flamebeard, the wind went out of his sails.

Flamebeard stood taller and was built like a smokestack. The pirate had stripped down to his waist. He must have been a few inches short of seven feet. He didn't appear to be in the best shape, but plenty of muscle was packed underneath the thick skin of his chest and shoulders. He sliced his cutlass from side to side. The blade was curved, broad with a keen razor edge. He moved it like a part of his own arm.

He spat black juice on the floor. "Are you going to pull that steel or pee your pants, land dweller?"

Peeing his pants was the avenue Abraham was more likely to take. He had no idea what had compelled him to boldly stroll across the room to the center arena with iron in his limbs. He did it, though. That was certain. Something had possessed him. But standing before Flamebeard sobered him. His eyes slid over to his men. Horace, Bearclaw, and Vern stood nearby with their arms crossed over their chests and a wary look in their eyes. Sticks stood against the bar, leaning with one elbow resting on the edge.

*Oh Lord, what am I doing? This pirate is going to butcher me.*

"Quit stalling. Pull your steel, coward," Flamebeard said.

Abraham's right hand crossed over his body and fastened on the hilt of his long sword, Black Bane. Slowly, he drew the weapon out of the sheath. The blade scraped quietly out of the scabbard. Its dark gray shone dully in the faint light of the tavern. He took a deep breath, hoping that would fill him with courage. It had no effect.

*I'm going to die.*

The corner of Flamebeard's mouth turned up in a knowing smile. "It's too late to surrender now." He brought his sword down and lunged with the speed of a fastball.

# 20

Abraham swatted Flamebeard's sword thrust aside with a swipe from his own blade.

The sharp ring of metal on metal filled his ears.

In a split second, his boots, which might as well have been fastened to the floor, were moving. That wasn't all that moved. The rest of his body did too, particularly his sword arm. It moved with a mind of its own. His sword crashed against the pirate's cutlass. It became a rigid metal snake on the attack.

Flamebeard backed away from the intense strikes. Using the range of his long arms, he slashed hard from side to side. Metal smacked against metal, parry after parry. The sting of the strikes raced from Abraham's hands up and through his shoulders. Somehow, he hung onto a sword that the larger man's blows should have ripped from his fingers. Thrusting and striking, he pushed the pirate back toward the corner.

*How am I doing this?*

Abraham wasn't trying not to do it, but he knew he wasn't doing it. His sword expertly moved in directions he never could have anticipated. His mind seemed to be trapped in a body not his own.

Flamebeard slid away from the dangerous range of Black Bane. He grabbed a chair by the leg and used it for a shield. Black Bane whittled down the chair stroke by stroke, hacking it into flying pieces. Flamebeard hurled the seat of the chair at Abraham. At the same time, the pirate lunged. "Die, land rat!"

Black Bane sang. *Slice!* Abraham cut Flamebeard's sword hand off at the forearm. Blood spat out of the stump.

Flamebeard let out a howl. "Impossible! No one douses the Flame!" The pirate took a knee and pulled a jewel-encrusted dagger from his belt. "No one!" He stabbed at Abraham.

Black Bane flashed before Flamebeard's eyes, and the pirate dropped the dagger. His head fell from his shoulders and rolled across the floor and into the bar with a *thud.* Flamebeard's big body fell over backward, blood pumping out of his neck.

A dead quiet fell over the raucous gang of pirates as they stared at their fallen leader.

"No one's ever defeated Flamebeard before. No one," one pirate said. He had a red cloth cap tied on his head in skullcap fashion. He wore a sleeveless jerkin and carried a short sword in his hand. "Only witchery could have done this. Flamebeard was the greatest sword of the seas."

Sticks made a callous statement: "You aren't at sea."

Abraham couldn't tear his eyes away from the man gushing blood on the floor. Flamebeard's body spasmed. Some fight was yet in him. Then his body went still. The blood no longer pumped out of his mutilated body. The leak turned into a drip. Abraham doubled over and vomited.

The pirates' hard eyes filled with fire. The one wearing the skullcap said, "There is more of us than them. Pirates don't lose to the land dwellers. Avenge our captain, Flamebeard." He lifted his sword high. "Kill them!"

Two pirates brandishing sabers chased Sticks into the back corner of the room. They were ugly men, built like rugged fishermen and missing many teeth. The one with a hawk nose with a ring pierced in the left nostril licked his lips and said, "Give yourself up, girlie. We'll all have at you one way or another. Make it easy on yourself by making it easy on us."

Sticks snaked two throwing knives out of her bandolier.

"Oh, those are very shiny toothpicks," said the other pirate, with a mane of hair past his ears. He shot her a grin. "Come and pick my teeth with them."

She flicked her pair of daggers upward. They stuck in a beam in the ceiling. The pirates' eyes locked on the knives, and they started laughing. The one with the nose ring dropped his eyes. Sticks jammed the daggers into his chest and the other's.

"You clever witch!" he spat just before he died.

Those pirates were dead, but the melee had begun. The clamor of battle reached a new crescendo inside the tavern. The pirates were hacking away at the rest of the Henchmen, who were brawling side by side for their lives.

Horace rammed his dagger hilt-deep in a pirate's belly.

Bearclaw swung his battle-axe into a man's chest. With a crunch of bone splintering a volcanic eruption of blood spewed from the pirate's busted chest.

Vern fought on his knees, with his long sword striking through pirates' legs and abdomens.

A pirate peeled away from the flock and flanked Horace, who was anchoring the right side of their defensive row. The bulky Horace—his arms locked up with another man's—didn't see the pirate coming. Sticks flicked a throwing knife from her hand. It hit the charging pirate right in the jugular. She searched out her Captain. He'd gotten separated from the group. A sea of men were coming at him from all directions. Fighting them all off would be impossible.

"Horace!" she shouted. "Get to the Captain!"

# 21

In one moment, Abraham was puking his guts out, and in the next, he was fighting for his life. He hadn't even processed everything that just happened. As in a dream, he'd slain Flamebeard. He saw it but didn't feel it. It just didn't seem real. Adrenaline kicked in next. Suddenly, he felt everything as if it were his own body. He had the vomit to show for it.

That was when the pirates came. Sweaty, greasy, and angry, the dangerous gang of sailors attacked in a wave of destruction. At that point in time, all of it seemed very real. Abraham's own self-preservation kicked in. The fight became real. Either he died, or they died.

Abraham let out a wild howl. He thrust his sword through a pirate's clavicle. He ripped it out and chopped down another pirate. He spun away from a sword chop that would have split his head. He countered the pirate's swing by cutting his sword through the man's ribs. With the bottom of his boots mopping through the rising blood on the floor, he cut three more men down.

Abraham wasn't the only one swinging victory after victory.

Horace, Bearclaw, and Vern, wearing their tunics over chain-mail armor, overmatched the unarmored pirates. The trio burst through the ranks with wroth force, piercing skin and chopping through bone. Over a minute later, the fight was over. Two surviving pirates dashed out the front door.

The blood-spattered Henchmen panted for breath as they looked over their fallen enemies. The dead pirates' wounds were ghastly. Abraham counted fifteen in all. Leaning with his arm braced against a wall, he threw up again.

"How do you fare, Captain?" Sticks asked. Specks of blood covered her face like freckles. Fresh blood stained her dagger-filled hands.

He gasped for breath and said, "There's no explanation for it."

The stench of new death wafted into his crinkling nose. He didn't dare another look at the slain. He'd seen more than he cared to see. It never looked so bad in the movies.

"I need some fresh air," he added.

Horace met Abraham at the doorway and pushed it open. He stepped aside and said, "Good fighting, Captain."

Abraham nodded at the bald warrior, whose beard was caked in blood. Once he got outside, he sucked in a lungful of air. He took several deep breaths and held out a hand. It was as steady as a rock. Inside his mind, he was shaking like a leaf. He couldn't believe his body wasn't trembling.

Iris and the two Red Tunics hustled over to the group. They all carried packs over their shoulders, and their arms were filled with sacks of goods.

Her soft eyes were as big as saucers. "What in the world happened?"

Bearclaw slung the blood from his axe onto the stones on the street. Blood dripped from a gash across his forehead. Another wound bled freely above the knee. "Seaweed-sucking pirates crossed the Captain. That's what happened. They paid for it."

"You need care, Bearclaw," Iris said. She put a handkerchief on his head. "Hold that."

The Red Tunics' packs were full to the brim with supplies, and they carried another between them. Their gaze jumped from bloody man to bloody man. One of them swallowed.

"Do we have everything that we need?" Abraham asked.

Iris nodded.

"Get the horses ready," Abraham said to the pack bearers. "We need to get out of here."

The waitress from the tavern came outside. Blood stained the bottom of her skirt. She was trembling like a leaf. Without looking at Abraham, she said, "Sire, my lord says that you did not pay for your meal. It's fourteen shards of silver. Forgive me for asking."

"Huh... oh." He looked at Sticks. "Pay her twenty."

Sticks's eyes lit up. "What? But their fish stew made you retch."

His eyes narrowed on Sticks. The fire in her eyes cooled. "Aye, sir." Emptying a purse full of small coins into her hand, she counted out twenty silver shards. The coins were the size of nickels and shaped like guitar picks with symbols stamped on them. "Here. Go. Tell your greedy lord that we might come for him next."

The bar maid curtseyed, turned, and vanished back inside the tavern.

"You're going to need to be stitched up, Bearclaw," Iris said to the bearish warrior.

"I'll heal just fine, but you can put those soft hands to work on me if you wish," Bearclaw replied to the pleasantly plump woman.

Iris smiled. "As you wish."

"Captain." Horace nodded down the street. A group of men had gathered several blocks down. They carried lanterns and were gesticulating in their direction. "The death of Flamebeard will travel fast. He has as many friends as he has enemies in the inlet, many of them prominent people."

It became clear that Horace, and most likely the others, had intimate knowledge of Flamebeard that Abraham had yet to recall. He had no doubt that the loud-mouthed pirate left terror in his wake, and Abraham had killed him.

"It was a fair fight," Sticks said. "None should have trouble with us. Flamebeard had it coming. He's a scourge of many."

Scowling, Vern said, "The sea folk won't take the word of strangers over the word of sailors. No doubt, the pirates' lies will catch fire and spread. They'll all come after us by the hundreds. We need to get to the horses and ride, before the *Captain* almost gets us killed again."

"Watch your tongue, Vern," Sticks warned.

"I can speak for myself," Abraham said. He stared Vern down. "Is there a problem?"

Vern shook his head. "No, Captain. I still breathe. It's good."

"Good. Keep it that way."

With the heat of battle still racing through his body, he didn't feel like taking any crap from anybody. He'd just killed half a dozen men or more. At least, he thought he had. One thing was sure—it all felt real. Leading the group, he headed down the road, following the steps that led into the city and back down toward the stables. The Red Tunics were leading the horses out of the stables when they arrived. Everyone mounted, Iris doubled up with Bearclaw. The pack bearers doubled up on her horse with one another.

Torch- and lantern-bearing sea folk had formed a blockade at the stable's exit.

Abraham turned his horse around. The citizens were blocking off the back entrance too. Scores of hard-eyed people were cramming the entrance. The Henchmen weren't going anywhere without another fight.

# 22

Abraham stood with his hands on the rail of Flamebeard's galleon with the morning sun in his face. He'd never ridden on a ship that had sails, or on any large ship, for any matter. Now, he was the captain of a pirate ship. As it turned out, the citizens of Seaport were very grateful that Flamebeard had been slaughtered. The pirate and his gang of surly men were a menace. Since Abraham vanquished Flamebeard, he also had rights to his ship and his men. He swore several pirates into his service. The others, loyal to Flamebeard, were imprisoned. Apparently, the Henchmen, accompanied by the sailors, could handle the sailing of the ship.

Flamebeard's galleon was named the *Sea Talon*. It was every bit a pirate ship if there ever was one. Grand in design, the ship had three masts and white sails with flame colors woven into the fabric. The Red Tunics hustled over the decks. They climbed the ratlines and managed the sails. The decks were scrubbed with mops and brushes. Everything was done under the orders of the elder Henchmen.

Back at Seaport, he'd sold the horses and wagons. The

Henchmen loaded up the frights and stuck them in the hold. That was Abraham's decision. No one questioned it, but no one gave him a pat on the back either. But in the past day, he'd slain a notorious criminal and a host of men, and now he had a galleon and all its treasures, plus Flamebeard's cutlass, to show for it. His fingers drummed on the railing.

*Wait until the king sees this.* For some strange reason, he felt good. *Whoever King Hector is.* He still couldn't picture the man's face.

Sticks brushed up against his arm. "Good morning, Captain."

"Good morning. I was beginning to think that all of you were avoiding me."

"Never. We've been busy manning the ship. It's no easy task to undertake, but it's all in good order now."

"I'll say. And we'll make it back to Kingsland much quicker. Tell me: why didn't we take a ship to begin with?"

"The frights didn't run on a ship. They fled on foot."

"Oh, I see. Sorry."

She showed him a puzzled look.

Abraham got the feeling that Ruger Slade wasn't a man who ever apologized for anything. He needed to bear that in mind.

The waters of the Sea of Troubles were choppy. Ahead of him was nothing but water. Behind him was the coast of Titanuus, a few miles away. He pointed west. "Do we have maps of what is out there?"

"Captain, there is nothing out there but the Elders. Only the boldest of fishermen travel beyond eyeshot of the coast."

"Why, will they fall off the edge?"

She tilted her head and gave him a perplexed look. Then that vanished, giving way to her normal, expressionless face. "No, the Elders will consume them."

He realized again that he should have known what she was talking about but didn't. But for some reason, he knew many other things that he hadn't before. He'd never sailed on a ship, but he knew what to call the three masts—the foremast, main mast, and mizzenmast—as well as the many decks—the main, forecastle, quarter, stern castle, charter, and poop. Belowdecks were the cargo hold, infirmary, brig, stores, and galley. He felt as though he'd been taken on a tour and was remembering everything.

He rested his elbow on the railing and said, "Let's go to my cabin to talk."

The captain's quarters was a twenty-by-twenty room with three windows in the back. A queen-sized bed was covered in linens and silks fit for a king. A small table for two was fastened to the floor for eating. A desk and chair sat against the wall. Two wardrobes and several wooden chests and strongboxes sat on the carpet-covered floor.

Sticks started undressing.

"No, I didn't bring you here for that," he said.

"Why else would you bring me here?"

"To talk."

She shrugged. "There isn't much else to do out at sea. You'll change your mind soon enough." She put her bandolier back over her shoulder then sat on the edge of the bed, crossed her legs, and put her hands on her knees. "I'm all yours."

Abraham knew what she meant. She was as frisky as he was and toying with him. In his new body, he found her hard to resist. Then he caught a glimpse of Jake's backpack on the bed among the pillows, and it brought him to his senses. He closed his eyes.

*It's not real. It's not real. It's not real. For God's sake, it's not real!*

Home. That was where he needed to be. He needed to be riding the lonely highways, living the life of a truck driver, and sorting his life out one day at a time. He took the position that whatever was going on wasn't real—it just felt like it. He decided to take the approach of a gamer. He was an avatar or a player. He'd have to ask questions to find answers about what he needed to do.

Was it like the computer games he'd played as a kid? Ask questions that were simple and easy. Find out what you can. Move up to the next level. Complete the mission. Find your way home again. He opened his eyes.

Sticks hadn't moved an inch. Her pretty eyes remained on his. "Seasick?"

"No." He sat down beside her. "Tell me about the Elders. Tell me about Titanuus. Tell me about this world."

"Your questions are very strange. I know that you are not the same, but you still fight like Ruger Slade. If you hadn't slain Flamebeard, I'd have been worried. The men were starting to doubt. I was too." She shook her head and grinned. "You tore up Flamebeard. That was a sight to see. No one will doubt you—at least, not for a while." She touched his cheek. "And I like the new you. The old you was an ass. I hope this one stays." She leaned toward him.

The skin of his neck heated up. The rocking of the ship cutting through the waters further stirred the desire within him. He kissed her. She kissed him. It didn't stop.

# 23

ABRAHAM LAY BESIDE STICKS, WHO WAS LEANING BACK AGAINST THE pillows, the sheets pulled up over her chest. With his head on the pillows, he stared at the cabin ceiling. Their impulsive, lustful act left him feeling ashamed of himself, but this time wasn't as bad as the last time.

*I'm sorry, Jenny. I couldn't control myself.*

Sticks's tomboyish good looks and enchanting figure were more than enough to break any man. He knew. He was used to hearing stories of sexual triumphs and failures in testosterone-filled locker rooms. He didn't figure he knew any man, single or married, who could turn down a woman like Sticks. And with his body and hers, that made the tryst all the more compelling. He still wasn't sure whether he was performing his own actions or the actions of Ruger Slade.

"Do you still want me to tell you about the Elders and Titanuus?"

"Huh...? Oh, yeah." His fingers pinched the top of the sheets to cover his chest, like a frightened kid listening to a scary bedtime story. "Go on."

"Give me a moment." She crossed the room to a bar mounted against the wall. She took a bottle of port from the rack below it. "May I?"

"Sure. It's all ours now."

She filled a glass goblet with the chocolate-colored port and sniffed the bouquet. "Flamebeard must have had a refined palate. Would you like a glass?"

He held up his hand. "No thanks."

She sat back down beside him. "Titanuus is the name of a slain celestial giant whose body formed our world. He battled through the cosmos, against Antonugus, the Star Slayer." She took a long sip and cradled the glass to her chest. "Here, on the waters of this world, they stood toe-to-toe, fighting for the destiny of the universe. Antonugus carried a sword made from star fire. Titanuus was no match for its power. Antonugus gravely wounded Titanuus. He stabbed him right in the heart. He chopped Titanuus's arms off and one of his legs. Titanuus fell into the waters of the deep, watching Antonugus take to the stars, singing in victory. He pumped blood into the waters, giving it new life as he died. That's how the world was formed. That is how the Elders were born."

"That's a captivating story," he said, thinking of the map he'd seen. It did resemble the body of a man with arms and a leg cut off. The top of Titanuus even featured a large bump that could be taken for a head. "Wouldn't that make this giant a thousand miles tall? It seems preposterous."

She shrugged. "There is no way to truly measure the largest or the smallest of anything."

"So, what happened to the arms and leg that was chopped off? Did they float away? Wouldn't they make islands or something like that?"

"The Elders ate them," she said.

"And the Elders are giant people?"

She shook her head. "No, they are sea monsters. Gods to some. They live far out in the sea. They swallow ships like this whole. That's why the ships never sail out of sight of the shoreline. They never come back."

He raised a brow. "Has anyone ever seen one of these sea monsters?"

"Yes. But that was eons ago. I will tell you this: ships that sail too far into the Sea of Trouble do not come back."

He made a quiet applause. "Yay." He didn't mean to be rude, but the story, though intriguing, was little more than a fairy tale told to frighten children. It was little different from the Greek or Norse myths he'd read as a boy. But to Sticks's credit, the monsters did seem bigger. He scratched his ear. "Well, thanks for telling me. Now everything is making a lot more sense." He rolled his eyes.

"Captain, I can sense your sarcasm. I assure you that my story is true. Everyone knows it."

Abraham slid out of bed and started putting his clothing back on. "I'm sure they all do believe." Putting his shirt on, he turned toward her. "Do you think it's possible that, farther out in the sea, is another land like this?"

Her forehead wrinkled. "No."

"I see." He tucked his shirt into his trousers and slid his boots on. At least he had a better knowledge of the world he was in. Now, he had no doubt it wasn't real, no matter how real it seemed. For example, his cabin was stuffy and had a musty smell. The featherbed was comfortable but the sheets smelled. Thinking about sleeping in them gave him the willies. He lifted the sheets and asked, "Can I get these cleaned?"

Sticks gracefully slid out of the bed toward the wardrobe. She opened the wardrobe double doors. A red coat hung inside, along with other shirts and trousers and a stack of linens and towels.

"I'll have a retainer reset your room," she said.

By *retainer*, she meant a Red Tunic. That's what they called them. He'd recently caught on to that. Apparently, he called them Red Tunics. As far as Abraham could tell, they were part squire and part fraternity pledge, but without all the fun. He had a lot of friends who lived in frat houses when he'd played college baseball for two years, during and after high school. He made the rounds, and the pledges would serve the brothers, hand and foot, at least when it came to cleaning the frat houses and serving the drinks.

As for the senior Henchmen, like Sticks and Horace, the retainers called them what they were, Henchmen—that or "sir." The retainers strived to become Henchmen, but Abraham got the impression that they were expendable.

He snapped his fingers, making a loud pop. "Ah, I get it."

Sticks gave him a curious look. "Get what?"

He didn't say it, but he thought of the red-shirted security officers from *Star Trek*. Every time they showed up, they died. The man before him, Eugene Drisk, must have had a sinister sense of humor or been a Trekkie.

"Nothing." He pulled his shirt open, revealing the brand of the king's crown. "As long as we are going to be at sea for a few more days, you might as well tell me about this."

# 24

STICKS PULLED HER SHIRT COLLAR DOWN AND OVER, SHOWING HER brand. As far as brands went, the skin was puffed up, but the detail, unlike most brands, was crisp. It didn't look like a burn or scar, much the way other brands did.

"All of the Henchmen wear the King's Brand. Not the tunics—they want to earn the brand. It's an honor. The adepts all have the brand. You really don't remember?"

"I can't say I do."

"You branded me. You branded all of us." She moved to the back side of the bed and stared out at the endless waters behind the window. "You seem to take pleasure in it. You were all smiles when you did me years ago."

"I'm not a nice man, am I?"

She started tying her hair into ponytails. "Are you going to let me speak freely? I don't want to be disrespectful and earn a whipping. Or be cast overboard like chum for the sharks."

"I've whipped you?"

Abraham prayed he wouldn't remember that. It seemed an unnecessary thing. The Henchmen were warriors, killers. They turned seasoned pirates into chop suey. No ordinary man would cross them after seeing that.

"I promise I won't whip you. I've never whipped anybody. Well, not in my world."

With her steady gaze on his, she said, "You are self-centered, arrogant, cruel, and malicious. You've killed your own men for speaking out against you. But they respect you even though our travels haven't been going so well. They are safer with you than without you. They don't have a choice, either way."

Abraham buckled on his sword belt. The boat rocked hard to the right. He danced a step back. Sticks grabbed hold of the headboard.

"Whoa! The floor's dancing." Spreading his legs out, he steadied himself.

They were definitely in a spot of choppy waters. Dark clouds now covered the sea as rain came down.

"If I branded all of you, then who branded me?"

"King Hector." Her shoulders swayed side to side with the jostling of the boat. "It's a great honor but not publicly known. You are marked for a reason. If you are captured, the enemy will see the mark. They will kill you or torture you. No, they will torture then kill you. That's why, at all costs, we avoid being captured. The mark is a death sentence even though it's a great honor to die in the service of the king. It's a better fate than what was already set aside for most of us."

"So the brand creates loyalty. That's interesting." He scratched the black whiskers on his chin. "We can't turn traitor because we'll be killed for it by the king or by the king's enemies. We are his property."

"Death before failure. We are all a living and breathing death sentence." She drank her wine. "The brand has powers too. It can stop a heart or summon a sky demon to anyone that deserts or is disloyal. It can bring luck, too."

"That's doesn't sound right," he said, rubbing his brand. "More stories to scare you. Besides, you said that the Henchmen were loyal to me."

"You, Horace, Vern, and Bearclaw have been together a very long time—before I met you, back when you were the old Ruger and not the new one that took over a few years ago." She finished off her port. "The king branded you, and you branded them. It's a longer story."

Even though thinking about it was grim, at least he had a clear understanding of what the brand was all about. He hoped it was another piece of the puzzle and that knowledge would lead him back to his world. He'd know who his troops were, too. The mark formed a brotherhood. All of them served the same king. They had the same mission. They were a team. He could relate to that. If there was one thing he understood, it was winning.

*The King's Brand. It sounds like the name of a cigarette company. Maybe I'll be able to use it in the real world one day.*

She finished braiding her ponytails and hung them over her shoulders. She approached him, touched his face, and asked, "Would you like a shave? You always liked it before. You'll want to look presentable for the king when the time comes."

"Do I shave me, or do you shave me?"

"Dominga shaves you. At least, that is your preference."

Of the ten Henchmen, he'd only gotten to know half of them. Seven were men. He knew Horace, Bearclaw, and Vern. The other four he hadn't become acquainted with. Three were women. He knew the faces of Sticks and Iris, but Dominga he didn't know. He remembered a few riders with their faces partly covered in cowls when he'd encountered them at first. He could see only their eyes. One was small, and he assumed it was a woman even though he could have been wrong.

"I'll wait," he said. "We still have a few days at sea, and I'm used to a fuller beard anyway."

"As you wish, Captain. Do you care if I move topside?"

"It's raining."

"I know, but I think you could use some time to yourself. I can send a retainer to set your bed."

He nodded. "No. Dismissed."

Without a word, Sticks departed.

Strangely, it felt natural to dismiss a woman he'd just slept with. The words came easy. Either he was getting used to becoming a captain, or the body he hosted was taking over. His fingertips tingled. He picked up Jake's backpack and hugged it tight and fell backward onto the bed.

*Lord, please tell me I'm not losing my mind.*

# 25

## The Past

ON A HOT AND HAZY DAY IN BRADENTON, FLORIDA, IN THE SPRING OF 2009, Abraham had recently signed a multimillion-dollar contract with the Pirates as their star pitcher. The Dominator, a name coined by his heated flock of fans, had come into his own. He pulled into the LECOM Field parking lot, driving a brand-new 2009 Chevy Kodiak truck with a smile as broad as the windshield.

Many of his teammates met him in the parking lot and checked out the new set of wheels. A lot of guys bought sports cars ranging from Ferraris to Porsches. Most of the bigger players could barely fit into the cramped cockpits of their European cars. Some of them were smart enough to buy a bigger Rolls-Royce or Mercedes. Abraham wanted to be different. He wanted big. He wanted roomy. He wanted American diesel. The Chevy Kodiak that Abraham rolled up in caught the attention of all of them.

The Kodiak was a vehicle true to its name. The midnight-black-edition turbodiesel king cab decked out in chrome made all the other cars look like kids' toys.

Buddy Parker, star outfielder for the Bucs, flicked up his black hand and whistled. "Woo-wee, now that's the perfect redneck vehicle. I'm going to get me one of them. I didn't even know they made 'em that big. No, I'm going to get two. Let me drive it."

"No, you have enough trouble keeping all four wheels of your cars on the road," Abraham said. "But when your Mercedes breaks down again, I'll be happy to tow you."

Buddy laughed.

He and Buddy had come into the league at the same time and hit it off pretty well. Buddy was from Alabama, a country boy raised on the farms, who knew more about running a farm than he did baseball. He talked about cows a lot but hated chickens. He had a five-hundred-acre ranch not far from his hometown. Once a year, he would have a massive team party and made the rookies milk the cows.

Jake hopped out the back door of the cab. The sandy-haired eight-year-old jumped up into Buddy's big hands. "Buddy! How many home runs are you going to hit this year?"

"One hundred," Buddy said. He always said that.

"That's impossible," Jake said. "Even Hank Aaron couldn't do that."

"No, but I'm going to try. You just watch and see. Buddy Parker and Abraham Jenkins are going to make some noise this season. This year, the P in *Pirates* stands for pennant!"

"Can I get a little help climbing out of here?"

Jenny asked. Abraham's wife climbed over from the passenger seat into the driver's. She wore a black Polo one-piece tennis dress that showed off her great tanned legs. Her light-brown hair was long, straight, and pulled behind her ears. A lot of people told her she looked like Diane Lane. Abraham told her she looked better.

Buddy set down Jake and hustled over to the truck door. "It would be my pleasure to help the most beautiful woman in Florida."

She let Buddy pick her up and set her down. She gave him a big hug and a kiss on the cheek. "Thanks, Buddy. My husband forgot to bring the fire-truck ladder."

Buddy tossed back his head and let out a gusty laugh that the entire parking lot could hear.

"It's not that high." Abraham pointed at the steps on the side. "You just have to step on these things, baby."

"I know dear, I just wanted Buddy to put his strong arms around me." She winked at Buddy.

Buddy kept on laughing and shaking his head. "Anytime. Anytime."

She walked over to Abraham, rose on tiptoe, and kissed him. "Just teasing."

"I know. But be careful. I'm not sure Buddy knows."

Jake grabbed Buddy's hands. "Come on. Take me to see the rest of the guys. I want to make fun of their errors and batting averages. Some of them really stunk last year. They need some motivation."

"You got it, kid." Buddy and Jake waved and walked away. "We ain't going to win no pennant if they are playing that way."

With her arms wrapped around Abraham's waist, Jenny asked, "So how am I supposed to park this thing at the shopping mall?"

"You aren't going to stay for practice?"

"Just teasing. I'm not going to spend all of *our* money yet. I'll wait until the end of the week."

"Just leave me enough to buy an airplane."

"I'll think about it."

He leaned down to kiss her perfect waiting lips.

*Knock! Knock! Knock!*

*Knock! Knock! Knock!*

Abraham's eyes snapped open. The dream from his past was

gone. He found himself staring up at the wooden ceiling of the *Sea Talon*'s captain's quarters and cradling Jake's backpack.

"Oh no."

Sticks entered the room, accompanied by Horace. Both of them were drenched.

Horace closed the door on the storming rain. "Pardon us, Captain, but we have a problem."

The ship rocked hard to the left, half rolling Abraham out of the bed. He set his feet on the floor, set the backpack down, and rose. "Don't tell me we're taking on water. Or we're lost." He wiped the saliva from his mouth. The dream must have put him in a very deep sleep. He didn't even remember feeling tired. "How long have I been asleep?"

"Hours," Sticks said.

Beyond the windows of the cabin were nothing but stormy seas and sheets of black rain.

"Is it still daytime?" he asked.

"Yes."

The boat rocked side to side.

He faced them and nonchalantly said, "Okay, tell me what has happened. And it better not be one of those sea-monster stories. I've been in the belly of a tunnel, now of a ship, and I don't want to wind up in a fish belly like Jonah."

"Who is Jonah, sir?" Horace asked.

"Never mind. Just tell me what happened this time."

"It's the frights, Captain. They've escaped," Sticks said. "And two of your men are dead."

# 26

HARD RAIN HAD SOAKED ABRAHAM HEAD TO TOE BY THE TIME HE made it from his quarters belowdecks. The brig was located two levels below his cabin. It was an empty jail cell, made from iron bars that the rich sea-salt air had crusted over. Two Red Tunics lay outside the cell in pools of their own blood. Using a lantern for light, he bent over for a closer look. Their throats were torn open. They looked like an animal had attacked them.

The ship rocked.

Abraham caught one of the support beams, steadied himself, and stood up. "How could the frights have gotten out of there?"

The brig's door had a simple lock-and-key mechanism, and it wasn't damaged. He saw no sign of the key either.

"Who has the key?"

Horace pulled a key out of his pocket. "I have this one. Vern has the other. He's searching for the witches. These are the only keys that I'm aware of. And no one was in the brig when we boarded. The keys were inside the brig, Captain."

"Bring Vern down here, and find those witches," Abraham

said. "There isn't any place to go on this ship. How hard could it be for them to hide? I want the ship searched from belly to mast."

"Aye, Captain." Horace hustled out of the room. His big feet pounded topside up the steps.

"This isn't what we needed. This stinks," he told Sticks, looking for some sort of affirmation. "Who in their right mind would have let the witches out?"

"The frights practice crafty ways of evil. They can beguile the mind if one is not careful. They should have been gagged," she said. "Women's words can be deadly."

"They can say all they want, but they can't make a key for the lock out of thin air." He stepped into the cell and looked for anything out of the ordinary. The hold was barren, free of any cots, chairs, or blankets. "Didn't they have shackles on?"

"Yes. But Vern took them off. He said if the ship sank, we didn't want to lose our prisoners to the sea. They'd need to swim."

"We aren't going to sink." The ship bucked up on a wave and crashed down again. Abraham corrected himself. "We probably won't sink." He made a disgusted look. The creepy frights on the loose opened up a nest of butterflies in his stomach. "If they were in shackles, we should be able to hear them from miles away. And this is a boat. I'm pretty sure chains on wood make a very noticeable sound."

"We'll find them, Captain."

"Will you quit calling me Captain when no one else is around!"

"Yes, Cap—" She closed her mouth.

Inspecting the lock, he asked, "How dangerous are these frights? I know a sword can take them, but they are strong as a wildcat. What do they do?"

"Evil magic," she said.

"Great." Abraham wasn't really sure what he was searching for in the cell. The danger was out of the cell, not in. But after having watched every episode of *CSI* twice, he felt as though a part of him knew what it was doing. *Who do I think I am?* CSI Titanuus. *What kind of trace am I looking for?*

Horace returned with Vern. Horace had the younger warrior by the nape of the neck. "Here he is, Captain."

"Where's your key, Vern?" he asked.

"It was stolen, Captain. I swear it." Vern spoke with desperation. The haughtiness he usually carried was gone. "The moment I heard the frights were out, I checked. It was gone. But I swear on my sword I didn't let them out." He looked down at the sword on Abraham's hip. "I swear it!"

Horace shook the man. "Quit whining like a dog. You're a Henchman!"

Vern clammed up.

It became perfectly clear by the tension in the quarters that the old captain would have killed Vern without a word.

Abraham dropped his hand to his hilt. "Vern, where is the key?"

"I swear I don't know. Captain." He blinked rapidly. "I'll help you find them."

Abraham squeezed his hilt. Part of him wanted to cut Vern down, but that part wasn't him. It was Ruger Slade, possibly taking control of him. He moved out of the cell. "Horace, lock him inside. And don't lose the key."

Horace closed Vern inside the brig. He twisted the key in the lock and tucked the key inside his tunic.

A pair of dark figures entered the tight quarters, Tark and Cudgel. They were a pair of well-built black men with light eyes that gave them a ghostly look. Tark had a beard, and Cudgel was bald. They wore tunics over the chain mail of the Henchmen. Stooped over, the lengthy Tark held out sets of shackles and irons. "We found these, Captain. Up on the poop deck. Didn't see the frights, but we'll find them. We always find them."

Tark and Cudgel were the company's scouts that rode out in front. Abraham didn't remember meeting them before, but he knew exactly who they were the moment they showed up. They were brothers but not twins. He wasn't sure, but Tark appeared to be the older, judging by the modest gray follicles in his hair and beard. They looked heavier in their wet armor but had sleek, wiry frames underneath. They carried long swords and daggers like the others.

Abraham cast a backward glance at Vern.

"I didn't even have the keys to the shackles. The retainers had them," Vern said.

Cudgel wiped the water from his face and asked, "What are your orders, Captain?"

Abraham had to think about it. Tracking down murdering witches was a new experience. Commanding a bunch of strangers who appeared to be a bunch of natural-born killers was a new adventure too. He thought of the only thing he could do. When the team had a problem, they would all gather in the locker room. "I want every Red Tunic and Henchman topside now!"

# 27

The company lined up in the torrential sheets of rain. The only persons not in the lineup were Horace and Vern. He stood on deck, controlling the rudders from the ship's wheel. Every other man and woman stood on the main deck, hip to hip, at parade rest with their hands behind their back. The Henchmen formed the first row. The Red Tunics made up the second.

Bearclaw anchored the line of Henchmen. Sticks was next, followed by Iris, Tark, and Cudgel. Beside Cudgel was a smallish woman with her face wrapped up in a cowl. Abraham pulled the cowl down around the woman's neck and looked into the very pretty face of a petite black woman. Her kinky locks of hair rested on her shoulders. Her soothing light-blue eyes were captivating. That was Dominga, an out-of-place beauty, and he couldn't blame her for covering up.

With the hard rains drenching his face, he said, "I'm going to need a shave later."

Dominga nodded. He found it refreshing that she didn't call him *Captain*. He moved in front of the last two Henchmen and stood between them.

*How old are these guys?*

The last two men in the row were a pair of surly graybeards. He looked down at them. Neither man looked fit enough to wear the armor or swing a sword. Their unkempt beards enhanced their shabby appearance. They could have passed for Nick Nolte from *Down and Out in Beverly Hills* on his worst day.

Abraham eyeballed both of them. "Have you seen any witches?"

The two Henchmen spoke at the same time. "Nay, Captain."

Each man had a sword strapped to his back. Around their waists were assortments of pouches, purses, small daggers, and knives. The looked like homeless soldiers. Suddenly, Abraham recalled both of their names: Apollo and Prospero. The noble names fit the soggy, bearded faces like lipstick on a pig. He shook his head and walked to the back row.

A wave crashed over the starboard side of the craft, soaking every boot above the toes. The Red Tunics and pirates stood firm.

Abraham marched by each and every one of them. They were a motley group, tall and short, long haired, short haired, men and women. They wore swords and hatchets fit for a hero of a hermit's village. The best thing they had going on for themselves were the red tunics they wore like a badge of honor. He looked a young woman dead in the eye. Her unkempt hair hung over her pie-shaped freckled face. She had big dimples in her cheeks.

"Do you know why your tunic's red?" he shouted above the winds.

"Aye, Captain. To hide my blood from my enemies!" she brazenly shouted back.

"No." He touched her chest. "It's to make you easier to see than me!"

The row of Henchmen chuckled in the wind.

"Stop laughing," he ordered. "One of you... One of us, perhaps two, is a traitor. I aim to find out who it is and make an example of them." He studied the face of every man and woman in the ranks, hoping he'd pick up on something.

The hardened company didn't bat an eye. His efforts were looking like a waste of time. In front of the group, as time passed, he started to feel silly. He needed to make an impression on them. He needed to shake them up. He drew his sword. "I know who it is. With my sword, I'll kill who it is unless I get a confession."

Heads turned side to side. Some daring looks were cast toward Abraham.

He walked behind the retainers and, one by one, laid his sword on their shoulders. "Duck. Duck. Duck. Duck." At that moment in time, Abraham couldn't explain himself. He was caught up in it. Like a superhero whose identity transformed the moment he donned a costume or screamed "*Thundercats*" or "*Shazam*," he was in it. "Duck. Duck. Duck."

*It's not real. It's a game. Or a figment of my imagination. Just kill one of them. See what happens. After all, you are a pirate.*

He stood behind Apollo with his sword pressed against the man's back. "Tell me, Apollo, did you free the frights?"

"No, Captain," the man said fearlessly.

"Do you know who did?"

"No, Captain."

"You know what, Apollo? I think you are lying. And what's the penalty for lying?"

"Dying, Captain," Apollo replied.

With a dark glimmer in his eye, Abraham said, "That's right. Apollo never lies to the Captain."

"Gurk!"

Abraham twisted around. One of the Red Tunics standing behind him had the front end of a harpoon sticking out of his chest. A sinister shriek-cackle from the depths of hell erupted from behind the dying man.

The retainer crumpled onto the deck. Behind him, a thin-lipped, red-eyed witch had a wooden smile on her face. "Ship sail. Ship wreck. Ship burn above the deck," she said.

Abraham buried his sword hilt-deep in the witch's chest.

Her eyelids fluttered, and she repeated the same words again: "Ship sail. Ship wreck. Ship burn above the deck!" Her pink-red eyes locked on Abraham's. In a dying gesture, she reached for his face and said, "Kingsland is doomed, otherworlder. You cannot save it! The king is d—"

*Crack!* Bearclaw split the witch's head with his axe. Ripping it out of her skull, he said, "You can't let them talk so much." He pointed upward.

The rain stopped. The wind stopped blowing.

Abraham lifted his gaze. The top of the ship's center mast was burning like a torch.

# 28

LIKE A GIANT'S MATCH, THE MAIN MAST BURNED. THE FLICKERING flames jumped onto the sails. The fire wasn't normal, as men would know it. The flames were a mix of blue, green, and red that crackled and hissed with a life of their own.

"There, Captain!" Bearclaw pointed at the mast.

Halfway up, the last of the frights clung to the wood. Vinelike tendrils jutted out of her body, making for additional appendages. Her hands and feet became sharp wooden claws. The flames in her eyes were the same as the burning mast's.

"Get the crossbows!" Bearclaw yelled.

"Red Tunics! Get the lifeboat in the water before this ship turns to a pillar of fire!" Abraham ordered.

The lifeboat sat in the middle of the main deck. The retainers scrambled into action.

"Where's my crossbow?" Abraham shouted.

"Coming!" Sticks said. She darted away and disappeared belowdecks.

Above, with a radiant pink glowing in her eyes, the fright

chanted. The fires spread. The rain-soaked ship sails began to smoke. The flames ate the fabric.

Flatfooted, Abraham gaped at the bizarre occurrence. The bony witch had created a catastrophe. Sticks reappeared and put his crossbow in his hands. He took aim at the hag on the center mast and fired.

The bolt zipped through the air right on target. The hag slipped around the mast like a scurrying insect, and the bolt buried itself in the large post.

"Bring her down! I want her alive!"

Bearclaw and Tark shot bolts from their crossbows. Both of them missed and started reloading.

"She is quick!" Bearclaw said.

The flames consumed everything they touched.

The Red Tunics started to lower the lifeboat into the water.

Abraham loaded another bolt into his crossbow. Eyeing the hag, he moved underneath her and aimed. He squeezed the trigger, and the bolt launched straight and true. The hag slipped around the post again, and the bolt hit the wood with another *thunk*.

"Stand still, you freaky cockroach!"

Bearclaw and Tark shot again and missed. They reloaded. So did Abraham.

Apollo and Prospero climbed up the ratlines toward the fright. Three retainers followed them up the ropes, making a line that trailed behind them. The passed spears up to the surly Henchmen. Prospero stabbed the witch in the leg, and she howled like a banshee.

"She bleeds! She'll die!" Prospero roared. Off-balance and clinging to the ropes, he poked at the hag, who nestled on the other side of the post. She had nowhere to go with the flames roaring several feet above her head and working their way down.

"Bearclaw! Tark! I'll shoot first, forcing her left or right. You have to nail her after that," Abraham said.

They nodded.

He locked his eyes on the hag latched to the center mast. She might dodge one bolt, but she couldn't avoid three of them. They created a half circle around the mast. Abraham stood in the middle, took aim, and fired. The fright scuttled left.

Bearclaw fired, and the bolt sailed true, hitting her right through the chest. She flung her arms outward. Tark slid around the pole and fired. His dead-on shot ripped through her skull, passing through one side and out of the other. She cackled maniacally. In a single bound, the witch woman leapt like a spider from the main mast back to the mizzenmast.

Abraham rushed toward the mizzen and bounded up the steps. By the time he got there, Sticks, Dominga, and Cudgel had climbed the mast using pairs of heavy gloves. They engaged the fright. The witch's tendrils coiled around their arms and legs. Sticks had a vinelike tendril around her neck. With one hand, the fierce woman clung to the witch's hair. With her other hand, she stabbed with a dagger.

With Sticks, Dominga, and Cudgel collapsing in on her, she could not withstand the brutal assault. The Henchmen, using small knives and daggers, chopped the hag away from the mast. The witch tumbled through the air and hit the planks, unmoving. The bold Henchmen climbed down with clawed animal skins on their hands, covering their fingers.

"Nice gloves," Abraham said.

The Henchmen huddled over the dead witch. The magic flames extinguished, but the damage was done. The tops of the masts were gone. All the sails on the main mast had been either chewed up by the flames or fully consumed.

Sticks cleaned her dagger off on the dead witch's clothing. She sheathed it and said, "The king won't like this. He wanted them alive."

"At least we have the bodies," Abraham said.

"They'll rot before we make it to Kingsland. No one will recognize what is left. The frights soil the earth from where they came," she replied.

"Toss them overboard, then," he said.

"We'll handle it, Captain," Cudgel said. He and Dominga hauled the body down the stairs and tossed it into the sea.

Abraham found himself alone on the sterncastle deck with Sticks. "Seeing you climb up that pole and taking it to the witch was incredible. This is one brave crew."

"Bravery won't do us any good now," she said. "Our mission has failed, and we drift further out to sea."

# 29

THE *SEA TALON* DROPPED ANCHOR. AT LEAST FOR THE TIME BEING, they weren't going anywhere. Abraham shouldn't have any sea monsters to worry about, either. He looked over the bow. The Red Tunics had the lifeboat in the water, ready to go. The shoreline was so far away he could barely see it. The sudden storm had taken them farther out than they were. He had decisions to make.

*What in the heck do I know about sailing, anyway?*

The center mast was toast. The sails on the other two masts were burned.

"What do you think, Horace?" he asked the meaty brute standing to his left.

Sticks stood to his right, watching the retainers climb back onto the main deck.

"The lifeboat will get us back to shore in a couple of trips. But the sails will function once we sew them up and catch wind again. It will be slower going, but it will do."

"Great. We're sitting ducks in the meantime."

"Pardon, sir?" Horace said.

"Nothing." Abraham changed course. "Is Vern still secured?"

"Aye, and whining like a hound. Permission to gag him."

"No. Whiny or not, I'm not so sure that he is to blame for all of this. But someone is, and they are still on this ship, aside from the Red Tunics that died. Take a head count. I want to make sure we aren't missing anyone else. Including me."

"Aye." Horace lumbered away.

With her elbows resting on the rails of the bow and her eyes cast toward the sea, Sticks asked, "Were you going to kill Apollo?"

"I don't know. I felt that was what my old self would have done. Am I right?"

"You've killed Henchmen and retainers before, so it was a good acting job. I was convinced you would go through with it."

"Well, don't expect mercy from me all of the time. I have a feeling I'll do things that are unpredictable."

"You're doing a fine job keeping the men on their toes. That's what matters most. Keep taking command. You have a knack for it."

That was easy for her to say. As for him, he didn't have a clue if what he was doing was right or wrong. He just made the best decision he could think of at the time. With no one else taking charge, he didn't have a choice. His fingers drummed on the ship's railing. He had a half smile on his face, remembering when he'd played Dungeons & Dragons. He and his friends confronted a hill giant. They all had different ideas on how to kill it. They emptied the toolbox, trying to bring the ten-foot brute down. Joe wanted to keep the giant alive so he could enslave it. Troy's goal was to decapitate it and mount the head on his war wagon. Tiffany ended up levitating the giant while Arley shot lightning bolts at it.

While all of that was going on, Alvin and Laid sneaked into the giant's lair and stole the treasure and hid it from the other party members. They were all so mad at one another that no one spoke or played again for months. In a way, what was going on now wasn't much different. Abraham made the best decisions he could, given the situation. He couldn't have cared less about treasure. He only wanted to wake up in his bed or truck cab again.

The black brothers, Tark and Cudgel, approached. With sweat dripping down his bald head, Cudgel said, "Captain, I think we have enough material to make sails. The boat might move at a crawl, but it will move."

"How long?" he asked.

"At least a day, maybe sooner."

"Make it so," he said. *Oh great, now who am I? Captain Picard?* His thoughts drifted to the other task at hand. *Who let the frights free? Who are the traitors among us?* All the Henchmen fought their guts out against the sea frights. They risked their necks to save the ship. He felt guilty for considering killing Apollo. Of course, the man couldn't be a real person anyway. It wasn't possible, so it didn't make any difference. But the old warrior had proved that his salt was as worthy as any. He fought without fear and with fire in his eyes.

Horace came back. "Ten Henchmen. One captain. Seventeen retainers. Twenty-eight. We started with thirty-one. Three retainers slain since we took the ship."

Abraham's past knowledge blossomed. He remembered traveling with a much larger group, as Sticks had suggested earlier in their travels. They'd had twenty Henchmen, forty retainers, and himself. Sixty was a large group. Now, they were less than half of that.

*I can't believe we've lost so many. No wonder they don't care for me. I'm getting them all killed.*

"That will be all, Horace. See to it that all our efforts are on the sails. I want to be sailing in the morning."

Horace departed.

For the rest of the day, the Henchmen and retainers went about their business as though they'd sailed a thousand times before. Abraham followed along with just about everything that everyone did. The sun set. A fog rolled in, and the sea vanished underneath the floating cloud.

He slept a lonely, restless sleep, tossing and turning between the dusk and the dawn. Sticks didn't stay with him. He wanted her there but didn't. Perhaps that was what made him so restless—either that or the horror he'd experienced the last few days: pirates, witches, and blood. The gruesome scenes appeared in his dreams, twisting them into nightmares. He wrestled internally with the events that he'd never seen or experienced before, things he'd done with the body that was not his own. Who was the man in Ruger Slade's body before him? He had a corrupted mind and dangerous intellect. That was one cruel, self-serving bastard. *I don't want to become that guy. I've got to be me.*

Abraham crawled out of bed and swung his feet to the floor. He rubbed his puffy eyes and yawned. He looked out the back window. The fog had lifted, and the sun shone on the sea. It shone on the sea and something else—ships full of stalwart, sullen-eyed, bare-chested men.

# 30

ABRAHAM JUMPED INTO HIS GEAR. HE HEADED TOPSIDE AND MET UP with Horace, Bearclaw, and Sticks on the top deck. Two small galleys were there, with long oars in the water and no sails, at the fore and aft of the ship.

Buckling on his sword belt, he asked, "Who are they?"

"Buccaneers," Horace said.

"Well, if they are Tampa Bay Buccaneers, they shouldn't be a problem." He smiled.

No one else did. The rest of the company crowded the fore and aft of the ship from the lower decks.

"I take it that these buccaneers aren't here to help?"

"No, those oarsmen are the same as the vicious looters in Flamebeard's gang but worse," Horace said.

Abraham made his way to the back rail. The galley there had thirty strapping men sitting at the oars. Their skin was bronzed by long hours in the sun. They had red-and-white war paint all over their bodies and not a friendly face among them. At the fore of the ship, only one man stood. He had a long red-and-black braided ponytail that started on the top of his head and ran down the length of his back. The rest of his head was bald. He wasn't a big man but was built more like a middleweight boxer, and he carried a cutlass on his hip. No war paint was on him.

Abraham put his hands on the rail and asked, "Can I help you?"

"I am Totem, chosen leader of the Sea Savages," said the man with the ponytail. He gestured at the *Sea Talon* with his hand and spoke slowly, like an Indian from poorly done cowboy movies. "You sail a fine ship. It is a gift to us, from the Elders. We will take this gift. You will be our prisoners. You will be our feast." His smile showed a mouth full of teeth filed down to a point. He clapped his hands, and all the men behind the oars bared their teeth. "Give yourself up. We are hungry."

Abraham lifted a finger. "Uh, could you hold on a second, eh, Totem? Oh, and by the way, I am… Ruger. I'll be right back." He turned to his company. "Are they buccaneers or sea savages?"

"The same. We call them buccaneers, and they call themselves sea savages," Horace said. "They aren't very big. We can take them."

"No, but there are sixty of them, and I don't want to lose any more men," he said.

With a wary look, Bearclaw said, "That never stopped you before, Captain."

Whereas the Henchmen hadn't said much of anything at all before, now they'd become bolder—either that, or they loosened up.

Not sure which, Abraham said, "Sounds like that tongue of yours has a mind of its own. I'd hate to think that with your own mind, you questioned your captain."

Bearclaw's chin sank into his neck. "No, sir."

"Go to my quarters and fetch me one of Flamebeard's chests."

"Aye, Captain." Horace hustled away. He returned in a minute with a heavy wooden chest.

"Follow me," Abraham said. He moved to the back of the boat, looked down at the buccaneer, and said, "Totem, I think you have it all wrong. You see, I've spoken with the Elders, and they told me that you are supposed to pick up your gift." He looked at Horace. "Open the chest and show it to him."

"But Captain—"

Abraham gave him a hard look.

"Aye." Horace showed Totem the chest.

Totem shuffled backward. He stomped his boots on the deck, threw his head back, and let out a wild shriek. The sea savages jumped up on their benches with spears in hand and pounded the shafts on their seats.

"Huntah! Huntah! Huntah! Huntah!" they chanted. The same fully aroused cry went up from the other galley. "Huntah! Huntah! Huntah!"

Totem stopped screaming and lifted his sword in the air. "We accept the Elder gift!"

# 31

After three more days of sailing, they made it to King's Bay without incident. King's Bay was the water north of King's Foot on the west shoreline. They docked the ship at one of the major port cities that ran along the leagues of coastland hugging the huge bay. They had no issues docking the *Sea Talon* though many eyes widened upon its arrival. Since they didn't bear the banners of the king's enemies in Tiotan and Bolg and paid the port fees, they had no issues with the king's port authority. Only those who didn't behave themselves in Kingsland had problems.

Abraham couldn't have been happier to be on land again. As a matter of fact, he got rooms for everyone at the seaside city called Swain. It was very much like the pictures he'd seen of Mediterranean cities that crowded the southern Greek and European shores. The buildings were made from big blocks of whitewashed stone. The rooftops were colorful. Seabirds squawked in the air and from lofty perches on the roofing, made from clay tiles.

The food and wine was good, and the people, who wore colorful, loose-fitting shirts, trousers, or robes, were friendly. He filled himself with sweet wine and food and retired alone in his room for the evening. It was a quaint room, ten feet by ten feet, with a bed, strongbox, and a long table against the wall with two candles on the tabletop beside an open window.

With a lot on his mind, he stared out his small cottage window overlooking the docks. Early evening had come, and the massive docks were a hive of activity. Sailors and soldiers were there in full armor. More big ships, galleons, brigandines, and galleys were there. Some were merchant ships, and the others were from the king's war fleet. Abraham didn't know how he understood all of that, but he did. All of it was vaguely familiar to him. The king's banners flapped from posts in the streets and on the top masts of the ships. One huge flag was mounted a hundred feet high on a small island of its own, like a memorial, between the docks. He couldn't take his eyes off the silky banner waving in the winds.

The king's banner was a flat golden lion head wearing a crown with six horns, with the white feathery wings of a bird for ears, on a royal-blue background. The crown on the lion's head brought back childhood memories. Abraham thought of the Cowardly Lion in *The Wizard of Oz* and King Moonracer from the Island of Misfit Toys.

*This can't be real.*

The seafaring citizens delighted themselves at the night festivals and ceremonies of lights going on. Colorful paper lanterns fueled by candlelight floated into the sky as in a Chinese festival. The people were a healthy mix of men and women, not so much different from home. It might as well have been a regatta at Three Rivers back in Pittsburgh but without the sternwheelers. Exhausted, he closed his shutters, took off his gear, and lay down in the bed. As soon as his head hit the down-filled pillow, he was fast asleep.

*Knock. Knock. Knock.*

Abraham opened his eyes. One eye was buried in his pillow. Bright daylight shone through the cracks of the shutters and onto his face. The bustling of commerce could be heard on the outside docks. The seabirds were squawking. The waves crashed against the shoreline and rattled the docks. That was the first night he'd slept through. No dreams. No disturbances. That would have been great, except for one thing. He was still in Titanuus. He rolled up and put his bare feet on the floor.

"Come in."

Sticks entered the room with a bundle of clothes. She closed the door behind herself. "You should have locked your door."

"I didn't realize it had a lock." He stretched his arms high and yawned. His body was alert and ready to go. "I slept like a baby. Must have been the wine."

"Swain is well-known for being a great place for rest despite the heavy activity. They say that the King's Bay is blessed. The sea wind caresses us all like babies."

"So I take it that you slept well too?"

She unfolded a cotton shirt, flapped it once in the air, and tossed it to him. "I don't sleep as well alone as I do with you."

"Sorry. I just needed a night to myself." He slid the shirt on then caught the clean trousers she threw at him. "We aren't engaged or anything, are we?"

She cocked her head. "Engaged? No. People like us don't get engaged. That's for royalty. We aren't royalty."

He stood up and slipped into his trousers. He grabbed his belt, which hung from the bedpost, and fastened it through the loops. He wondered when belt loops had been invented. He stuck his finger through the loops. "Do all pants have these?"

"No, you had a tailor sew them in. Your preference."

He rubbed his jaw. *Interesting.*

*Knock. Knock. Knock.*

Sticks opened the door. Dominga entered. The petite black woman with very pretty eyes carried in a bowl of water and set it on the table. She had a towel around her neck and a straight razor in her free hand. She smiled at him. "Are you ready for your shave, Captain?"

"I guess."

"You'll need to take that shirt off," she said.

"But I just put it on."

Dominga whispered in Sticks's ear. The expressionless Sticks lifted a brow.

"What?" he asked.

"We need to get you cleaned up." Sticks helped him out of his shirt.

"Why the sudden change?" he said.

She tossed the shirt onto the bed and said, "Because the King's Guardians have arrived."

# 32

FROM HIS WINDOW, ABRAHAM COULD SEE KNIGHTS IN SHINING armor riding on horseback in the streets. He counted twenty in all, in columns of two. Each of them wore a full suit of glistening full-plate armor. Their full helmets were fashioned like lion faces, each with a plume of lion hair at the top. The horses moved at a slow trot as they pranced down the stone road. They carried the banner of the king on a flagpole in the front and in the back.

Abraham swallowed. The King's Guardians were a formidable group who rode tall in the saddles and carried an air of superiority about them. The citizens that stood in the streets quickly hustled out of the oncoming horses' pathway. Some of them cheered the knights and applauded, but not all.

A group of miscreants dashed into the streets with their hands loaded up with rotting food and fish. The gangly group started hurling the waste at the knights. The filthy muck splattered on the King's Guardians' shiny armor.

The rabble-rousers chanted, "Death to the king! Death to the king!"

The horses came to a halt. The lead knights' helmets turned

toward the rank assailants. The miscreants hurled more foul scraps and shouted curses. The knights in the front row spurred their white horses, and the gallant beasts charged forward.

The miscreants couldn't hide their shock-filled faces. A raw-boned man beat his chest and screamed at the charging knights. The rest of them scrambled away.

The first knight trampled the miscreant standing in his path. The second knight ran down another man. The merciless guardians chased down and trampled four more troublesome people though the streets and returned to their ranks. Not one citizen stood within fifty feet of the knights after that.

Crammed in the window beside Abraham, Dominga said, "That's what those dirty little lawbreakers get."

"The King's Guardians don't take any crap from anybody, do they?" Abraham said.

"No. An assault on his men is an assault on the crown itself," Sticks said.

The train of knights started riding out of town.

"Dominga, get him shaved. We don't want to keep the King's Guardians waiting."

Dominga gave Abraham a quick shave and quietly departed, leaving him in the room alone with Sticks.

With an arched brow, he said, "So I'm supposed to meet up with the King's Guardians, and they escort me to him."

"Yes, but with a great deal more discretion." She ran her fingers over his smooth face with a very soft touch. "The arrival of the King's Guardians is the way the king is letting you know that he knows you are here."

"How could he know that?"

"The king has eyes and ears everywhere. We are a part of that body. The moment we docked, I'm certain a rider or a pigeon delivered the message."

"I didn't think anyone knew who we were," he said.

"The king's allies do. I'd assume some of the king's enemies, too. Either way, the king is expecting you. May the king find favor with you, Ruger Slade." She gave him a goodbye kiss on the cheek and moved away.

He grabbed her hands. "Wait, aren't you coming?"

"There is a different path for the rest of us. If all works out, we'll meet you back at the Stronghold, the same as we always do. If not, it's been a pleasure serving the crown with you." She pulled free of his grip. "Goodbye."

Like a ghost, Sticks vanished on the other side of the door. Abraham sat quietly on his bed, scratching his head. *What in the world is going on now?* Sticks was the only person he could talk to. Now, she was gone. He jumped up and opened the door to see no sign of anyone in the hallway. He went back into the room, buckled on his sword, slung Jake's pack over his shoulders, and went down the steps to the main tavern floor. He expected to see the Henchmen and the Red Tunics having breakfast. Instead, the tavern was empty of any occupants—no serving girls at the tables and no bartender behind the bar. It was like an abandoned saloon in a ghost town but without all the dust.

Abraham made his way down the staircase. The boards groaned underneath his feet. He stopped at the bottom of the steps on the main floor. His nostrils flared. The smell of food cooking in the kitchen wafted through the room, but he still saw no sign of anyone. He wandered into the middle of the room.

Eyes narrowed, he said, "Hello?" The nape hairs on his neck rose. His hand fell to his pommel. He turned back toward the staircase.

Underneath the staircase was a small round table he had missed. A man was sitting in the chair behind the table with a long sword lying on top of it. He wore a traveling cloak with a silk collar. Black leather gloves covered his hands. He had the striking features of a nobleman, feathery black hair and a clean shave, but a white scar ran from his bottom lip to his chin. He had a scowl on his face.

"Feeling edgy, Ruger?" the man asked. He shoved the table back and stood. The man was lean, as tall as Abraham, and wearing a coat of blackened chain mail underneath his cloak. He picked up his long sword. The weapon was as well crafted as Black Bane. A lion head was fashioned on the pommel. He picked up his sword and walked toward Abraham, cutting the weapon's tip across the grime-stained planks of the floor. "I've been waiting for this a long time."

## 33

"Go ahead, Ruger," the man said. "Slide out that steel and see what happens. There's nothing I'd rather do than put your head on my father's platter."

Abraham's fingertips needled the handle of Black Bane. The contempt in the man's dark eyes clearly showed that they knew each other. He just needed a name. It was on the tip of his tongue, but he couldn't retrieve it.

He stalled. "I think we both know that if I drew, not only would I not be dead, but you would be dead."

"Puh," the man said. With a fine swordsman's grace, he slid his sword into his scabbard. "Father will have your head soon enough. Let's go."

*Father*. The man had said it twice. That implied he was King Hector's son. A lightbulb memory moment flashed in his mind. This man was King Hector's son, Lewis. Lewis had a long history with the Henchmen too. He hated them. He hated everyone who was not royalty. A new tide of information flowed though Abraham's brain. He closed his eyes and shook his head. He staggered to the bar as a migraine came on.

"What is the matter, goat lover? Are you having a spasm? That's what happens when you are in the presence of greatness," Lewis said.

With spots flashing in his eyes, he said, "I'm fine. But apparently, you aren't doing so well if the king sent you to greet me. What did you do this time, Lewis? Get caught screwing in the stables?"

Lewis sneered. "Watch your tongue, dog. Besides, I'd never be caught dead with some barefoot milkmaid like you."

"I wasn't talking about a milkmaid. What I was talking about has hooves, not toes."

Lewis slapped his hand hard on Abraham's shoulder. "Oh, Ruger," he said mirthfully, "the time will soon come when I'll see you gutted open or hanged. We'll see what clever words you have to say then. But in the meantime, you should watch your words, Henchman." He patted Ruger's face with his hand. "Come on, now. Let's get on the journey. I can't wait to hear all the details of your latest plunder."

Thanks to the new flood of memories, he was able to put more pieces of the strange world together. Lewis was one of King Hector's children. He was also the commander of the King's Guardians. He wouldn't be in that role if he wasn't worthy. Lewis was a knight with great expertise, as good as any.

Lewis also detested anyone not of royal blood. That was why no commoners were in the room. That was why the King's Guardians didn't hesitate to trample unruly peasants either. He had a very cavalier attitude, and so did his men. That was a big reason that he hated the Henchmen. It was a big reason that everyone who wasn't royal hated him. He was a grade-A spoiled jerk, but he could back it up.

Abraham stood up straight, looked him in the eyes, and said, "Lead the way, Guardian Commander."

Lewis snorted. He led them through the back, where two white stallions waited. The horses had the King's Brand on their left hindquarters. It was the type of crown that Abraham had. They climbed into the saddle and rode out of town. This was customarily what Ruger Slade did at the end of all his missions. At some point, he'd be escorted back to the king's castle, known as the House of Steel.

The show of the King's Guardians served as a distraction. The knights routinely made their rounds to the cities in Kingsland. No one knew when they were coming or going. Sometimes they escorted the Henchmen, and sometimes it was someone else. The king could send anyone he wanted—clerics, mages, spies, or merchants. One way or the other, once the Henchmen made it back to Kingsland, the King would know they were there. Only beyond his borders did he have no control.

In Kingsland, all roads led to the House of Steel. The road they were on had ankle-deep wagon ruts in some places. The sprawling countryside was rich in tall grasses and wildflowers that spanned as far as the eye could see. Rich farmland and cottages were spread throughout the territory. After an hour of riding out of town on a stifling day, they caught up with the King's Guardians and continued to ride behind them.

After a few more hours, Lewis—dabbing his forehead with a satin handkerchief—broke his silence. "Your mission was to return with several frights, and you didn't return with any." He huffed a laugh. "And now, my father's patience has run out. This latest failure will be catastrophic for you and your hapless men. Frankly, I'm glad to see it over with. I never understood why my father chose a rogue like you to begin with."

Abraham didn't reply.

"That's it. No clever remarks," Lewis added. "Did a cat catch your twisted tongue?"

Abraham thumbed the sweat from his brow and said, "I'll tell the king I did my best. If he doesn't like it, I guess I'll get what's coming to me."

"You'll get the guillotine. That's what you'll get. All of you!" Lewis tossed his head back in laughter. "Oh, how I hope to see it."

"If you think that you could do so much better, then why didn't the king send you to retrieve the frights?"

"You know full well that I have asked. My knights are more than qualified to handle these ridiculous missions." Lewis removed a glove and fanned himself. "What was the mission before last that became such a debacle?" His dark eyes brightened. "Ah, I remember. You were supposed to destroy a supply bridge in Tiotan, which you successfully did. But it was the wrong bridge, wasn't it?"

Abraham wasn't certain, but the words rang true.

Lewis went on. "And then there was a simple matter of retrieving the Ozam Tablets in the Dorcha territory. What happened there? Hmm? You brought them back in pieces and lost parts of them. Those were priceless artifacts. They contained historical information that was vital to the restoration of the crown. And what about the Shield of Puran? Consumed by a fire worm."

Abraham shifted in his saddle. The truth behind Lewis's sneering words stung. His mind started trying to put pieces of the memories together. He needed to talk to Sticks about what had happened on those missions. That was when he remembered something. His chest tightened. *Oh no.* Until he met with the king, all the Henchmen would be imprisoned.

# 34

BARACHA WAS THE NAME OF THE PRISON CAMP WHERE THE Henchmen were taken. It was a high-walled facility made from tremendous stones. Shaped like a hexagon, the Baracha wall stood fifty feet high and had only one entrance, a small iron portcullis. The only way out was either through that portcullis, or over the wall, which was heavily guarded. Baracha meant "place of misery" in the old language.

Sticks crinkled her nose as she fanned flies away from her face. The prisoners—sweaty and grimy—carried an unavoidable stink. The high walls of the Baracha kept the wind out, making it worse. The camp was one hundred yards from wall to wall. A lot of prisoners walked the yard. It was crowded, but the Henchmen clung together, keeping their backs to the wall. The men made a wall around the women, but the catcalls hadn't stopped since they entered.

The skies rumbled. The clouds were turning dark.

"A bad rain is coming," Cudgel said. He held out his hand and twisted it up and down. "In about an hour. Maybe it will wash some of the stink out of here."

"I doubt it," Sticks mumbled. She was squatting beside Dominga and Iris.

All of them covered up the best they could in their blankets. That was the only thing the prisoners were given when they entered. It kept prying eyes off them.

"It's only going to turn this dung hole into a mudhole. It always does."

The prison yard was packed dirt. No grass grew. With over one thousand people walking about, no vegetation would survive. No cells, dungeons, walls, bars, or chains existed. Each prisoner was on his own. They were treated like animals. Many newcomers didn't survive the first day because they were beaten to death and thrown into the pits below the Wall of Defecation. That was the southwest wall, converted into a massive latrine fifty feet long. A creek of sludge at the bottom washed excrement out to sea. It was the last place a woman wanted to be without an escort.

"I've got to go," Dominga said.

Sticks rolled her eyes. She'd been a Henchman a long time. This wasn't her first visit to Baracha either. She'd lived here briefly and in the king's dungeons. But this was Dominga's first time. She was a Red Tunic who'd only made her way up to Henchman on the last mission. She wasn't a former prisoner, either. She was a volunteer who started at the bottom, like the rest. Pretty but tough, she'd somehow made it.

"Come with us," Bearclaw said. Vern, Tark, and Cudgel joined him.

"I need to go too," one of the retainers said. She was the young pie-faced woman with a lot of freckles and dimples in her cheeks. Twila was her name, the only other woman left besides Sticks, Iris, and Dominga. She held her blanket tight around her body. Her hands trembled.

Tark waved the women over, and the men escorted Dominga and Twila away.

As soon as the group started walking away, the vulgarity came out from the surrounding prisoners.

Sticks shook her head. *Animals.* She did a head count of who was left: Horace, Bearclaw, Vern, Cudgel, Tark, Iris, Prospero, Apollo, and Dominga. Including her, that made ten of them, plus five Red Tunics. The rest of the Red Tunics and retainers had fled the moment they heard the word *Baracha*.

Aside from the Henchmen, plenty of rough characters were wandering the prison yard, hardened men and women, and others just pitiful. Most of them were waiting on their sentencing, but if they died, that made the entire process a lot simpler for the courts. Baracha made a fine crime deterrent, but too many troublemakers couldn't help themselves. If threatened, the Henchmen could hold their own. But some had died in Baracha. Sticks just hoped their wait wouldn't be too long.

Horace slid into Dominga's spot. Squatting by Sticks and Iris, he asked, "Do you think we are going to make it out of here this time?"

"I don't know. It seems like we've been getting by on borrowed time. After this last debacle, I think the king's grace will end for us," she said.

Rocking back and forth on her heels, Iris said, "Oh, don't say that. I'm facing life in prison for my mysticism. I only use it to help people."

Sticks scanned the crowd and saw the top of Bearclaw's head. Many lust-filled eyes were following the group. Baracha was the worst place for a woman to be. One had to be a very bad woman to get there. But they had their gangs in the yard too.

"It's death or the dungeons for us," Sticks said.

"At least we'll have our own room. Even though the grave is a very small one," Horace said.

"Yeah, if we have a body left to put in the grave," she said.

Iris plugged her ears. "Oh, don't say that either."

Horace chuckled. "So, what is your take on Ruger? He's not been the same since the tunnel."

"I don't know," Sticks said.

"Of course you know. You slept with him."

"So?"

"I'll sleep with him," Iris said. "I'll get a lot of information out of him."

Horace shook her head. "So you'll sleep with him and not with me?"

"You aren't Ruger, or even close," Iris said.

"What do you mean?" he objected. "I'm all man. I might not look like Ruger, but I've the same iron-made muscle under these puffy arms."

With a subtle neck roll, Iris turned her nose away and said, "It's not that."

"Well, what is it then?" he asked.

Sticks held a hand up. "Can the two of you do this some other time?"

Horace harrumphed and said, "I've been at this for over five years. Two good years, three bad ones. I probably know him better than any. Sticks, you know him second best. But I think something is wrong with him. Like before." Horace spoke quietly. "Do you think he's possessed?"

Sticks knew Horace knew him as well as she. Horace was a former Guardian like Ruger. They'd ridden together for years before the Henchmen. So had Bearclaw and Vern. The rest of them were convicts and hopeless misfits. They were an expendable resource given a new purpose to serve the king. The missions went well at first then started to slide backward a couple years ago. She told a white lie. "I think he got his courage back."

"I think it's too little, too late," Horace said. He looked about. "The king will be done with us."

"I hope not," Iris said.

"Hope isn't for people like us," Sticks replied.

Bearclaw, Vern, Tark, and Cudgel returned with Dominga and Twila. The women had deep frowns on their faces.

Horace moved aside and let the women take their place by the wall. "That was quick."

"That's because we didn't make it." Bearclaw turned toward a large unsavory group of men and women marching straight toward them. "They stopped us."

Horace looked at the ugly group of thugs. "What do they want?"

"They want to swap women."

# 35

King Hector's castle, the House of Steel, was built on a bluff overlooking the Bay of Elders. The castle itself was nothing short of magnificent. It was one hundred thousand square feet of living space made of block stones, archways, and pillars of marble. The walls were blocks of white marble with golden and rusty flecks. The pillars and archways were black with swirls of gold and bronze in them. The hallways had carpets running the length of the floor. Great tapestries depicting stories of Kingsland's history adorned the walls. The stories they told were astonishing. Mighty fire-breathing beasts and heroes that looked as if they were hewn out of rock decorated the tapestries. The forces of light battled the invasion of darkness. Colossal beings with armor made of stars battled in the heavens. Abraham lost his breath looking at the detailed scenes, amazed that someone could sew something with such accuracy.

*How in the world do they do this?*

"Keep your unworthy eyes off of my father's tapestries," Lewis said. He shoved Ruger in the back. "Eyes on the floor, servant dog."

Abraham dropped his gaze to the floor and let Lewis lead him through the castle. The haughty prince marched on with his chin up in silent triumph. Lewis hated Ruger. It took a while for Abraham's mind to recollect exactly why, but when it came to him, he found it perfectly understandable. Lewis had crossed swords with Ruger once. The prince had the ugly scar on his lip and chin to show for it.

*I'd hate me too.*

With the King's Guardians posted all throughout the castle, he and Lewis traveled alone. They made their way to the parapets that made a pathway around the castle. From the top of the west wall, he could see the sprawling city of Burgess. A road of stone as wide as five wagons ran down from the castle to the grand capital city. The sprawling city stretched out for miles in a grid of well-built buildings and cottages. Beyond that city were farmlands. North and south of the castle were docks, beaches, and a harbor bustling with activity and commerce. From the castle's point of view, Burgess was perfect, but that was far from the truth.

The House of Steel's spires were another marvel of brilliant architecture. The six stone columns surrounding the castle rose a hundred feet high and were capped by twisting spearlike steel tips that shone in the sunlight. The House of Steel's gigantic flag hung outward from the top neck of the tower, flapping in the brisk ocean winds. But that wasn't why the king's castle was known as the House of Steel. Abraham's neck rose upward. It was called the House of Steel because of the gargantuan sword stuck downward tip first in the middle of it.

With the bottom end of the crusted-over sword standing fifty feet higher than the tips of the towers, it dwarfed everything else about the castle. The pommel had cross guards angled forty-five degrees downward. The blade sank into the top of the castle and vanished into the building. The gargantuan blade's steel showed a petrified look of gray stone covered in the gritty element carried by centuries of the salty sea winds. It was forbidden to touch the

Sword of Stone. The Sword of Stone, according to the legends, was the weapon of Titanuus, buried in his leg after the celestial, Antonugus, defeated him. Seabirds nested in the hilt. Droppings and grit were all over the massive stone.

"Will you keep pace?" Lewis said. "You always gawk every time you see it. After you've seen it once, I don't see how you would ever forget. It's nothing but a poop stand now."

Abraham hustled up to Lewis. They rounded the southern wall toward the east side, where the king would be waiting. The east side was the safest place for the king, out of the view of his enemies. The backside of the castle was protected by two hundred feet of sheer cliffs, making it virtually impenetrable—not to mention the fleet of ships guarding the king's harbor and the soldiers who patrolled the entire castle. The King's Guardians in the castle numbered over one hundred. The king's personal soldiers numbered another thousand. He commanded an army over thirty-five thousand strong. They patrolled Kingsland cities, but the largest host of them were stationed at bases protecting the King's Foot and the border mountains between Kingsland and Southern Tiotan.

Two of the King's Guardians stepped aside, allowing entrance to the king's grand terrace, which overlooked the Bay of Elders. Lewis and Abraham approached a man wearing a garish blue-seafoam-colored robe with lion's fur around the shoulders. He had his back to them, his gaze fixed toward the sea. Abraham's heart started to race. Sweat gathered on his brow. He was in the presence of the king.

# 36

STICKS SLID UP THE WALL. SHE HAD A SMALL BROKEN PIECE OF STONE in her hand. This wouldn't be the first prison scrap she'd been in, and it probably wouldn't be the last. Hanging back, she let Horace do the talking. He'd stepped to the front, facing the gang of goons who outnumbered them two to one. "Who is demanding a swap?" he asked.

A man pushed his way through the net of greasy bodies. He wore a cloak with a hood covering his eyes. A strange symbol was carved into his cheek. In a silky voice, the man said, "Why, that would be me, Horace. Baracha welcomes you back."

Horace stepped forward and glowered down at the man. "Save your pleasantries for some other fool stuffed inside these walls, Shade. Be on your way."

Shade lifted a finger. Unlike everyone else in the prison camp, his hands and clothing were clean. "Ah, ah, ah, I think that you would be wise to listen to me, you bearded egg. My offer is very generous. As you can see, I'm offering six of my finest maidens for only two of yours."

He stepped aside to show off the six ugly women he was

talking about. Two of them were a pair of old crones, white eyes blinded by time, staring aimlessly and leaning on canes. The other four were flabby whores with hungry smiles that offered mouthfuls of missing teeth. They blew kisses at him with puffy lips.

"They will keep you warm when the winter comes."

Horace crossed his arms over his belly. "We won't be here for winter."

Shade rolled his neck. "Are you sure? As I understand it, you will be here for a long while. Take my offer. It's the best one that you will get from me. I offer protection. You don't want to be free game. Even men of your strength cannot overcome the sheer weight of superior numbers."

Horace looked down at Shade, who wasn't very tall but was fairly well built. He stepped on Shade's clean boots. "You're starting to piss me off, maggot. Begone."

Shade pulled his feet free. "You shouldn't have done that!" He didn't hide his irritation. "Be wise, and make a deal with me. If you don't, you won't be left alone. Not ever."

"It is not our decision to make," Horace said. He stepped aside. "I'll tell you what. If the women that accompany us are willing to make the swap, then who are we to stand in your way. Go ahead. Ask them yourself, worm."

Shade eased his way forward two steps past Horace. He cleared his throat. Addressing Dominga and Twila, he said, "Ladies, it would be in your best interest to accompany me to a more suitable arrangement in the camp. You will need my protection. Word has it that you won't be leaving, or you will at least be here for a long internment." He touched his chest and bowed. "I'll personally see to it that you are well taken care of."

"Does that include me?" Sticks said in her dry voice. She walked right toward Shade and stood eye to eye with him. "Well, does it, Shade?"

The swarthy man's Adam's apple rolled. "Why, Sticks. I didn't realize that was you. I thought you were just another one of the boys. But, yes, I would gladly extend my offer to include you, but I'd have to take two of my hags, er, maidens back."

Sticks grabbed him by the gonads and squeezed. "How about you stay on your side of the camp, and when we walk, you look the other way?"

The Henchmen chuckled with under-their-breath laughter.

Shade jumped away from her. "You will regret this misgiving, you plank-faced fool. I run this yard, not you!" He huddled inside the safety of his surly group and pointed his finger at all of them. "And don't you think for a moment that any of you are going to get out of here anytime soon. Not alive, that is. I have long ears. As long as any. The king is through with you." He started to turn around and turned back. "And make your own facilities. You are not welcome in mine!" Holding his crotch, he and his gang moved on.

Dominga stood beside Sticks and bumped wrists with her. "What's between you and him?"

"We have a history," Sticks said.

"It's pretty clear that he hates you."

"He hates all of us. He used to be a Henchman, but the Captain booted him out." That was only part of her story. Shade and Sticks had a deeper history than that, one she preferred to forget about. "He always gives us a hard time when we come back."

"Well, he's wrong, right? We won't be here that long, will we?" Dominga said.

"That I'm not so sure about. Shade might be a worm, but he doesn't make idle threats."

Near the middle of the courtyard, Shade had more prisoners gathering around him. He pointed in the Henchmen's direction. If he said something, he meant it. And he appeared to have taken control of one of the largest gangs in the prison. If he wanted them dead, he could probably get away with it. It would be a problem—a fatal one.

Heavy rain drops began to fall. Thunder rumbled in the sky.

Holding out his hand, Cudgel said, "The rain comes early. A bad sign."

A group of tall men with long ears and bulging trap muscles almost up to their ears broke away from Shade's pack. Not ordinary men, they were from a race of barbaric brutes called Gonds. They weren't good for much more than soldiering and farming. They were stupid but fought like their heads were on fire. Their impulsive urges got them in heaps of trouble. Now, eight of them were coming toward the Henchmen with their big fists swinging at their sides.

Horace cracked his knuckles. Vern clenched his jaws. Bearclaw cracked his neck side to side. Sticks rubbed her rock. In the background, Shade stood with his hands on his hips, smiling.

Horace breathed deeply in through his nostrils, and his broad chest expanded. "It looks like the dance is starting early."

# 37

Lewis dropped to one knee. "Hail to the King." He bowed.

Abraham felt Lewis's hard stare on him and awkwardly sank down to one knee. He was about to repeat what Lewis had said but bit his tongue. He kept his eyes down, the same as Lewis, who sent an irritated sideward glance at him.

Nothing was said in a strange moment that felt like an eternity. The soft footfalls of King Hector approached. Abraham could see the hem of King Hector's robes dusting the tops of his shiny brown leather boots. The knot in Abraham's throat tightened. The king had an aura that stood his hairs on end. It was a foreign experience. He was dying to look up but dared not. He didn't know why, but Lewis wasn't looking up either, and he was the king's own son.

"Rise, son," King Hector said in the polished voice of an English gentleman.

Lewis slowly came to his feet, and the king embraced him.

In a warm and fatherly manner, the king said, "I take it that your journey to Swain was without incident."

"There was some rabble that attacked the King's Guardians. They were taken care of, Father."

"You killed them?" King Hector sighed. "I hate to hear it. But they must be made an example of. Just tell me that they weren't Kingsland citizens. That's hard to accept. Tell me they were more infidel invaders."

"I don't know. One enemy of the crown is the same as the other, citizen or not."

The king rubbed his hands together. "Sometimes I wonder if my stern tactics are the problem," Hector said. He walked back toward the patio wall as Lewis followed. "I have gallows in every quadrant of the city. Traitors are hung every day. Still, with a sickness, they assault the crown. I don't understand how that can be. Not so long ago, it didn't use to be this way."

Abraham lifted his eyes. He could see the back sides of King Hector and Lewis. The king was smaller in stature. He had a full head of wavy and curly gray-brown hair and leaned heavily on his left leg. Abraham dropped his eyes the moment the king turned back toward him.

"I could stand here and gripe about my problems incessantly for a week. Heaven knows that I've lost enough sleep." King Hector sighed again. "But let's get to the business at hand. Rise, Ruger. Rise and kiss the king's hand."

As if propelled by an unseen force, Abraham did as he was commanded. He looked at King Hector, and his knees wobbled. He fought to steady himself as the king's soft eyes drew him in. The king's strong aristocratic features had softened with time. The formerly prominent jawline sagged. His easy smile showed a few crooked teeth. It reminded him of an English gentleman from a movie that he couldn't readily recall. The king wore a small crown and had a sizeable teardrop-shaped emerald around his neck.

"Are you well, Ruger? Your back bends like a bow," the king said.

Abraham broke out in a cold sweat. New memories were

flooding in. He and King Hector went back. Way back. Everything was jumbled together. "I'm sorry, Hector. I—*oof*!"

Lewis belted Abraham in the gut, doubling him over. "You mangy cur! You don't address the king by his first name!"

"Son, will you calm yourself," King Hector calmly said. "My servant doesn't look well. Perhaps it is the sickness from one too many failures. I don't see the need to quarter him over a slip of the tongue. At least not today. Besides, there is no one else around but us."

"Thank you for your mercy, King Hector," Abraham managed to blurt out.

Lewis had hit him like a heavyweight boxer. He could punch harder than he looked like he could, and the blow surprised him.

With a groan, he straightened his back. "I am sorry."

"I know you are, and you should be. After all, your last several missions have failed." The king clasped his hands behind his back. "Come, join me at the overlook."

"As you wish, King Hector," he said.

They stood at the patio wall together, gazing out over the sea. A sheer drop two hundred feet down led to where the waves crashed against the jagged rocks. Lewis stood behind Abraham's left shoulder, while the king stood at his right. He was certain Lewis would try to push him over.

"Look at all of those ships, Ruger," the king said.

At least one hundred warships were in the bay.

"The King's Fleet. The greatest fleet in all of Titanuus. At least it used to be. There was a time when the King's Fleet stretched all the way around the continent. Our territory was unlimited. But because of weak leadership, a spreading depravity, and faithless broods of people, Kingsland, once the capital of the entire world, has been pushed down to the bottom of the world like crap stuffed into a boot." He looked Abraham in the eye. "Dirty rotten scoundrels are taking over the world. My kingdom! We must stop them." He looked away and rubbed his temples. "Oh, my head hurts thinking about it. Lewis, will you get me something to drink?"

"Father, I will not leave you alone with this wretch," Lewis said. "I'll send a guardian."

"You'll do as I command! Go. I'm not a toddler that needs babysat. Go, son. Go."

Lewis gave Abraham a dangerous look and stormed off.

The king watched him go. "He's a good son. Loyal. More than I can say for the rest of them." He turned his attention to Ruger. "Now, tell me. Why is the best swordsman in the world failing me?"

# 38

THERE WAS AN OLD SAYING ABOUT GONDS IN KINGSLAND. *NEVER fight a Gond. Run like hell instead.* Aside from being as stupid as they were strong, the Gonds had animal-like endurance and a high tolerance for pain. Many of them pierced their bodies and had tattoos all over. That was what the Henchmen were up against now, a small host of rangy men who were more animal than man. The ashen-skinned men with cords of muscle from their toes to their chins thrust themselves into the Henchmen.

The rain poured down. Blood mixed with mud. Angry screams and howls of pain rose above the thunder. Big-fisted men swung their hearts out. Bone cracked against bone. Cartilage gave way. White teeth tore flesh away.

A blood-hungry crowd gathered around the brutal scene. Wagers were made.

Sticks slipped into the fray. A Gond had Horace pinned down in the mud with his hands locked on the man's neck. She cracked the ugly Gond in the temple with a stone. The brute shook his head and made an inhuman, horselike whinny. She hit him again and again, trying to crack his skull open like an egg.

"Get off, you beast!" she yelled.

The Gond punched his elbow back into her ribs.

She collapsed on the ground, clutching her sides, the wind knocked out of her. Her ribs felt busted.

Horace twisted free of the Gond's grip the moment the savage took his hand away. He locked up the Gond's wrist and applied pressure. Bone snapped. The Gond's jaw dropped open. Horace slammed his elbow into the man's chin, breaking the jaw and knocking the barbarian out. He crawled over the mud to Sticks.

"Get your scrawny arse away from here. They'll break you in half." He shoved her toward the frenzied crowd.

Another Gond jumped on his back and bearhugged him from behind. Horace hip tossed the man into the mud and kicked the man in the ribs.

Sticks rolled away from the danger. Horace was right. The Gond would break her in two. She was a great fighter with her daggers, but without them, well, hand-to-hand combat was not her strong point, especially against huge men who could squash her. But she wasn't going to sit around and watch, either. She scooped up a handful of mud and slung it in the eyes of Horace's attacker.

Horace got the Gond in a headlock and squeezed with all his might. "Well done, sister. Well done!" His jaw clenched. The barbarian picked up the beefy man and slammed him hard into the ground. "This one kicks like a wild mule! Smells like one too!"

---

Vern squared off with a Gond who fought with his mouth wide-open. The fit fighter jabbed punches into the Gond's face and ribs. The Gond smiled stupidly at him. Vern, not known for strength, hit him with everything he had. "I suppose you're too stupid to know when to fall down." He landed a right and left in the man's chin. Then he pulled back, shaking his hands. "What are you made out of, rock?"

Like a wild ape, the Gond lunged at Vern. His fingers tangled up in Vern's hair. The Gond headbutted the smaller man, and nose cartilage gave way. Blood dripped down into Vern's mouth. The Gond unleashed a relentless assault of hammer fists on him. Vern's legs turned to noodles, and he flopped face-first in the mud. The Gond kept whaling.

---

Bearclaw's kidney punch dropped a Gond to one knee. His fierce chop to the neck got the Gond clutching at his throat. He grabbed the man by the face and jammed his thumbs into the barbarian's eyes. The savage prisoner twisted away. Bearclaw let out a wild howl and chased after the savage, but his legs were tackled. He hit the ground hard as two Gonds jumped him then pounded him with hammerlike fists.

---

Five Gonds fought against Cudgel, Tark, Prospero, Apollo, and the other four Red Tunics. Prospero and a Gond were yanking at each other's beards as they headbutted each other. A Red Tunic jumped onto the Gond's back and bit his earlobe off.

Cudgel and Tark wrapped up the legs of a Gond and held on for dear life. The Gond whaled away at their backs. A Red Tunic latched himself onto the Gond's arms. The Gond slung him into the mud with a flick of his arm.

The other three retainers were getting manhandled by one lone Gond. The Gond busted two faces together. He picked another retainer up over his shoulders, slammed him hard into the ground, and stomped on him.

---

The ugly battle went back and forth, up and down, blow for blow, with feet sliding and faces eating mud for another minute. Then a bansheelike howl started, and the crowd fell silent. The Gonds broke off their attack.

The prisoner guards on the wall were swinging cowbell-shaped whistles that were attached to ropes over their heads and made the shrill sound of a siren.

Prison soldiers entered the prison yard, wearing plate-mail armor and open-faced helms. They carried spears and jabbed them into anyone who didn't clear their path.

One prisoner, a man well past his prime, ran into their path. He dropped to his knees with his fingers clenched together. They told him to get out of the way. He shook his head. They gored him. Order was restored.

Sticks counted forty Baracha soldiers. In addition to the spears, they had swords on their hips. They had the worst job a soldier could have in guarding a prison. They were ready to take a poke at anyone who crossed them and often did. She rubbed her ribs.

Horace wiped the mud from his face and huffed for breath. "Never thought I'd be glad to see them."

"Me either. What's wrong with all of you? I thought we were tough. You all got the crap kicked out of you," she said.

Prospero spat a tooth out of his mouth. He reached inside his mouth and pulled out another. Apollo did the same.

Cudgel was doubled over with his hands on his knees, sucking for air. "I hate barbarians." He huffed another couple of breaths. "There's no fear in them. Just stupid."

"Agreed," Tark said as he held a hand against his swollen face.

Two retainers dragged Vern by his boots over to the group. His nose was broken, his face bloody and swollen.

Sticks looked down at him and grimaced. "Did you even try to fight?"

Vern pointed a shaking finger at her and said, "Still prettier than you."

Bearclaw took a knee by Vern. "He won't be able to fight anytime soon. Shade is far from finished."

Sticks looked across the yard. Through the rain, Shade caught her eye and waved.

"Yeh, he's going to take us down one Henchman at a time." She looked at Vern. "At this rate, we won't last a week."

# 39

"*You're the King's fool now!*" Abraham saw those words in his mind as though they were written on a chalkboard. They were the last words Eugene Drisk had said at the tunnel, the mystery man who disappeared through the portal. Suddenly, the words came to mind and haunted him like the king's weary eyes.

"Where would you like me to start, uh, Your Majesty?" he asked.

King Hector tilted his head slightly over and looked deeper into Abraham's eyes. "Have you lost your edge, Ruger? And be honest. I don't have time for games. I have five kingdoms that want my head on a platter. A city of ungrateful citizens burgeoning to rise up. Tell me—do I need a new Henchman? Should the king's sword be somebody else?"

"Er... no." The pride of a ball player came out of Abraham. He would never sit down if he could pitch the winning game. "Absolutely not."

"What happened to those frights? They should have been an easy mark. Just put them in irons, and they are powerless," the king said.

"On the ship, they somehow escaped and wrought havoc. I can't explain it, but we killed them. Their bodies deteriorated. They were tossed into the sea." He held the king's stare. "But I defeated Flamebeard and brought the *Sea Talon* as a prize. I have his sword to show for the effort."

King Hector arched a brow. "Interesting. Flamebeard is renowned for his pillaging and swordsmanship. He's also worked for and against my crown." He stuck his bottom lip out and tilted his head side to side. "My crown is better off without his treachery. So you turned him into chum, did you?"

"He lost his head."

The king chuckled. "Despite that victory—and a new prize for my coffers—you still failed me, Ruger."

"I'm sorry. I did my best."

"Sorry. *Sorry* is for the weak. You are not weak. You can't be. And it sounds like you've lost control of your own men. Clearly, you have a traitor… or many. Have you executed any of them?"

"No. Until I prove otherwise, I assume they are innocent. I'm investigating."

The king shook his head. He walked down the parapet wall and sat on the edge. His shoulders sagged as if the weight of the world were collapsing on his shoulders. "In the streets, they call me the Ruthless King. Me. Ruthless. Yet they are the ones that are breaking the law. You can't have a country without laws. I enforce them. Without laws, there is no Kingsland. Without Kingsland, there is no law. There is only chaos. That's what thrives in Tiotan and Bolg. Hancha is no better. Their people are slaves, for all intents and purposes. My people are free, yet they complain."

Two seabirds landed on the wall near the king. He reached into a leather pouch and flicked bits of bread and seed at them. The birds pecked at the bits and flew away.

With his eyes fixed toward the Bay of Elders, the king said, "In the beginning, there was only one kingdom. Kingsland. It rested on the very heart of Titanuus. All of the races and creatures of the world were united. For centuries, we lived in peace, but over time, pride eroded even the best of us." He looked at Abraham. "My ancestors, in their efforts to please everyone, allowed this kingdom to be pushed aside, down to the bottom of Titanuus's foot. The people wanted new kingdoms and new leaders. They wanted to do it their own way. Before long, there wasn't one king to rule over the world but many." He waved his hands in an aggravated manner. "For the longest time, they fought each other, but now, they have all decided to fight against me. Somehow, Kingsland, the most orderly nation, is the problem."

Abraham started putting the pieces of the puzzle together. He'd heard the king's stories before, and he'd heard the stories from others. Ruger Slade had plenty of memories of them. Kingsland, the shiny star in Titanuus, was on the cusp of extinction. It was the last kingdom of the old world, where there had been order and peace. A dark poison had spread everywhere else, polluting the lands and devouring good people. All this had been done to insidious effect via a new cause of false righteousness spreading from generation to generation. The New Kingdom was what the movement was called. It promised glory for all but brought only strife.

King Hector had needed a long time to figure out what was going on. His ancestry had failed to protect the crown. They appeased their allies, not realizing they were enemies, and gave away their lands. They trusted the growing countries would do the right thing, as Kingsland always had, but that would not be the case. Each country fought to obtain more power. They used spies, espionage, sabotage, and marriage for their own personal gain. Alliances were made and broken. Skirmishes and battles raged.

As the situation got more out of hand, King Hector realized he had to do something. He had to fight fire with fire. He had to send spies into the other lands, so he created the Henchmen. They would be a nameless bunch of renegades who would spy and sabotage for the kingdom. For years, their missions were very successful, but lately, they'd hit a wall. And Abraham was their leader.

"There are so few that a king can trust," Hector said. "A man's oath is not as strong as it used to be. Men, women, pfft... They all lie for personal gain. They say practically anything. Ruger, I saw a light in you that others did not see. You proved me right, but lately, that light has been gone. I don't know what happened. You were my finest knight. The best sword. A renowned defender. And you deserted. Years of service, and you left. Why, Ruger? Why?"

Abraham wished he had the answer to that, but he didn't. It was another one of those fuzzy spots in his mind. If he had to guess, he would assume it had something to do with the body transformation. But one thing that did come to mind was that desertion by a King's Guardian meant certain death. Yet he lived. He was hated for it.

"I can't explain it, My King. I lost myself."

"Yes. Yes, you did."

More seabirds landed on the wall. The king tossed out more crumbs.

"You've had long enough to redeem yourself. But now, as much as I hate to do it, this experiment is over. I can no longer justify the risk. I'm disbanding the Henchmen." He stood, approached Abraham, fingered his emerald pendant with one hand, and put his hand on his shoulder with the other. "And I'm sad to inform you that your death sentence will be executed. Tomorrow. Guardians!" The knights who guarded the entrance to the terrace hustled over in their plate-mail armor. "Take him away."

# 40

The king's condemnatory words took Abraham's breath away. Even though he was in the body of a fighting man, he had no will to strike. He stood dumbfounded. Everything around him turned into slow motion. The wings of the birds flying away from the wall flapped in a weird form of stop-motion. He could hear the metal-shod feet of the King's Guardians marching on the stone patio at a very slow rate. His head twisted toward the entrance to the terrace, leading back into the castle. A two-step stair led up to it. Three figures came through the billowing curtains of the archway's entrances. An older woman was being escorted by two men. One of the men was Lewis.

*The Queen!* Abraham dropped to a knee. It was Queen Clarann. She wore silk sleeping robes. Her hair was pulled up and braided. She wore a small diamond-studded tiara. Her pretty face appeared ashen and wrinkled. She shuffled when she walked with the men standing close by but not touching her.

Each of the King's Guardians dropped to a knee and bowed also.

The king rushed over to greet her. "My love, you should not be outside when you are so sick." He took her hands in his. "Please, stay in bed. You need your rest."

"Oh, I've been inside long enough." Queen Clarann let him kiss her on the cheek then brushed him off. "I want to see that sea one last time before I go."

"Don't say that," King Hector said. He fastened a hand around her waist and escorted her to the wall. "But if that is your wish, I will not deny it." He shot an aggravated look at the other man on the patio. "Viceroy Leodor, my queen is ravaged. When will you get this disease under control?"

"The Sect works at it day and night, Your Majesty. We come closer by the day," Viceroy Leodor said. He stood tall, wearing cream-colored robes trimmed with purple. He had a beak of a nose, bright, close-set eyes, and a sunken chin. He spoke in a respectful but forced manner. "But this disease is no ordinary disease. It is a curse. My healers and potion makers work endlessly to resolve the matter."

Queen Clarann sat down on the wall and groaned. She still had a spark in her eyes and strength in her voice. "Please, no more of those disgusting concoctions. I'd rather die now than swallow another." She stuck her tongue out. "Blecht."

"Don't say that, Clarann. I would not want to go on another day without you." King Hector spoke in a soft and soothing tone. "You are my wife. You are my life."

She touched his cheek with her trembling hand. "Hector, you have been good to me, but don't be so dramatic. It unsettles my stomach. You will always be more husband than king to me. That is more than any wife can ask for. But the citizens need more king than husband. I am holding you back. If my time comes, it comes."

"That is nonsense. You are far from full of years, unlike me. I will find a cure for you," Hector said.

"Don't be silly. Look at me. I look like I'm a thousand years old. I don't want to live my last days looking like a mummy." She brushed a withered hand across his check. "I'm sorry, Hector. I know this isn't fair to you. You never could have imagined this when you took such a younger bride. Now, I'm haggard and ugly."

"That is outrageous. You are as beautiful as ever."

She chuckled drily and rolled her eyes at him.

"Leodor!" Hector shouted. "This madness has gone on long enough. Certainly, you have some inkling that will end this disease. This is Kingsland. Anything is possible, or I am not the king!"

"Your Majesty," Viceroy Leodor said, "the only possibility is the egg of the fenix. Its yolk is said to cure anything. But as you well know, all of our expeditions to retrieve it have failed. And no one has sighted a fenix in decades. There are myths and legends, but that is all that we have."

The king stood. "No, they are not. My father saw one himself. They live if he says they lived." He clenched his fist. "If there is an egg to be fetched, we will have it."

"Father," Lewis said, "we have lost over five hundred men and women on these expeditions. The territories take them before they even arrive. It is a fruitless quest. Certainly, there is another way."

"What?" Queen Clarann asked. She started into a fit of coughing.

Hector, Leodor, and Lewis converged on her with outstretched hands.

"Oh, back away," she said, with steely resolve. "Hector, what news is this. You are sending men and women to their deaths, chasing after a silly legend for me." She grabbed Hector's hands in hers. "Hector, I know you love me, but I won't have you sacrificing lives of our loyal people on my account. That is foolishness."

King Hector stroked her cheek. "My dearest, you are the queen. The people are your humble servants. It is their duty. A kingdom must have a king and a queen. And selfishly, I need you."

"You'll have another queen. After all, there was one before me. I'm sure there will be one after. It's customary," she said.

"She didn't hold a candle to you. You know that." Hector kissed her hands.

Abraham noticed Lewis glowering at his father.

"Her sudden death was a tragic accident," Hector continued. "But I think it was destined to bring you and I together."

"Oh, don't say that, Hector. I feel so guilty. That's probably why I have this awful curse. It's payment to the Elders." She coughed. "Promise me you won't send any more to their deaths."

King Hector stiffened. "As you—"

"I'll do it!" Abraham blurted.

"Shut up, dog!" Lewis stormed over and kicked him in the gut.

# 41

Abraham fell on all fours. With a groan, he fought his way back to his knees.

Lewis kicked him in the ribs. "Stay down, you walking, breathing, and sniveling wretch."

As tough as Abraham was, a kick in the ribs and gut still hurt like hell. On hands and knees, he spat out more words. "I can retrieve the egg. Please, one chance for redempt—*oof*!"

Lewis laid into him once more.

Squinting her eyes in Abraham's direction, the queen said, "Who is this man? And quit kicking him, Lewis."

"He is no one, my dear," the king said. "It's some finished business that I'd concluded when you arrived. Guardians, remove him immediately."

"Give me one chance, King Hector. Let me redeem myself. I beg you."

While listening to the conversation, Abraham had had a two-part inspiration. It was one part fear and one part *This has to be a part of a module or something*. If Titanuus was a fictional world wrapped up in his imagination, then maybe a scenario needed to be played out. Perhaps saving the Queen would lead him back home. He didn't know, but he knew that he had to act, or he would die in the king's gallows. The Guardians hooked their arms under his arms and began dragging him away.

"I can do it," he said. "I will do it. I swear it!"

The queen narrowed her eyes at Abraham. "Hector, don't I know this man?"

Hector opened his mouth.

She cut him off excitedly and said, "Ruger. Is that you?"

"Yes, Queen Clarann! Your devoted servant."

"Guardians, let him go," she said. "What is the meaning of this, Hector? I thought Ruger was dead." She eyed him. "Hector? Explain."

"I'd rather not, but I will," the King replied. "You know that Ruger deserted the Guardians and we lost sixty-five men. Several years ago, he resurfaced. I had him arrested." He eyed Abraham. "He deserved nothing less than execution, but I showed mercy. I gave him a choice: death or be branded as the King's Henchman."

Queen Clarann's mouth hung open. "Being a Henchman is a death sentence. Why didn't you tell me that a new sword had been branded?"

"There are more important matters. Besides, Ruger has failed his missions. I'm executing his death sentence tomorrow."

Lewis smiled. "An excellent decision, Father."

Queen Clarann stood up and teetered over to Ruger, her eyes shining like blue suns. She put a hand on his chin and lifted his head. She looked him over. "I was heartbroken when you deserted. But I am glad to see that you live. You were a true and faithful servant." She looked back at King Hector. "Is he still the best sword? If so, you'd have him killed?"

"Pfft, he's not the best sword, Mother," Lewis said. "I am."

"Oh, please. You are good, but your sister Clarice is better than you," she said.

Like a whiny snot, Lewis said, "She is not."

Queen Clarann held Abraham's face with both hands. With her thumbs underneath his eyes, she stared at him with eyes that looked as if they could see into his soul. "Give him one more chance. Grant him the expedition."

"Dearest, please, leave this business to us," Hector said. "There is much that you don't know. I will send out better men than him."

Lewis strutted forward, smiling with dignity. "Yes, Mother. I will go."

"No," she said. "You will send Ruger."

"One lone man will not be enough. It is an arduous journey. He will only desert us again," Viceroy Leodor said. He licked the sweat from his pale lips. "And men like him are not equipped for such an adventure. They are fighters. They need a group of skilled workers capable of finding the fenix and knowing how to handle it as well. I wouldn't venture it without the skills of priests and mages. It's a full-fledged campaign."

"I'll figure it out, Your Highness," Abraham said. "I have many Henchmen."

"Just do your best. Serve the kingdom, Ruger. Come home again."

She touched his cheek and looked right into his soul, and a spark that came straight from her fingertips went through Abraham's heart.

"Redeem yourself," she whispered softly in his ear. "Be brave, old friend."

The king rushed over to her side and took her from Abraham. "She's exhausted. Viceroy Leodor, take her back to her quarters." He kissed her cheek. "I'm coming along shortly, dear. Rest well."

"I'm tired of resting. I want to do something else besides sleep," she said.

Viceroy Leodor led her away. "I'll have the servants draw you a revitalizing bath."

Abraham wasn't certain where he stood. The queen might have a sharp mind, but she seemed so fragile. He feared that her words didn't have any weight. He waited as the king chewed his bottom lip while watching her go. He could tell by the worry in the man's voice and the look in his eyes that he truly loved her.

With a sigh, the King turned and faced him. "It looks like you have another chance—a futile one at best, but a chance."

"Father, this is outrageous," Lewis whined. "There is no fenix. It's a fool's quest. By tomorrow, Mother will forget about it. Put this traitor in the guillotine and get it over with."

"One day, when you have a wife that you love, you'll do anything for her. If she wants Ruger to seek out the egg, then so be it."

"Mother doesn't care about the egg, Father. She likes him like a loyal old hound"—Lewis sneered at Ruger—"and is granting him undeserved freedom. That is all. She is feeble and overly merciful. You know what Leodor says. He's done all that he can. There is no hope for her. She is strong. She understands that."

Shaking his fist, Hector said, "I need hope. This mission will give it to me. Ruger, if you pull off this miracle, your death sentence will be waived. And I will show you my gratitude."

Lewis stiffened. "Father, you can't trust him. He's a washed-up swordsman. His men are thugs. Let me and my men handle this. It might be lunacy, but for Mother, it would be an honor. We are the best hope that you have."

Hector shook his head. "You are not seasoned in the ways of the world beyond the border, son. I appreciate your offer, but no. You are the Captain of the King's Guardians. I need you here. Rise, Ruger."

Abraham did so.

"These are dire times. Bring that egg back to me. I know it exists."

"I am your Henchman. I'll do whatever it takes." He looked the king in the eye. "Death before failure."

Lewis laughed. "I'm certain that you'll soon experience both of them soon enough."

# 42

Below the House of Steel were dungeons. Abraham was kept in a cell. He was the only one there. Made from blocks of stone and bars of steel, the drab place was clean aside from the cobwebs in the corners. Not even a guard was posted, or rats crawling along the floor. In his cell was a cot, a small pillow, and a bucket. He sat on the cot, lay down, and weighed his options. His situation was getting more uncomfortable and tenser. Since he'd arrived, he escaped one dire situation only to fall into another. The king meant business, but Abraham liked him. He liked the queen too. She was a salty woman, like his grandmother, who didn't let anything get by her. He wanted to help them. He didn't know whether he or Ruger wanted to help more. Something more seemed to exist between Ruger and the queen that he didn't comprehend. Her gentle touch jolted his heart. He wanted to go home, but he wanted to help them too. He'd gotten caught up in their lives. Now, he had to try.

In the meantime, he needed to figure out what was really going on in his mind. Everything he saw, tasted, or touched had been real. If he didn't know better, he'd swear that he had indeed been transported into another world and another body. But that was impossible. He'd seen movies like *Total Recall* and understood the basic concepts of virtual reality, but this was ridiculous.

Plucking at his lips, he said, "Am I Neo? Is this the Matrix?" He rolled onto his side as a multitude of new memories filtered through his mind. He felt as if a jump drive of information had been loaded into him. He recalled various sword-fighting styles: high guard, wrath guard, ox guard. People, places, and things crossed through his thoughts. Some of it was crystal clear, but the rest of it was fuzzy, as if he was sharing his mind with another person, or his had been transplanted into an android. "I just want to drive my beer truck again."

"What is a matrix?" an invading voice said.

Abraham sat up. Viceroy Leodor stood on the other side of the cell's bars with a curious look in his eyes and tapped his fingers on the bars. Abraham had a natural aversion to the bald and chinless man.

"It's a name for a puzzle," Abraham said.

"Life is a puzzle." Leodor looked at Abraham with a deep and spacey gaze. Then, he casually leaned against the bars. "Especially yours. Once again, you have escaped a certain death after failing another mission. I don't know if I should be more impressed or irritated."

"Why would you be irritated?"

"You're a Henchman. Less than a goat. You irritate me."

Abraham stood. "Ah, but I wasn't always a goat, now was I? I was the king's finest knight," Abraham said, probing Leodor. He knew who he was but thought he knew him better. "Was I not?"

Leodor's frown deepened. He stuck a key in the lock and twisted. "I want you to know that despite my love for the queen, I hope that *you* don't make it back. You have been nothing but a waste of time the last several years. I've supplied you with your needs. How many of your Henchmen and precious Red Tunics died this time? Forty."

"Thirty-eight." The amount jumped right off his tongue, and he felt guilty for saying it. "Why are you keeping tabs on me?"

Leodor rolled his eyes and stepped aside. "That's my charge, fool." He narrowed his eyes and looked deep into Abraham's own. "It seems that wound on your head rattled your gray matter." He let Abraham pass and led him out of the dungeons. "Based off my count, you've led over one hundred seventy-five people to their deaths."

"Hey, it comes with the territory. And like me, they volunteered for it. They took the King's Brand—nobody forced them. It's the same as any soldier." He didn't mean to say it in a callous manner, but it came out that way. He wasn't sure why. But he remembered his father telling him that the moment you sign up in the military, you sign your life away. "Maybe our odds would be better if you joined us?"

"Pfft. I'm in the business of saving our kingdom, not destroying it. Now, if you don't mind, keep your tongue bridled. Walk with me and listen. There is much that you need to know about the fenix egg if you are going to have a chance at finding it."

Abraham clammed up. But a voice inside himself wanted to shoot his mouth off. He wasn't sure whether it was himself or Ruger. After all, he had liked to talk a bunch of smack back in the day. It came out naturally. And if this was a fantasy or dreamworld, he saw no reason not to be whoever he wanted. He followed Leodor through a labyrinth of concealed corridors behind the castle's main walls and listened intently to the uppity man's words.

"The last two campaigns started at the same time. One campaign started at the top mountains north of Titanuus's spine, and the other campaign started at the bottom. The goal was to meet in the middle. The fenix or fenixes nest in those peaks. That's what the legend says. But it's thousands of square miles of treacherous terrain. Not to mention the other unexplored phenomena and creatures that indwell the Spine." Leodor stopped, spun on a heel, and faced Abraham. "Better men and women than you have boldly taken on this quest. None of them have come back. Of course, they may have fallen prey to our enemies, but more than likely, the Spine took them. I think that it will take you too."

"Thanks for the pep talk. It's no wonder the kingdom is doing so well."

Leodor shook his head and led Abraham up a long narrow flight of steps that twisted into one of the six outer towers. Halfway up, they entered a small enclosed room lit up by a pair of torches in brackets. The king stood inside with two Guardians and his son, Lewis. They were looking at a square table with Jake's backpack lying on top of it.

# 43

NIGHT FELL UPON THE BARACHA PRISON YARD. ON THE INNER RING halfway up the walls were huge torches in brackets. The guards on the top of the wall shimmied down ropes and lit the torch fires. They provided little illumination and created a darker spot in the middle. That was where Shade and his gang lurked. They waited in the shadows, like prowlers, waiting for the Henchmen to make a move.

The Henchmen huddled together against their section of wall. They were damp from the hard rain, which had finally stopped. The mud that they'd rolled in was caked and dried on their clothes.

Horace sat beside Sticks, clawing the mud out of his beard. Vern lay on his back, groaning from time to time. Bearclaw, Cudgel, Tark, Apollo, and Prospero stood guard, keeping their eyes peeled for another assault by the Gond. The Red Tunics, aside from Twila, stood with them.

"We can always attempt an escape if we have to," Horace said. "I'd rather die outside of these walls than inside here. I don't care if I only make it five feet." He looked at Sticks. "You're small enough to disappear. We can make the distraction."

Digging her rock into the ground, she said, "There is nowhere to go. Might as well stay here. I gave my word as a Henchman."

"We all did. But I'm not going to let Shade get the best of us." Horace cast his gaze outward. "He's a snake and a liar. Cost us two missions. He should have been dead, along with the others."

"I've got a shovel ready for him," Bearclaw said. He turned around. "When they come at us again, I say we all put our efforts on the biggest Gond. Take him down, and it will weaken the others."

Horace shrugged his heavy shoulders. "It will buy us time. It's sound enough. You, Cudgel, and Prospero do it. I don't think Vern will be able do anything. Maybe we can hurl him at them."

Vern groaned as he rolled onto his side and said, "Funny. Feed me to the dogs, why don't you?"

The heavyset black warrior Cudgel walked up on Vern and glared down on him. "You should be fed to the dogs. You let those witches out. You betrayed us, the same as Shade did. I ought to bust your melon open myself." He pointed a chubby finger at the incapacitated man. "Two of my brothers are dead because of you. There were four of us. Now, only Tark and I live!"

"I didn't do it!" Vern moaned and grimaced. "I swear it. By my brand and on the Elders, I didn't do that!"

Sticks kicked Vern in the backside. "Sure you didn't. Why would a liar lie about that?"

"I'm the best sword, after the Captain. You need me."

"Yeah, look at you. You're a real fine fighter, all curled up in the fetal position," Sticks said. All the Henchmen chuckled, aside from Cudgel. He turned his back toward the yard.

"I'm a swordsman, not a brawler. And I fought my guts out against the Gond." Vern winced. "Forgive me for not being born an animal."

"The rest of us fared well enough," Horace said.

"That's 'cause you're built like a chimney. Heavy as one too," Vern fired back. "And let me point something else out to you brilliant bunch of sages. Don't you find it funny that Shade, who was blamed for the prior calamities, wasn't around for this one? Maybe the Captain got it wrong. Maybe we all did, because the same stench of treachery lingers without him."

Sticks and Horace exchanged a glance. Vern was right. Shade had been the fall guy for the prior failures, but failures continued to happen. Now they were blaming Vern. If they were wrong about Shade, they could be wrong about Vern. When Shade had come on board, the well of success ran dry. Now, it was still happening without him.

"Vern's right. It could be any one of us," Sticks said.

"Yes, it's Vern," Horace said. "But Shade is still a snake. I never liked him before, and I don't like him now. He's come after us anyway."

"Well, forgive the man for holding a grudge. And it ain't me!" Vern said. He rolled over. Dominga was sitting with her back to the wall, looking at him. "See something you like, don't you?"

"No, I see a man with a face like a rotten tomato," Dominga said.

"You really know how to hurt a man when he's down." He turned away. "I guess I should have expected as much from one of the Captain's whores anyway. But you're missing out. My sword's just as big and shiny as his."

"Pig," Dominga said.

Vern shrugged. "I'm not a pig. I honestly and sincerely find you attractive. I couldn't say it before when the Captain was around. After all, he hoards all the girls, the same as everything else. But, seeing how we aren't going anywhere, I might as well spill my guts out. Dominga, I love you."

The pretty ebony-skinned woman had to fight back a smile.

Vern smiled through his busted lips. "I knew you liked me." He closed his eyes. "All women like me."

Sticks caught Dominga picking her lip and trying to hide a grin. *The little she-devil does like him. I'll be.* Vern wasn't bad. They'd been riding together a long time. He did his work. But he had brought up some illuminating points about Shade and Ruger. Ruger did hog everything, from the loot that they recovered to the women he bedded. He hadn't always been that way. He'd changed. Now, he'd changed again—for the better, she hoped. But they all still had the same problem—someone was betraying the group and making it look like an accident. *But who?*

"We've got company," Bearclaw said.

Shade approached with a larger group of goons. "Good evening, friends. I was strolling the yard, and I had a change of heart. I decided that I would give you one more offer: two of my finest ladies for just one of yours. I'll even let you pick which woman though I think Sticks is very much on the cusp between a man and a woman." He peeked at her. "I think it's the clenched brow that brings out the brooding man in her. But, like a prize sow, the woman of your choice will be well taken care of. You have my word."

Horace stood up and faced Shade. "Are you going to fight this time or talk?"

Shade spread his hands out. "I don't need to fight."

Horace threw a punch at Shade. The rogue slipped it, backed into his gang, and said, "Take them!"

# 44

King Hector held up Jake's backpack and asked, "What sort of satchel is this, Ruger?"

It was a good question but hard to explain to someone who had not seen the likes of it before.

"A backpack," Abraham said. He rubbed the back of his neck. "For storage."

The king turned the backpack around in his head. He shook it. "Something rattles inside. Listen to me. This isn't the first foreign object that I've come across. I've seen other strange things not designed by anyone in my kingdom. Our enemies are developing new weapons to use against us. This might be one of them." He shook it again. "What is it? Where did you get it?"

"Your Majesty," Leodor said with his hungry eyes glued on the pack, "if you will allow me, I will be happy to use the Sect's resources to garner more information about it. The delicate services of the Zillons will unravel its mysteries." He reached for it.

King Hector pulled the backpack away like a child. "I don't want the Zillons to unravel the mysteries. I want Ruger to tell me." He narrowed his eyes at Ruger. The emerald pendant hanging on the king's neck sparkled. "That's an order from your king."

A strong force attacked Abraham's mind. The fighter inside him battled against it, but something was pulling information out of him. It dug for the truth. A new layer of perspiration broke out on his forehead. He wiped it away. With the king's intent stare haunting his soul, he reached for the pack. He decided not to fight it but to give in. He reached out and said, "All right, you want to know that truth."

"Yes." The king handed him the pack.

"Well... You can't handle the truth! But here goes." He pointed at the face of the badge stitched into the pack. "That's a Pittsburgh Pirate." He slung it over his shoulders, adjusted the straps, and buckled the fastener around his belly. "That's how this works." He took off the pack and unzipped it. "These little teeth make a zipper." He zipped it back and forth really fast. "It makes a very distinct sound."

King Hector, Leodor, and Lewis stood with their mouths agape.

"Now, wait until you see this." Abraham dumped the contents of the pack out onto the table.

The three other men made a noticeable *ahh* and crowded the table like flesh-eating vultures with eyes the size of saucers.

Abraham had stuck a few items into the pack over the years, but he never removed what was Jake's. He wasn't sure what all was in there, but his heart melted the moment he saw his picture on a baseball card. His throat tightened, and his jaws clenched.

The king's delicate hands rummaged through the foreign hoard. "What are these marvelous items?" He picked up a half-empty container of orange Tic Tacs and shook it. His eyes brightened. I know what this is." He put it to his ear and shook it. "It's a music box. I like it."

Abraham would have laughed if his heart wasn't swelling like a biscuit baking inside his chest. His picture and his boy's belongings got to him. He swallowed the lump in this throat and picked up a book. "This is a coloring book. Those robot things are called Transformers." He picked up a box of thirty Crayola crayons. "These are painting sticks." He opened the lid. "See all of the pretty colors." He tossed the box to Lewis.

Lewis swatted it away with an appalled look. "Father, these items are bewitched. I wouldn't touch them."

Abraham picked up the flashlight. It was yellow plastic with black ends. "This tube is a light, but it doesn't work." He started picking up and explaining one item after the other. "This is bubble gum. Long overdue homework. An unpaid electric bill. A bottle opener. An autographed baseball from Buddy Parker. A Zippo lighter and a pocket knife." He choked up. He and Jake had been planning a camping trip that never happened. He'd given those items to Jake. They were Jake's grandfather's.

Still filled with wide-eyed wonder, the King said, "How do you know the names of all of these things?" He picked up a multicolored cube. "What is this? It has so many teeny tiny gem-colored tiles." He hefted it in his hand. "And it's so light."

"It's a puzzle." He took a deep draw through his nose and took the cube. "Allow me. He started twisting the square. "It's a puzzle. You have to get all of the same colors matching on all six of the sides. It was created by the great wizard... uh... Rubik."

"What happens when you solve it?" Leodor said.

Abraham decided to have some fun. "Well, legend has it that whoever solves it will be granted a wish. But only the person that solves it."

When Leodor reached for the cube, King Hector snatched it away. "I will solve it." He started twisting the cube like a madman. "Hah! Look at that. I have three white ones in a row. This will be no problem."

"Your Majesty, it sounds dangerous. Perhaps you should let me work on it for you," Leodor pleaded.

"Nonsense. It's mine." King Hector held his audience's attention another ten minutes as he stuck his tongue out of his mouth. Finally, he hopped up and down and said, "This is impossible."

"Again, I will solve it for you, Your Majesty," Leodor said.

King Hector set the cube down on the table. He tapped it with his finger and said, "If anyone touches this cube that is not me, I will cut off both of his hands and feed them to the hounds." He poked his son in the chest. "That goes for you, too." He picked up Abraham's baseball picture. His head tilted. "What tiny people must have painted this strange portrait. Who is this man?"

Abraham looked the king dead in the eye and said, "That's me."

# 45

The king held the baseball picture up to Abraham's face. "No, that is not you. And I don't understand why you said that, either. What are these strange symbols on the miniature painting?" He handed the picture to Leodor. "Can you interpret them?"

"No, but I will research it using the resources in the Sect's library the first chance that I get," Leodor said.

King Hector picked up a small black frisbee and flipped it with his fingers. "You have a great deal of explaining to do, Ruger. I don't understand how you came to knowledge of these objects. I need answers, clear and concise and not gibberish."

Abraham decided to spill his guts. "Your Majesty, I'm from another world. My name is Abraham Jenkins. That's my name on that card"—he pointed at it—"and my mind is inside the body of Ruger Slade. I don't know how else to explain it."

Lewis's sword whisked out of his sheath. He stepped in front of his father and held his long sword in the high guard position. "He is possessed, Father! He should hang!"

With an appalled look, Leodor said, "I agree. This devil should not be allowed to live within the walls of this castle. He must be executed."

"No," King Hector said calmly. "Son, put away your sword. I want to hear more about what this man—Abraham, is it?—has to say."

"But Father—" Lewis objected.

"Do as I say!"

Without taking his eyes off Abraham, Lewis sheathed his sword.

"Your Majesty, that would be quite foolish. He is a demon that can speak only lies," Leodor warned. "We must be rid of him."

Abraham swallowed.

"Perhaps," the king said as he tossed the frisbee up and down. "But at this point, what do we have to lose? The queen is dying. My enemies are chomping at the bit. We need something. An edge. Perhaps he can provide it."

"I agree with the viceroy, Father. Don't allow this," Lewis said.

The king pulled up a stool sitting underneath the table and sat down. He waved his hands over the objects on the table. "We have a vault that contains more objects like this. I collected some of it. The rest was inherited. Sometimes one shows up in the fairs, and my personal merchants bring it to me. But none of it makes sense. And when we come across these possessed people, what do we do? We kill them out of fear without acquiring any new understanding of what they are about. I think that it's time that we changed our tactic. Perhaps this is why our enemies have the edge. These otherworlders are on their side. It's time to change the tide."

Leodor's expression tightened as he stiffly shook his head. "Your Majesty, this is dangerous. As your chief advisor, I advise against it."

"That has been noted! If you object, then you may leave. Lewis and I can handle this… unless you want to leave too, son?"

Lewis jaw muscles flexed. "I'll stay. But if a demon climbs out of that body, I'll split him in half."

The king extended his open hand and said, "Go ahead, Abraham. Tell me about yourself. I'm eager to hear it."

*What have I got to lose? This isn't real either way. Besides, maybe it's therapeutic.*

Abraham opted for the truth and told the king everything that had happened after he drove into the East River Mountain Tunnel. By the time he finished, his limbs were weary. He was exhausted.

The king didn't say a word. He sat with his arms crossed, rubbing his emerald pendant between his thumb and finger. Finally, he said, "That's one whale of a story. It rings with truth. But I'm not sure what to make of it."

"Me either," Abraham said. "It's either true, or I'm dreaming. Or maybe we are all dreaming."

King Hector arched a brow. "Hmm... I see what you mean. The queen has many dreams. Wild ones. She tells me all the time. She won't let the scribes write them down because she doesn't want people to think that she was crazy. But maybe dreams are real. Who is to say? So the moment you took the sword, you changed. And another man appeared and disappeared through a mystical portal."

"Yes, sir."

"It's *sire*," Lewis said.

"A ring of light. Leodor, has the Sect reported anything about this?"

"I'll look into it."

"And this other man you saw. You said he was unfit," the king said as he took the baseball card from Leodor. "Not a well-knit man like this."

"No, King Hector. He wasn't fit at all. He was shabby looking. Older. Like Leodor but fatter and shorter."

Leodor looked as though he'd swallowed his chin.

The king chuckled and eyed the baseball card. "You have the look of a warrior though the clothing is very strange. Perhaps this other man was not fit for Ruger's body. That might have driven the failures. But with that said, Abraham, I have a question for you. You want to return to your own world, don't you?"

"Yes."

"I don't see how that fits into my service," the king said. "Your body is mine to command, but the mind is someone else's. I don't think that this can work out."

"King Hector, I gave you my word that I would try to find that egg. I'll keep it. If I return, I vow to continue to help you if you will continue to help me."

The king scratched behind his ear and said, "That sounds fair enough. I'll honor it."

"Thank you, Your Majesty!" He kissed the king's hand. "You won't regret it."

"Just bring back that egg." The king stood. "What about our men? What will you tell your men?"

"Nothing. The truth. I don't know."

The king laughed and tossed Abraham his backpack. "Let's hope this campaign doesn't end before it's started."

# 46

VICEROY LEODOR MADE HIS WAY TO THE HOUSE OF STEEL'S archives. He was alone. His fingers twitched at his side as he moved quickly down the stairs, past a dozen wine cellars, and in through the wooden doors that led to the archives. It was a musty room with a vaulted ceiling and book shelving stacked twelve feet high. Large candles burned on the study tables spread out over the stone floor. Racks of scrolls sat against the walls as well. Inside were several scribes writing down the daily records with quill and ink. They wore blue robes with white collars.

"Get out," Leodor said firmly.

Five bookish men stuck their quills in their ink jars and hustled out. They closed the creaking doors behind them. The doors rattled shut.

Leodor made a quick pass through the premises. No one else was around. He headed to the back wall and passed underneath an archway, where a small door was blocking passage. He removed a key from underneath his robes and opened it. The room inside was pitch black. He muttered an arcane word. A soft yellow light illuminated the room with the quavering power of one hundred candles emanating from four globes that were attached to the top of a brass pole.

The room was a ten-by-twenty rectangle with a small rectangular table evenly centered in the middle. Wooden shelves full of books lined the eight-foot-high walls. Small cobwebs filled the empty corners of the cedar shelving. Tiny bugs and spiders crawled away from the light and disappeared into the cracks and crevices.

These were the oldest archives in the kingdom, eons old, but well-preserved in the cool dry climate. They contained records of the history of man near the beginning of time. They talked about life in Titanuus when only one kingdom existed. However, the language was ancient, forgotten, and very few could interpret it. The scribes would work on it slowly, but it was hardly a priority.

Leodor's hands rifled through a pile of scrolls stacked up neatly at the end of the farthest bookshelf. He'd studied in the archives for decades and knew them better than anyone. He controlled the scribes too, keeping their discoveries to himself. He kept his own enlightenment private as well. He slipped a small scroll out of the bottom of the pile. It was made of lamb's hide and bound by a leather cord. The scroll had a silky touch to it. He took it to the table and unrolled it.

It contained ancient script, but he could read it. It had been written during the era when all kingdoms were one, ages before. It told the story of King Ruoff and the Crown of Stones. It was the same crown worn by King Hector today. Six settings remained empty, made for six gems. The emerald in King Hector's pendant was one of those gems. King Hector's oldest ancestor on record was King Maceadon. He'd had five selfish children and one good. At their prompting, he agreed to bless each with a kingdom. He passed each of them a stone set in its own crown in his feebleness before he died. He gave his emerald stone, a crown, and Kingsland to his youngest and good son. The other five siblings were jealous and corrupt. King Maceadon's children and their children's children drifted further apart. King Maceadon's bloodline became so foul that only the good bloodline could be traced back to King Hector. Led by strife and greed, the new kingdoms continued to divide. Their true heritage was lost, along with their crowns and stones. In their anger, they all turned against the Kingsland, ruled by the youngest brother, and forced him from the main lands, south, to where the House of Steel resided.

Leodor traced his finger over the lettering. He mumbled the ancient text in his own language.

"Six stones. One kingdom. A crown with sturdy horns. Six stones unite all kingdoms. One land. One people. One king. One home. Six stones, the life of Titanuus. Six stones to rule the throne. Six stones to unite the world."

He knew the saying like the back of his hand, but more was there to be read. It told how the stones were meant to be together, working as one. But a devoted group of men and women hid the stones so that no one would ever find them again. Their location was kept secret for eons and their location finally lost. Only King Hector still had the one made from emerald. At least, that is what they all believed it was.

Leodor's fingers traced over the ancient lettering. He read aloud. "When the eyes of the other worlds open, the stones will reveal themselves." He rolled up the scroll and tapped it on his chin. "To tell the king or not to tell the king... That is the question."

# 47

INSIDE BARACHA, THE HENCHMEN BATTLED THE GONDS IN THE night. Cudgel and Tark latched onto a Gond's massive legs like ticks, while Bearclaw choked the man to death. The strategy proved futile. The superior numbers of Shade's gang overwhelmed them. Horace had both of his arms locked up by two men, while a third brute beat on him like a drum.

Prospero and Apollo were both facedown in the dirt, taking hard kicks to the ribs.

Bearclaw was the last to go down swinging before he succumbed to the thrashing.

Shade and his gang hemmed Sticks and the other three women against the wall. Vern crouched in front of them. He held his ribs with one hand and balled up a fist with the other. "Why don't we settle this between me and you, Shade?" Vern said. "Man to man!"

"Step aside, you fool. I'm not going to get my hands dirty on account of you." With his hands concealed in his cloak, Shade eased toward Vern.

Vern threw a hard punch.

Shade snaked his neck out of the way and drove a knee into Vern's ribs.

With a loud groan, Vern crumpled to the ground.

Sticks slipped into Shade's blind side, dropped low, and punched his ribs.

Shade fell onto both knees. Clutching his sides, he said, "Will one of you idiots contain her?"

Two Gonds pounced at her.

She kicked one that was missing his ears, in the crotch. The barbarian didn't wince. With a swipe of his heavy hand, he snatched her by the hair, yanked her up to her toes, and head-butted her. Painful stars exploded in her eyes, and her legs became noodles. She swayed but didn't fall on account of the Gond holding her up by her hair.

She looked up at the Gond and said, "I thought you mindless cow turds had standards."

"Uh huh," said the second Gond with tattoos all over his face just before he punched her in the gut.

The wind exploded out of her. As she gasped for breath, they let her fall to the ground.

Shade squatted down beside her and said, "Ah, looks like someone is bonding with her new lovers." He patted her on the head. "Good for you, Sticks. The Gond appreciate a humble woman. You'll make an excellent bride for the entire tribe."

The prison sirens whistled in the air. On the other side of the prison yard, the guards, spears in hand, charged toward the fight. They dug their spear butts into Shade's gang and the Henchmen with merciless force. The gang of Gonds dispersed.

Shade backed away from Sticks. As spears were pointed at his chest, he held his hands up high. "Heh, heh, heh." He grinned down at Sticks. "The guards won't care forever. Your time is almost up. Like them. Your numbers dwindle." He tipped his head at two dead Red Tunics who lay facedown in the mud. Their necks were twisted unnaturally toward their shoulders. "Bye... for now."

The pale-faced commander of the Baracha guards was the only one not wearing a helmet. He wore blackened plate mail, with the commander's eight chevrons stamped on the chest. Wolf fur was woven into the shoulders, and it made a short cape behind his back. He carried a studded mace with both of his hands. His face was ugly and pockmarked. His greasy brown hair was combed over. He spat tobacco juice on the ground and asked, "Which one of you goatherds is Horace?"

"I am," Horace said. He was on his knees with his hands sunk into the muddy ground. He pulled them out with a sucking sound. "Can I help you, Commander?"

"Yes, you can. You can round up your bastards and get your fat belly out of my prison." The commander spat juice on the ground. "Well, what are you waiting for? A wagon?"

With a groan, Horace came to his feet. "Aye, sir."

"Sergeant, see to it that they are properly processed." The commander looked down at the two dead retainers. "Are those your dead?"

Horace nodded.

"Drag them out unless you'd like me to have the Gond bury them for you."

"No, thank you. I'll take care of it." Horace picked a Red Tunic up in his arms. Bearclaw crawled out of the mud and hefted the other dead man over his shoulders. Escorted by the Baracha guards, Horace led the Henchmen toward the prison's portcullis exit.

Shade's gang beat their chests and jeered. Hundreds more prisoners joined in. Shade marched alongside the Henchmen, shouting at them with bitterness in his voice. "You'll be back! All of you! Tell Ruger I'll be waiting for him too! Tell him the Gonds will be waiting! Next time, all of you will pucker up and kiss my fanny!"

Sticks didn't look back. She held her stomach as she hobbled through the front gate with a growing headache.

Once outside of the prison yard, the Baracha guards returned all their gear to them. The commander pointed down the road and sent them on their way. Sticks trudged down the road with her chin dipped. Her headache was awful. Everything was sore. Everyone in the company moved at a sluggish gait, their shoulders sagging.

"Where to now?" Sticks asked Horace.

"I'm not sure. The Stronghold, I suppose," he replied. With the dead man in his arms, Horace took the lead.

They made it one hundred yards up the road when Horace came to a stop. At the top of the rise, a rider on a horse waited in the moonlight. The midnight rays glistened on the man's breastplate. It was Ruger Slade.

Slowly, the company slogged up to their captain and cast their weary eyes on him.

Sitting tall in the saddle, the strapping sword master asked, "What's the matter with you guys? You look like you just ate a mouthful of donkey dung."

The Henchmen exchanged glances with one another.

"Pardon, Captain," Horace said.

Ruger Slade's black horse nickered and stamped its hooves. It had a white patch of hair on the top of its snout and was geared up with a black leather harness and saddle.

"Easy, boy. Easy." He looked at the dead man in Horace's arms. "A sad thing seeing a Red Tunic becoming a dead tunic. Let's go make a hole and bury them."

The Henchmen followed Ruger Slade for miles, all the way to his stronghold south of Burgess. It was a small fortress built from natural stone, three stories tall, complete with battlements at the top, with its back against a steep hillside of rock. It was surrounded by acres of rich farmland and a small lake. A red barn with stables lay nearby. Livestock grazed. Hired hands slept in the surrounding storehouses. It was Ruger's home and the Henchmen's stronghold, a place that rivaled the lands of the local barons of Burgess.

They stopped at a graveyard overlooking the lake. Dozens of headstones were in the field. Horace and Bearclaw grabbed shovels and started digging. All the Henchmen took turns, even Ruger.

Sticks dug in disbelief. They hadn't buried a Red Tunic or Henchman in years. The old Ruger had stopped doing it. Now, the new Ruger dug and even said a few words.

"Ashes to ashes, dust to dust. May our brethren find a heaven where their steel does not rust."

# 48

Abraham woke in total comfort. He lay in a down-filled bed, dressed in soft cotton. He was so comfortable he didn't want to move. He was sunk in, paralyzed in bliss. He didn't even remember having gone to sleep the night before. He didn't want to open his eyes.

*Please let me wake up in the most comfortable hospital bed ever.*

His nostrils flared. Somewhere, coffee brewed. The early birds chirped their morning songs. A breeze ran through the room, carrying the smell of baked bread to his nose.

*Grandma?*

When he was a boy, he would visit his grandmother in the country and stay a week at a time. Every morning at the table were flaky oversized biscuits stacked a mile high. That was decades before. He knew it couldn't be but wished it could.

A gentle hand caressed his chest. Soft, sweet breath touched his face. A nubile body brushed up against him. A sensual leg crossed over his.

*Uh oh. Dare I look?*

He thought at first that it was Sticks. But her touch wasn't so soft. He thought of his wife, Jenny. He wished it could be her but knew it couldn't be, for she was dead.

*Perhaps I'm still dreaming.*

He opened his eyes.

A gorgeous woman with piles of jet-black hair lay beside him with a smile in her gorgeous eyes. She ran her thighs up and down his. She said in a sensual voice, "Good morning, Captain." She kissed his shoulder with lips as soft as rose petals. "Did you sleep well?"

"Uh… I think so," he said, trying to recall her name.

From behind him, a second body wrapped him in a warm embrace. Lips kissed his back and neck. He thrust himself up into sitting position. Another woman lay on the other side of him. She was identical to the other one with the beautiful raven hair and dusky skin. They could have easily passed for the supervixen Hispanic and Italian movie stars he'd grown up watching.

"Wow."

"You fell asleep so quickly last night that we didn't get to have any fun," the one who woke him up said as she sat up beside him. She wore a short black nightgown that showed off her natural curves. Her hand worked its way down his chest. "Are you ready to have fun now?"

The other woman was dressed in pink. She looked underneath the furs and said, "I think he is."

With all his teenage fantasies suddenly coming to life, he needed every ounce of willpower to say, "No. Just, wait, uh, please, ladies." His heart raced like a galloping horse. He knew Ruger's body was about to take over, and he couldn't let that happen. "It's just a dream. Just a dream. Don't worry about it," he mumbled.

The door opened to his room. A third woman entered, carrying a serving tray. She wore a sexy white medieval teddy designed like the others. She was another identical twin.

*Triplets! Now I know it's a dream.*

The woman in white set down a platter of food on the end of the bed, with a mug of steaming coffee, a stack of what looked like crudely made pancakes, a pile of scrambled eggs, and cooked ham. "Captain, you must be very hungry from your journeys. You did not eat last night. Let me feed you, as I always do."

He was hungry, and not just for food. He gazed at her full breasts, swallowed, tore his eyes away and asked, "Sophia?"

"Yes," the woman in white said.

He pointed at the one in black. "Selma."

"Yes, Captain? What is your wish?" Selma replied.

He turned to the one in pink. "Bridget."

Bridget kissed his fingers. "You named me. You can rename me."

A new wave of memories came back to him. Viceroy Leodor mentioned setting the old Ruger up with property and servants years before. The triplets were a special gift. A lot of Ruger's history continued to pour back into his memories. The Stronghold was a fine piece of land that used to be the property of a retired Guardian. Leodor had the power to gift it to Ruger. Or perhaps, Ruger—or rather, Eugene—demanded it. He wasn't entirely sure. But based off the evidence, Eugene shamelessly took advantage of all the comforts that this fantasy life had to offer. He took a long look at the beautiful women surrounding him.

"Oh lord, I am Mudd."

"No, you are the Captain," the dreamy Selma said innocently.

Selma wore black, Sophia pink, and Bridget white. Eugene must have made them always dress in those colors so that he wouldn't mix them up even though each of them did have their own unique mannerisms.

*At least he didn't name them Blossom, Bubbles, and Buttercup. That would have been really weird.*

Abraham slid out of the bed and covered himself with a blanket. He was still grimy from his early adventures.

Bridget tugged at his blanket. "You need to bathe. The hot springs await, as always." She pulled her shoulders back and made a perky smile. "I will join you!"

He pulled away and headed for the window. The room took up the entire third floor of the Stronghold. It had wardrobes, chests of drawers, Persian-like carpets, and closets. The outer walls were solid stone, but the interior walls of the other rooms were wooden. The home had many modern aspects. He guessed it had five thousand square feet inside the rock. Outside were botanical gardens, hedges, a working farm, and at least a dozen hirelings that he could see breaking a sweat in the morning sunlight. With a great pond, its own hot springs, eye-catching gardens, and voluptuous women dwelling inside, it was nothing short of a medieval Playboy mansion.

*This is ridiculous.*

He crossed the room and stopped in front of a mirror angled so that he could see the women lounging enticingly on the bed. He took his first long look at himself.

*Dang. Hugh Jackman, eat your heart out.*

His sculpted frame wasn't layered in mounds of muscles. It was a finely honed physical specimen with well-defined, rippling muscles. He towered with broad shoulders and a narrow waist. He might as well have been cast from molten iron. With strong angular features and a steel-hard gaze, long limbed and big handed, he didn't look anything short of the deadliest swordsman who had ever been. He had the scars to show for it. No wonder men feared him. He feared himself.

He heard the rattle of a wagon rolling and saw it outside, hitched to a mule. Hay was loaded in the wagon, along with tools to work the fields. Far off in the distance, Bearclaw was manning a plow in the gardens. Sticks drove the wagon out of the barn. Cudgel, Tark, and two Red Tunics were sitting in the back. They were out of their armor and in work clothing. Sticks caught his eye and looked away.

Abraham started toward the steps.

*What's this all about?*

"Captain, where are you going?" Sophia said.

"Yes, we've missed you. Come back to bed," Bridget added.

Abraham left.

# 49

"WHOA, WHOA, WHOA," ABRAHAM SAID AS HE TOOK THE MULE BY the reins and brought the wagon to a stop. He looked at Sticks. "We need to talk."

"Certainly, Captain," Sticks remained in her seat and looked him dead in the eye.

"Let's walk, and don't call me Captain," he said. "Cudgel, Tark, don't go anywhere. We'll be right back."

Sticks hopped out of the wagon. She was still filthy dirty from the prison yard.

He followed the pathway that led out to the pond. No one else was nearby. Last night, he hadn't told the group anything new either. He just acted according to what he knew about Ruger. And burying the dead was the right thing to do, with a proper burial, when people gave their lives for you. He'd learned that from his veteran father.

"I'm still fuzzy on a lot of things," he said. "I know places and some people, but I'm not sure how it all works. So fill me in. When we come back to the Stronghold, all of you sleep in the barns? The house is plenty big."

"We used to stay in the house, but you removed us a few years ago. You said the hirelings work harder when we are out here." She shrugged. "We all work hard out here. It's what we do."

"But you only supervise, right?"

"It depends on the mood you are in. You say you want the Stronghold to be... tasteful. You are very proud of your wine cellar and gardens."

"I have a wine cellar?"

"Below the house, beside the dungeon."

He stiffened. "I have a dungeon too?"

"Yes," she said with a straight face. "But you don't use it for prisoners. You enjoy other things."

"Ah geez, I'm a pervert. Or I was a pervert. Listen, Eugene was the pervert, not me." Tapping his chest with his fingers and looking right at her, he said, "I'm not a pervert."

Sticks shrugged.

Ruger's eyes were like a scanner that would identify things and fill in the blanks as he saw them. Ruger's mind would fill in some memory gaps, too. They walked out on a small dock at the pond. Ducks swam by. Facing outward, he said, "I was a real dickhead, wasn't I?"

"Dickhead?"

"A jerk."

She tilted her head. "You pull something hard? You are good at that."

By the blank look on her face, he knew she didn't understand. "No, let me see... Uh, I mean, oppressive, selfish."

Her creaseless forehead started to crinkle. She nodded. "Yes, very much so."

"Did I ever talk about my... inner self?"

She shook her head.

"Did I speak another name? Or call myself Eugene?"

"No."

Abraham couldn't blame Eugene for keeping it all to himself. Being trapped in a new body and in a different world was more than enough to drive a sane person crazy. He'd dreamed about such things as a teenager, but for it to actually happen was freakish. "Was the old me close to anyone in particular?"

Sticks took a knife out of her belt and spun it with a hand. "You preferred your privacy but indulged yourself in what you would call the flavor of the day."

"So I didn't have a favorite?"

She twisted her knife around, put it away, and shrugged. "You enjoyed new things. Pretty things."

"What about the me before the last me? What was he like?"

"You wouldn't be standing out here staring at ducks this time of morning. You'd be practicing with your swords. We'd all be practicing, and we wouldn't be gardening or farming, either." She kicked at the ducks that swam toward her. They quacked and swam away. "We all stayed in the Stronghold too, but not the retainers or hirelings. Plenty of room in the barns for them. They haven't earned the brand. Not all do."

Abraham scratched his cheek. He wanted to understand more about who Ruger Slade really was. *What happened to that man? Did he wind up in another body as well? Where is the real Ruger Slade?* "Tell me more, like, about my personality."

"Well, you were a knight once, the leader of the King's Guardians. So you were disciplined, stern, quiet. Those are the traits of a knight," Sticks said. "But, Horace, Vern, and Bearclaw know that old you better than I. They were Guardians too. Young and brave, they followed you after the first time you went crazy."

"Oh," he muttered.

She was talking about what King Hector had mentioned. Ruger Slade abandoned the Guardians, and many of them died. It sounded as though someone had jumped into Ruger even before Eugene Drisk did. Abraham wondered if that all had something to do with the sword, Black Bane.

Sticks continued. "There was always sadness. You didn't mix with the women like you do now and didn't engage in these casual conversations. You served the king, but it was all business. You conducted yourself with a heavy heart."

"So I wasn't much fun. But I didn't get as many killed then either, did I?" he asked.

"Many died, but no, not as many. You've never been afraid to put your Henchmen into battle for the cause. You would engage when what had to be done, had to be done. We've thwarted the plans of many of the king's enemies. We burned, we butchered any enemy of the king we came across. We've destroyed outposts, thwarted spy rings, purged the traitors from the sewers they hide in. You name it, we've done it. But we stopped getting our hands as dirty a few years ago."

"Dirty jobs, huh? I like that show." His stomach rumbled. "Have the Henchmen had breakfast?"

"A bowl of meal, as always."

Abraham didn't know any one of them very well, but he was disgusted by how they'd been treated. The Henchmen would have given their lives to him or the king. It was his crew now, and the time had come to make changes.

"Round the Henchmen up. It's time to break bread."

---

The first level of the Stronghold was a combination of kitchen, weapons training facility, and dining hall. During hard rains, they pulled the tables away and trained. They ate their meals there too, together, but that tradition had been abandoned years before. The second level of the building was a barracks made up of small beds and bunks, enough beds for one hundred soldiers to be quartered tightly together. At the top level was the Captain's quarters. It used to be divided into three sections, with two separate smaller quarters for the top sergeants. Now, it was only one room. Below the building was a dungeon, supply and weapons storage, and the wine cellar.

Abraham sat at the head of a long dark oak farm table, waiting for the Henchmen to join him. One by one, they came in the front door, with Bearclaw leading the way followed by Sticks, Vern, Cudgel, Tark, Dominga, Iris, Prospero, Apollo, and Horace bringing up the rear. Horace closed the door behind himself. Horace and Sticks sat at the head of the table, on either side of Abraham. The rest of the group took seats on the benches, spreading out but still filling only half of the huge table.

All the Henchmen were hard eyed, weary, and dirty. Prospero yawned and smacked his lips.

Horace broke the odd silence and said, "Good morning, Captain."

"Good morning," Abraham replied.

This was the first time he was able to take a really good look at all of them. Bearclaw had a fresh scab running down the length of his face. Vern's face looked like rotting pumpkin, and he wasn't a half bad-looking man to begin with, compared to the others. The rest were in better shape, all stripped down to muddy black tunics or shirts with long sleeves. Iris sent a warm smile his way. Cudgel and Tark looked at him intently with their smoky light-colored eyes.

Abraham scratched the side of an eye, unsure how to address them. He'd been a strong voice in his locker room, and words usually came easy, but at the moment, the uncertainty in their faces created doubt inside him.

He cleared his throat. "From now on, we all eat here. Together. Like we used to."

Bearclaw and Horace looked down the table at him. Prospero and Apollo pulled their elbows from the table. Dominga's tired eyes brightened.

"The hirelings are fixing breakfast. You can smell it, can't you?" he said.

Horace nodded. "Of course, Captain." He raked his fingers through his beard. "It all smells very good."

Abraham knew who these people were, but aside from Sticks, he didn't have a full grip on their personalities, aside from them being a fierce group of fighters. He felt as if he were in the locker room for the first time, meeting a new team. There was some awkwardness. He'd given thought to telling them who he was, as he had with Sticks and King Hector, but decided against it. He was just going to be who he wanted to be going forward, but he needed to break the ice with them. "From this point on, here in the Stronghold, let's all speak more freely with one another."

"But Captain, you told us if we didn't keep our tongues tied, you'd cut them out," Horace said.

"Well, after the latest lump on my head, I've changed my mind. So be yourself. That's an order."

A hireling woman appeared from inside the hidden kitchen galley. She was older, brown haired and bowlegged, with two metal coffee pots gripped in her leathery hands. She set the pots on the table as steam came from the spouts. Right behind her came another woman who could have passed for her daughter and had an innocent look about her. She carried a tray of clay mugs made with handles. The women set everyone up with a fresh cup of coffee, complete with cream and sugar that they made available. They vanished back into the galley.

The Henchmen stared blankly at their cups.

Abraham lifted his cup and said, "It's not Zombie Dew, but it will do. Drink up, everybody."

The hireling women brought out more platters of food: bacon, piles of ham and eggs, biscuits, ugly pancakes, and gravy.

The Henchmen heartily dug in.

Abraham was glad to see it. His grandmother had always told him that the best way to make friends was to serve them good food. Everyone liked good food. He enjoyed his own meal and the company. *The triplets' meal will have to wait.* Instead, his gaze was transfixed on the homeless-looking Prospero and Apollo, who were holding their plates up and licking them like hounds. *Clark Griswold, eat your heart out.*

Sticks carefully cut her food up with a knife and fork. Horace belched after every three mouthfuls. Vern chewed agonizingly slowly while Bearclaw stole food from his plate. He wasn't sure if they were a family, but they got along well enough with one another.

Abraham set down his utensils, deciding to take a crack at a little locker-room humor. "I'd like to share a joke that I heard long ago in a place far away."

Everyone stopped eating and looked his way.

Horace let out a final belch. "Sorry, Captain."

"It's fine," Abraham said. "So, a duck walks into a tavern and says, 'Hey barkeep, do you have any grapes?' And the barkeep says, 'No, I don't have any. Get out of here, you silly duck.' So the duck waddles away and leaves. The next day, the duck comes back and says to the barkeep, 'Hey, do you have any grapes?' Angrily, the barkeeper says, 'No. We only sell wine and ale here. Now, the next time you come into my tavern and ask me for grapes, I'm going to nail your bill to the bar.'" Abraham tapped the table hard with his finger. "'Now, get out of here, you stupid duck!' So the duck waddles out and leaves. On the third day, the duck comes back and says to the barkeep, 'Hey, do you have any nails?' The surprised bartender said, 'No.' Then the duck says, 'Well, do you have any grapes?'"

All the Henchmen looked at Abraham as though he were stupid, save for one.

Vern erupted in laughter.

# 50

After the plates were cleaned, no one said much of anything. The environment remained as stale as bread. Drumming his fingers on the table, Abraham said, "I guess you're wondering what the king said to me or why my head is still attached."

"It's not our business. You're the Captain, and you give the orders," Horace said with a nod. "I think I speak for us all when I say that we are thankful for the meal. Shall we take the fields now?"

With a bewildered shake of his head, Abraham said, "No. This company has another mission. We'll be departing by tomorrow, if not today."

The group exchanged curious glances.

Cudgel leaned over, put his elbows on the table, clasped his fingers, and said, "Another mission? So soon?" When Horace glared at Cudgel, he glared right back. "He said we could speak freely."

"He didn't mean that freely," Horace fired back.

"Yes, I did," Abraham said.

Rolling his thumbs in front of his chest, Vern said, "Ha ha."

"Don't disrespect the Captain!" Horace roared. He pounded his fist on the table and pointed at Vern. "You giggling traitor!"

"Back off, Horace," Bearclaw said. "I've known Vern since we were young men. I don't think he's the traitor. Not now. For all we know, you are the traitor."

"What?" Horace's eyes twitched. "You hairy black snake! It makes perfect sense that you'd side with him. You're in on it, too!"

Sticks jumped in and said, "We don't know any of that! The frights might have found a way on their own. After all, they wield magic."

"And probably give birth to men like Vern!" Horace said.

Grimacing, Vern pushed himself up off the bench. "Listen, you bearded turd, you can call me a lot of things, but you aren't calling me a traitor. I say we settle this outside. Sword against sword. You might last five seconds since I'm wounded."

With a heavy shake of his bald head, Horace said, "I'll take that challenge. I'm going to put you down, and I'll put you down next, Bearclaw!"

Dominga jumped up on the table and said, "You two idiots shut your buttholes! No one's fighting anybody!"

Vern looked up at her and said, "Pretty thing, you aren't stopping anybody, but you're welcome to try."

"Vern, you couldn't whip me right now," she said. "I'd beat the hell out of you. Horace will stomp a mudhole out of you. You know that. Just sit down!"

"Your words cut deeper than any sword. I have pride." Vern sat down. "You know."

Horace made a triumphant harrumph.

"What are you guffing at, Horace?" she asked. "Sit your buttocks down."

Horace blanched. He started to sit, but Sticks stood up and

said to Dominga, "You aren't anyone's leader. Horace. Sergeant. Me. Sergeant. You. Not sergeant!"

Dominga shrank under Sticks's hot gaze. Frowning, she did a back flip off the table and sat down at the bench. With the same fire in her voice she said, "The Captain said we could speak freely. What in Titanuus's tit do you think freely means?"

"I'm not sure what it means," Sticks said. She looked at Abraham.

Abraham smiled. "That's what I like to see out of my Henchmen. Some smack talk does the body good." He tapped the table with his fist. He'd been in the thick of his share of locker-room fights. "Real good. But I don't want anyone gutting anyone over a squabble." He showed his fists. "You can duke it out like brothers, but no weapons."

"But Captain, Vern betrayed us," Horace said.

"We've all ridden together a long time. Me, you, Bearclaw, and Vern were all the King's Guardians. You stuck with me when my failure happened. I don't think you'd betray us all now." Abraham shrugged. "Maybe things change. I don't know, but I'm not executing a man without proof or an admission of his crime. I don't know who freed the frights. It might have been one of us or one of them. Right now, we can't let it happen again. The slate is clean. We have to go forward. It's time for another mission. I can't make you get along. I can't make one believe the other. We're all going to have to trust that our actions speak for themselves. As for me, I haven't seen anyone here, or out there, do anything wrong. From this point on, the slate is clean."

The Henchmen exchanged uncomfortable looks. Some frowned, and others grumbled, expect for Prospero. His head was dipped onto his chest, drool running into his beard. He was snoring. Vern gave a stiff nod toward Abraham.

The bench groaned beneath Horace when he turned his body

toward Abraham and said, "Fair enough. So what did King Hector say?"

"Well, he wasn't happy that we failed to return the frights. As a matter of fact, he was so unhappy that he decided to execute my death sentence," Abraham said.

Iris clutched her hands to her chest and moaned. "Oh no."

Horace stiffened. Several sets of eyes at the table grew big. If Ruger died, the Henchmen would be condemned. All of them would go back to prison, and the former knights would be hanged. The rest would be forgotten. Their fate depended on the company's success.

"So, the king's grace ended?" Horace asked.

"Yes, but fortunately, the queen's grace has not," he said. "If it weren't for her timely interruption, I believe I'd be swinging in the gallows this very morning. She is still fond of me, and sadly, she is sick."

"The queen is ill? What is wrong with her?" Iris asked in a sweet voice.

"I don't know. She's rigid, aging rapidly. Her vibrant beauty has faded." He took a swig of coffee. "It made my heart ache, but she still had fire in her eyes."

Resting his thick forearms on the table, Cudgel asked, "Certainly the viceroy can cure her? He's well-known for his methods and ability to heal."

"Pah!" Iris's cheery expression hardened. "The Sect is not as they say."

"I don't know, but Leodor has been doing everything that he can." Abraham finished his coffee and set it down. "He sent two expeditions to the peaks in Titanuus's Spine to find a cure. One north and one south. They never returned."

"Well, of course not. Not many that navigate the Spine ever live," Bearclaw said as he picked his teeth with his fork. "What were they looking for?"

"The egg of a fenix. He says its yolk can cure anything," he replied.

Everyone at the table started laughing so hard that Prospero was jolted from his slumber. He looked around and joined in with the cajoling. Even the stoic Sticks broke out in giggles.

Abraham sat in stunned silence, bewildered by their amusement. "Why is that so funny?"

Horace wiped his eyes and caught his breath. "Sorry, Captain. We all adore Queen Clarann, more so than the king, but sending a campaign into the Spine to search for a creature that does not exist... Well, that's plum foolishness." He hacked out a cough and tapped his chest. "You were jesting, weren't you?"

"No. The king and the viceroy were dead serious. King Hector claims that he's seen the fenix."

"No one sees the fenix and lives," Bearclaw said. "So that would be impossible. So say the legends. Are you sincere? They really did send out two campaigns into the Spine?"

"That's what they said."

"A campaign like that is over one hundred men each, and none of them returned?" Cudgel asked. "That is a shame for the queen. I've cast my eyes on her twice before. She was very beautiful. She had the strength of an eagle in her eyes. If the mythical fenix egg was her only hope, then her situation is fatal." He rubbed his chin. "I wonder who the next queen will be?"

"Ah, I'm sure the king will find a woman that is just as beautiful. After all, he is the king," Horace said. He put his hands down on his knees and rocked back and forth. "So, Captain, we are sorry for the news, but tell us, what is our next urgent mission?"

Abraham swallowed as he scanned the eyes of all the eager faces. His mind, merged with Ruger's, didn't recall anything about the Spine or fenixes. The Henchmen's reaction revealed that he'd bitten off more than he could chew. *Oh lord, what have I agreed to?* He sipped from his empty coffee mug. "Uh, well,

King Hector wants to send one more campaign after the fenix egg."

With his hairy arms crossed over his chest, Bearclaw huffed and said, "Well, may the Elders favor them. What about us?"

Abraham intently looked at them all and replied, "We are the campaign."

# 51

Rolling her neck, Dominga said, "Well, somebody cut my jugular now."

"Yes, but shoot me with a crossbow first," Vern said. "Right in the heart, because without Dominga, I don't need it."

"Captain, tell me that this is not so," Horace said as he rocked back and forth on the bench. "We are soldiers. We use sabotage and espionage. We spy and gather information. Sure, we are expendable, but traversing the Spine to search for a fenix... That makes no sense. It's a suicide mission."

Everyone started to grumble and murmur. Prospero beat his head on the table. Apollo yawned. Sticks shook her head and chewed on her lip.

"Captain, we only have thirteen seasoned men left. Thirteen! Those expeditions had hundreds," Cudgel said. He wiped away the new sweat beading on his forehead with his forearm. "You've commandeered many more people, right?"

All eyes fell on Abraham.

"No," he said.

They let out a unified "Aaaaah!" and began shaking their heads and mumbling to themselves.

"It was either that or die. That would have been true for most of us," he said. "Henchmen, we are going after the fenix egg. That's an order."

"With only thirteen men?" Vern said. "The last mission we started with sixty. And now it's just us and a bunch of green tunics."

"Red Tunics," Dominga said.

"You know what I mean," Vern said.

"You bear the mark, Vern," Sticks said. "We all do. If he had to sail to the edge of the sea, we are bound to do it. No one forced any of us to take the King's Brand. It was voluntary."

"Yes, my brothers and I had such a great choice." Cudgel's nostrils flared. "Throw our lives away or rot in prison."

"At least you get fresh air," Bearclaw added.

"Not to mention that the king can release us from our pledge," Dominga said. "Can't he?"

"King Hector can do whatever he wants. It's just never been done before," Horace said. "Most of us die first."

"But you get a proper burial and your record wiped clean for fighting for the king," Sticks said.

"A fat lot of good that does our dead brothers," Cudgel said. He threw an arm over Tark. "We are the last ones. We'll never see my mother and father again."

Horace turned toward Cudgel and said, "Well, you shouldn't have been stealing from the king's livestock."

"We were starving. What else were we going to do? We were only children," the round-faced black man replied.

"Beg," Horace answered.

"Griping about the past isn't going to do us any good," Abraham said.

The hireling women slipped in from the galley, waddled over, refilled everyone's coffee, and disappeared back into the galley.

"Those campaigns were too big. A baker's dozen should work out better. Maybe we wouldn't have lost so many if we hadn't taken too many to begin with."

"It was your idea," Vern said with a stupefied look. "And what's a baker's dozen?"

"Thirteen. It means thirteen." He flipped his hand. "Listen, we are going to load up, take one small wagon, and head for the hills. There is no other choice that we have. Any questions?"

Cudgel lifted his hand. "We never go on a mission without at least one mystic. Who is going to care for our wounds and cast fire against our enemies?"

"You can let the dogs lick your wounds," Vern said.

"At least they'd like mine. They'd never touch yours," Cudgel fired back.

Vern rolled his swollen eyes.

"I can handle the wounds, mostly," Iris said.

Cudgel snorted.

"Who did we use before?" Abraham asked.

Sticks sat straight up.

Cudgel's eyes turned as white as the moon as he slammed both hands on the table. "Elgan did." He slapped his hands on the table again. He stepped over the bench as Tark did too. He stuck a finger at Abraham. "You might be the Captain, but there is something very wrong with you. I don't care if you slay me." The brothers stormed across the room, punched the double doors open, and exited with the door slamming behind them.

Abraham felt bad but remained poised. He wasn't going to remember everything. Mistakes would be made. He'd have to live or die with them. But this was what he had to do if he needed to find a way home. "Any other questions?"

No one said a word.

"Let's get ready then. Come on, Sticks."

# 52

On separate horses, Abraham and Sticks rode to Burgess. The king's city was surrounded by miles of sprawling countryside and white cottages with light-blue roofs. Several stone-paved roads led into the city, miles away. On the way in, they passed plenty of travelers coming and going on foot, on horseback, or on wagons. The city itself was far vaster than his view from the House of Steel's high walls. Hundreds of buildings, made with stone and mortar, stood over fifty feet tall. He also saw great cathedrals with massive archway entrances and stadiums for entertainment and contests. The storefronts showed off colorful wreaths and decorations on their doors. Goods were enticingly displayed in the windows. Hard boots walked over the wooden porches. Old men and women were seated on benches outside. The city was laid out like a small fantasy version of Pittsburgh, with a constant sea breeze that stirred free-flowing hair.

Most of the people wore robes of different fashions and fine linens. Many men wore long shirts and trousers. Feet were shod with either boots or sandals. Barefoot children raced through the streets. Everything appeared orderly, well laid out, and splendid, except for the bloodstained gallows set up at the entrance to every quadrant.

One block ahead, crows and pigeons fought on the gallows deck, where criminals, treasonous men and women, were hanged. Two soldiers wearing steel cap helms and leather armor and carrying spears and swords on their hips guarded the gallows. The gallows had two nooses strung up and one guillotine stained black from dried blood. The nooses swung in the wind. The gruesome structure's posts and beams creaked against the ocean breeze.

Two men still hung in the nooses. They wore no hoods, tongues hanging from their mouths. Abraham and Sticks rode by, watching crows pick at the flesh. The rank-smelling sourness of rotting flesh filtered through the air. The soldiers were working their way up the steps. They lowered the dead bodies, loosened the nooses, and tossed them over the side into a wagon.

"That's probably going to be me if I don't bring that egg back," Abraham said.

He hadn't spoken since they'd left. Neither had Sticks.

Crinkling her nose, she asked, "Why are we here?"

"I don't know. I just wanted to get away from the others. I thought that coming here might refresh my memories."

"Is it?"

"Well, I know where I'm going, at least." He looked back at the gallows they'd just passed. "The people don't seem very fazed by the killings."

"Their hearts only harden against the king—not all, just most," she said.

A pair of long-faced women wearing black robes walked right out in front of their horses. The one on the right held up two fingers, wiggled them, and asked, "Death to the king, or life to the king?"

"Death to you if you don't get your wrinkled ass out of my way." Sticks reared up her horse.

The women dashed across the street and vanished into a small cathedral entrance.

"That was spooky," he said.

"They are probably members of the Sect. They control everything in Burgess but without saying so."

"Yes, so they work for Leodor?"

"Or Leodor works for them. No one knows. None of them ever admit to anything though they claim to support the king. I don't think a one of them would ever take the King's Brand, though."

They traveled from one side of Burgess to the other, where the road led out toward the sea. Levees, docks, wharfs, and boats of all kinds could be seen all the way up the shoreline. Some men fished from piers, while others hauled nets out of small boats. Abraham led them down to the beach, away from the crowds. The horses made their way down onto the wet sand. Surges of foaming green waves crashed over their hooves.

"What's on your mind?" Sticks asked.

"I needed to clear my head. Beaches are pretty popular for doing that where I come from." He breathed deeply through his nostrils and exhaled. "I think that's the first real deep breath I've had since I've been here. I did have a good sleep, though."

"I bet you did."

"Oh, the triplets. Well, nothing happened in there—this time, anyway." He laughed and made a sheepish smile. "Something must really be wrong with me to miss out on that kind of opportunity when this world is not real."

"You didn't tussle with them?"

"Did you hear any tusslings?"

"No. I wasn't listening, but usually, we can hear it. Hmm."

Staring out at the distant fishing boats, he said, "Okay, before I lead us into the jaws of death, I need to make sure I understand my men and women. I'm pretty hazy on all of our history."

"Me and Dominga worked our way up. Dominga's new and

picked by, well, the other you. I came on because, well, I was on the run and had no place to go. You found me during recruiting Red Tunics. That was years ago. Horace—"

"No, don't tell me anymore. Horace, Bearclaw, and Vern were all knights like me." His eyes widened. "Ah crap, Prospero and Apollo are Guardians too, aren't they?"

"Yes."

"Oh man, when I lost my head, well, not me, but Ruger, they followed. They were to be punished the same as me. They weren't the only ones. So many others died." He leaned forward and patted his black horse's neck. "I recruited Cudgel and his brothers out of prison. They were young, barely men. Tark, Levi, and..." He squinted. "William were their names."

She nodded.

"And half of them died. Man, that hurts me. Do you know how many have died under my leadership?"

"One hundred and seventy-five Henchmen and retainers. Most of them retainers."

"You know this?"

"You used to keep a ledger. Now I keep it since you stopped doing it."

"And I've been doing this, how long, seven or eight years?"

"That's about right. I came on five years ago. I've been a Henchman for over three."

He shook his head. "Why would anyone volunteer to do this?"

She reached into her saddlebag, fished out two apples, and fed one to her horse. "It's a better life than farming or living in a prison. It's a chance for some nobody to serve the cause of the king. Not everyone can be one of the king's soldiers. Not everyone can find a place to work, either. It's a chance for status with promise of adventure, even treasure."

"I guess we are all a bunch of desperados in one way or another, I suppose." He opened his hands and caught the apple she tossed him. "It's no wonder we can't win if we are no more than a bunch of thieves and criminals."

"In the past, you brought the best out of all of us. We would fight hard for you, trust you before the change," she said. "They liked the old you. Besides, you used to say that everyone is a criminal in one way or another. Some get caught, and some don't."

He smiled. "I said that?"

"Years ago."

# 53

ON THE SHORELINE, BELOW THE CLIFFS THAT ROSE UP TO THE HOUSE of Steel, Abraham gathered the Henchmen. They were a formidable bunch, wearing black tunics over the chain-mail armor. All of them rode on horseback. The retainers, Twila and two young men, drove a two-team horse and wagon loaded with supplies. They also had three pack mules and five extra horses. The group looked as though they were ready for anything.

The King's Guardians, led by Lewis, approached from the south. Viceroy Leodor rode at his side. A dozen knights in full plate armor rode behind them. The sun shone on their lion-faced helmets. The lion's mane plumes billowed against the ocean breeze.

Abraham leaned over his saddle horn. Horace and Sticks were on either side of him. "You might want to make yourself scarce. You know how cavalier Lewis is."

"Aye, Captain," Horace said.

Lewis brought the Guardians to a halt with a raised fist. He and Leodor separated from the group and trotted up to Abraham.

With the sun shining in his face, Lewis said, "It's a beautiful day to begin a dreadful expedition. What a shame I can't be joining you."

"Seeing how I'm trying to save the queen, you might want to give me your blessing," Abraham said.

Lewis reached over and pushed Leodor's shoulder. "That's what the viceroy is for. Go ahead, Leodor. Give him the fool's blessing."

Leodor frowned. From underneath his beige robes, he removed a scroll. "Ruger or, well, what do you want to be called?"

"Let's keep it simple and stick with Ruger," Abraham said.

"Yes, yes." Leodor licked his lips and handed Ruger a scroll. "That is the same information that I gave to the other expeditions. There is a history about the fenix and the names of peoples that have claimed to have seen it. Many people still worship the fenix but will guard its secret well. I cannot say if there is any truth to what is on that scroll or not. But there is a grain of truth in every lie and legend. Perhaps the elders will be with you. We will pray long life for the queen."

"Long live the queen," Ruger said. He tucked the scroll in his saddle and looked at Lewis. "Is there anything else? I'm ready to partake in this dreadful journey."

Lewis gazed behind him. "You don't boast very many. Is that because you led them all to their deaths?"

"No," Ruger said casually. "Some of them deserted."

Lewis laughed. "Those must have been the smart ones."

---

"So, what load of dragon dung did you put on that scroll?" Lewis asked Leodor. Both men remained on their horses, watching Ruger lead his company up the shore. "I hope you at least gave them a nibble."

"I gave them enough information to keep them busy," the

clammy Leodor said. "And I'm certain that the result will be the same as the other two campaigns. Failure."

"It's a shame that you can't find a cure for Queen Clarann. She is a good woman. I like her."

"Sadly, some things cannot be cured. I fear that there is little hope for your stepmother. And I like her too." Leodor shifted in his saddle. "I really hate riding these things. They are so uncomfortable." He eyed the Henchmen. "I'm glad I'm not them. I'm not sure how they do it, how any of you do it. All of that armor must be very uncomfortable."

"You wouldn't say that if someone came at you with a sword. My chain and plate has saved me countless times." Lewis leaned over his saddle horn, his eyes intent on the campaign. "Is there any truth to the fenix and the powers of the yolk in the egg?"

"It is written. But proven… That's another thing."

"Tell me more about it."

"They histories say that the fenix is the spawn of the Elders, a truly magnificent and powerful creature. The images show part dragon and part monster, a great head and slavering jaws that can consume entire people. If one were to find it, we would not know. They would not survive the encounter. I think this will be Ruger's final journey."

"I don't know," Lewis said. "Sometimes I think the Elder of Luck is by his side. Even with eyes and ears on the inside, he keeps coming back. His last personality, well, that was manageable, but this one, this Abraham that speaks in his body now…" He shook his head. "He has an edge in his voice."

"I only heard desperation, my prince. He's still a far cry from the true Ruger that we know." Leodor jumped in his saddle as a seabird soared right over his head. "Bloody things. Why do they pester me so?" He composed himself, but his eyes searched the skies. "Besides, now that Ruger has lost his station and you have filled it, it becomes easier to fulfill the Underlord's demands. It's what you wanted, wasn't it?"

Lewis rubbed his hands together. "Yes. We should meet with the Underlord, shouldn't we?"

"Agreed. I will arrange it." Leodor cast a backward glance. "You'll have to separate yourself from the Guardians for a time."

"I know. That won't be a problem." The Henchmen faded into the shoreline. "I'll be curious what the Underlord has to say about this recent change in Ruger. The entire idea of different personalities taking over men's bodies is unsettling. Could such a thing happen to me?"

"I don't even think that the Underlord knows. But I sense change in the air. These possessed people are a sign of it." Leodor grabbed his reins in his soft hands. "And the portals that Ruger mentioned. That's another part in the puzzle. What unholy terror will come out of them next?"

"Humph." Lewis turned his horse around. "Holy or unholy, as long as it doesn't come after me, I don't care."

# 54

THREE DAYS OF RIDING PASSED BEFORE THE HENCHMEN ARRIVED AT what the locals called Titanuus's Crotch. They rode along the shoreline where they could and took the roads that snaked around the seashore cities of Southern Tiotan. At the moment, Southern Tiotan and Kingsland did not war with one another, but tensions were high. The Henchmen kept moving, camping outside the small towns that ran along the coast. Now they stood on the shores of Titanuus's Crotch, which was little more than a barren wasteland against the sea.

Abraham swayed side to side in his saddle. For the last several miles of riding, he'd kept his eyes fixed on the great mountain range called Titanuus's Spine. The mountains were leagues wide, and gargantuan hilltops rose beyond the height of the clouds.

*Oh my.*

This wasn't the first time he'd seen mountains like this. In West Virginia, hills were everywhere, but they weren't even above sea level. Titanuus's Spine was more like the Colorado Rockies, perhaps much bigger and longer. It reminded him of something else. When he was a teenager, his father had been stationed in

Hawaii, and Abraham took a trip to Maui. He and his friends took a mountain-biking trip up to the top of a massive volcano called Haleakala. The mountain rose over seven thousand feet in height, where a great crater waited in the middle. They rode their bikes down mountains and back through the clouds that waited four thousand feet below. They didn't stop screaming down the road until it bottomed out at sea level. Acres of pineapple fields greeted them on the journey home.

Titanuus's Spine appeared to be very much like that except its peaks were jagged and dreadful.

Abraham snorted in a deep breath and slowly let it out. "This sucks."

Evening started to fall. The Henchmen's faces were already weary. No one had said a word in three days, hardly. Even the chatter by the campfire had been muted, as if all of them were on a long, quiet march to death row.

"Orders, Captain?" Horace said.

"Let's make camp."

"Aye."

Once that camp was set, Abraham rounded up the company by the campfire. "It's time for a little fellowship by the fireside," he said.

The Henchmen gathered. Some stood, while others sat. As always, Horace and Sticks remained to his right and left. "That includes you Red Tunics, too."

The Red Tunics, the pie- and dimple-faced Twila, along with the other two young gangly men, slunk over. None of them ever spoke to the Henchmen, aside from acknowledging orders.

He held up the scroll that Leodor had given him. "I'm going to keep it simple. We're going to try and retrace the steps of the other campaign. Certainly, that large of a group won't be that hard to follow. And according to this writing, we'll need to ask the people that reside along the base of the Spine if they know anything about the fenix." He opened the scroll and stared at it. "Uh, it appears that there are several tribes, or villages, that worship it. And I don't think they would worship something that they haven't seen." He thought about his own faith. "No, wait, I take that back. Anyway, that's the plan. But I'm open to suggestions."

No one said a word.

"Come on. I know that at least one of you has something to say." He rocked back and forth on his heels. He patted the pommel of Black Bane. "Someone say something."

"Er… well, Captain," Apollo said in a very gravelly voice. He scratched his scruffy beard. "Seeing how we are about to journey into the mountains and face a certain death, would it be possible to unwind one last time? You know, wet our tongues on some rum and ale."

"You want to go on a bender?"

"No, I want to get drunk and maybe cozy one last night with a trollop." Apollo scanned the women. "Seeing how all of these prudes are spoken for."

Iris lifted her hand. "I'm not spoken for, but I wouldn't sleep with you for a thousand shards of silver."

Twila perked up. "I would." She shrank back down under the stares of the Henchmen. "Sorry."

"Is this where the group stands?" Abraham asked. "You want a night of carousing? Huh." He used a serious tone. "Do you?"

"I do," Vern said after a brief silence. "And we haven't had a break since our last journey. We came back with our arses in hand and were tossed in Baracha." He touched his black-and-blue nose. "Then you show up all smiles. So, yes, I would like to go on a *bender*, as you say."

"We need to have our wits about us. We can't traverse the Spine hungover and drunk. We need to be sharp," Abraham said. "With our luck, we're bound to be in a fight before we know it."

"I fight better drunk," Apollo said.

"Aye, me too," Prospero agreed.

"Great, I have team Nick Nolte on my side. Anyone else?" he asked.

Tark lifted his hand. So did Cudgel, Vern, and Dominga.

"Oh, I see what the problem is," Abraham said sarcastically. "We've been failing all of these missions because we've been stone-cold sober." He looked at Horace. The beefy man shrugged. "We all know better than that. Besides, we're at the mountain's bottom. There's nowhere to go and get your freak on. Sorry, Apollo."

Vern took the toothpick out of his mouth and said, "We aren't far from Hackles, Captain."

"Hackles?"

Horace whispered in his ear. "It's one of the last stops at the base of the Spine. We've been there some time ago. Perhaps half a league up the shoreline. We'll still be on course before we enter the mountains."

Abraham took a long, hard look into the tired eyes of his command. Some held his gaze. The others looked away. He'd seen faces like that before in the locker room after a losing streak. Sometimes, a team played hard, but it wasn't working. Sometimes, people just tried too hard, and it wasn't happening. Everyone was stiff and rigid. They needed a break. They needed to loosen up. They needed one last night on the town.

"Well, what are you waiting for? Get this camp broken down. We're going to Hackles!"

The Henchmen, one and all, let out a roar.

# 55

Hackles was a shabby seaport city where maybe ten thousand inhabitants thrived. According to local legends, it was the place where Titanuus had dumped his bowels when he died. The inky green seawaters were as foul as a dead sea. It was nothing compared to Swain in Kingsport. The rickety wooden buildings bowed and swayed against the wind. The floorboards on the porches creaked underfoot. Fishermen bandied about, singing songs about the sea, with jugs of wine hooked in their fingers. Others shuffled along, groaning about stiff backs and griping about the big fish they'd missed that day. The docks were small, and so were the vessels. The foamy seawater that beat against the rocks on the shore smelled strongly of salt and seaweed. Hackles was a rotten town.

The Henchmen loved it.

The tavern's regulars were a bunch of fishermen, mostly older, with thick beards and long-stemmed pipes. They grumbled and hunkered down over their drinks. Many eyes widened at the sight of the Henchmen, who came in with full armor and steel on their hips. Hackles wasn't much of a town. It was a place where many came for solitude, but it provided a little excitement from time to time when strangers passed through.

Within the hour, the Henchmen had nestled in. Apollo and Prospero practically dove into the first tavern they came across and vanished inside. The high-pitched squeals of women erupted from inside. Cudgel and Tark were the next to enter, followed by Bearclaw and Vern. By the time Abraham made it inside, all the men had giggling women sitting on their laps or hanging on their arms. The women's scant clothing revealed a lot of paint coating their nubile bodies. The body paint sparkled in the candlelight. The serving women brought tankards of ale and goblets made of steel. Apollo and Prospero opened their mouths wide, the women poured, and they guzzled it down.

Abraham took his seat at a corner table. Horace joined him.

Watching Apollo and Prospero, Abraham said, "And to think that they were Guardians once. Weren't they beholden to a higher standard?"

"We aren't Guardians anymore," Horace said as a curvy waitress set down two tankards of ale on the table. He gave her a nod and a wink and watched the sway of her generous hips when she walked away. "But even Knights celebrate victory, the same as others do. Including me. You remember that, don't you?"

"I think you've known for a long time that I'm not the same Ruger that you've always known," Abraham said.

Horace guzzled his beer. "Ah! What do you mean, Captain?"

"My strange behavior. Mannerisms. You know that I'm different."

Horace buried his chubby cheeks behind his mug and shrugged.

Ruger pressed the issue. "You think I'm crazy, don't you? And the men do too, don't they?"

"It doesn't matter what we think. You are the Captain." Horace set his goblet down and wiped his forearm across his mouth. "And I advise the Captain not to talk like this."

Abraham took a long drink of the warm and bitter ale. "This isn't very good. It tastes like boiled bark." He set it aside. "Horace, look at me. We have to talk this out. You and I were close once, right?"

Horace's neck rolled a little. "Aye, Captain. We all were, before the disgrace. We are loyal to you and the crown." He showed his intense eyes. "It doesn't matter who is in charge inside that body. We gave our word. We'll follow you to the depths of the ocean. Our word is honor. We don't need a brand to keep it."

Abraham rested his forearms on the table. "Even if I'm possessed?"

"Don't say that. I don't know what you are, but at least you have your spine back." He crossed his arms over his chest. "No pun intended, as you would say."

Ruger smiled. "I said that? When?"

"Not so long ago. Many times. You speak funny words time to time."

"Well, at least you are used to it."

Abraham thought he might talk more about who he really was but opted not to. The Henchmen were devoted men of their word. He was convinced that they would keep it.

"So that waitress gave you an approving look. Are you going to go for it?"

"Go for what?"

Abraham nudged the man. "Bed the woman. Copulate."

Horace's eyes were attached to Iris, who was sitting at the bar with Sticks and Dominga. They were all having a laugh. "No."

"You like Iris, don't you?"

Horace opened a hand and flung it outward. "What's not to like? She's a ravishing sight. I like the way the red in those auburn locks comes out in the sunlight. Her homely smile makes my heart sing."

"You should go talk to her."

Horace shook his head. "No. I've tried that. I've stopped that. She's a stubborn mule, that one."

"Have you ever tried to make her jealous?"

"What do you mean?"

Abraham reached out and grabbed a waitress passing by. She was the same one that had served them. He swung her around onto Horace's lap. He put a pair of silver shards in her hand. "Listen, gorgeous, you stay on his lap and make that woman jealous."

The curvy woman threw her arms over Horace's shoulders, hugged him tightly, and said, "My pleasure!"

"Captain! Captain!" Horace said. The waitress shushed him with a full kiss right on the lips.

Abraham grabbed his ale and giggled. If what was happening wasn't real, then he might as well have some fun with it. He drank. *I just wish the ale tasted better.* He left the table and crossed the floor. The tavern had two bars, one on the sea side and the other on the side of the Spine. Both bars offered large outdoor porches, making an excellent view of the Spine and the choppy waters in the Bay of Elders. He moved to the mountain side and took a seat on a stool, at the loneliest corner of the bar.

The Spine was nothing but black rock mountains jutting upward toward a dark-blue sky filled with faint, twinkling stars. He saw no sign of constellations like the Big Dipper, Draco, Orion, or even a North Star to go by. He sipped his brew. *This is not my world. Where in the heck am I?*

Sticks joined him. "Nice night."

He answered with his gaze fixed on the skies. "Yeah."

"So, will I be joining you tonight?" She put her hand on his arm. "It might be the last chance we have to enjoy ourselves, too."

He dropped his eyes to hers. Sticks had eyes as hard as stone, but a softer side of the woman waited deep inside. She was right. That night might have been his last time to have fun. He wondered if this was what it felt like before a soldier went to war, not knowing whether or not they would come back. He liked her. He didn't want to hurt her either. He took her hand and said, "Yeah."

She rose up on her toes and leaned in for a kiss.

A commotion of high-pitched voices came from the sea side of the tavern. The scuttle of boots rushed toward new screams.

Ruger and Sticks moved in behind a pack of angry fishermen, who started shouting obscenities. Another group climbed up over the porch railing. They were men and women, dripping wet from head to toe. Ruger got his first good look at the invaders. They were fish-like people with slanted black eyes, covered in skin like fish scales from head to toe.

"Myrmidons," Sticks said.

# 56

The myrmidons climbed over the railing one by one. Water slipped down their sleek bodies, making puddles on the plank floor. They walked like men, with green-silver scales and black fins for ears on their sleek heads. Their eyes were black, with large white pupils in the middles. Not a strand of hair was on any of them. They were all scaled, bald, and sleek. They wore strands of seaweed for dress and carried no weapons but had very long black fingernails and sharp, spiny ridges on their backs. They spread out into the tavern, bumping into everyone they passed.

"Watch it, fish-face," Cudgel said right after an oily-scaled myrmidon jostled his table and knocked over his tankard.

Abraham dropped his hand to his sword. "What is it about these seaside taverns?" he asked Sticks. "Every time I enter one, trouble comes."

"The myrmidons are nothing but trouble." She hooked her arm in his. "They'll go away. Just ignore them before they do."

"Are you sure?"

"That's what you always told us."

Abraham rubbed his eyes. He—or rather, Ruger—had recollections about them. The myrmidons were an ancient race of seafaring people, small in number, who kept to themselves in the caves along the seashore and the smaller islands. They were great swimmers and fishermen and still mostly men despite their amphibian appearance.

"I guess so," he said. "I just hope our crew doesn't get all riled up over them."

Very quickly, the myrmidons made their presence known to everyone in the tavern. They dragged away chairs and tables, creating their own spots. They kicked back, swung their legs on the tabletops, and leaned backward on two chair legs. The waitresses were pawed at and victim to bubbly-voiced catcalls.

A myrmidon who stood seven feet tall lumbered through the tavern. His large hands had webbing between the fingers, and he wore many large gold chains over his neck like a gangster. His long arm was hooked over a female myrmidon. She was a beautiful and sensual thing with a necklace of violet pearls that dangled down between her plunging seaweed neckline. She winked at Abraham. The male stopped and looked at Ruger. The small black fins above his earholes bent downward.

In a bubbly voice, he said, "Keep your eyes from my lady if you want to keep them." He showed his hand, which could cover Ruger's entire face. The black claws on the tips of his fingers extended another foot.

Abraham sneered and said, "Go back to your lagoon, ya goon."

The spiny ridges on the myrmidon's back flexed up and down like dominoes and rattled like a snake's tail. He pointed a quill-like fingernail at Abraham's eyeball. He waved it back and forth. "No, no, no, no. Don't taunt Flexor. It will be your doom." He pulled his hand back, and the fingernail retracted. Flexor and his woman strode to the bar and sat down.

"Flexor. What the heck kind of name is that?" Abraham said. "Sounds like a rubber toy or something."

"If we leave them alone, they'll leave us alone," Sticks said. "Let's take a walk down on the shore since the night is so nice."

"All right," he said.

He scanned the room. Despite the myrmidons' loud voices and raucous mannerisms, the Henchmen seemed to be fitting in just fine.

"Just let me have a word with the men."

Bearclaw and Vern were playing cards at a table with two women between them. Vern rolled his toothpick from side to side. Bearclaw studied his cards and didn't bat an eye.

Abraham leaned over Bearclaw's shoulder and said, "We have bigger fish to fry. See to it that our men don't get into any trouble."

Bearclaw nodded. "If the fish men don't bother me, I won't bother them."

"Make sure they don't bother you." He looked at Vern. "Or you."

"Can I bother them?" a pleasant-looking waitress with flaxen curls asked. She scooted beside Vern with both hands under the table, massaging Vern's thigh. Her green eyes were smiling at Abraham. "We don't get many brawny men in these parts."

"Just keep them happy." Abraham moved over to Horace.

The waitress Abraham had put on Horace's lap was sitting in a chair beside the husky warrior with her elbows on the table and chin on her hands. Horace was frowning like a bearded bullfrog.

"He's not very playful," she said. "Can I use this silver for something else?"

He shooed her away. "Sure. What's the matter, Horace?"

He followed his stare. Across the room, a myrmidon appeared to be getting flirty with Iris. The big country-girl smile on her face suggested she was enjoying it.

"Ah. Listen, it will pass. For now, make sure the company stays out of trouble." He blocked his view of Iris. "Do you got it? I don't want any steel drawn."

Horace leaned to the right and looked around Abraham. "I got it."

He slid through the room and had to change course because a pair of myrmidons swung their legs across the gap between the tables and blocked his path. They made bubbly laughing when he went around them.

He caught up with Sticks and said, "They really are a bunch of annoying jerks, aren't they?"

"Jerks? You mean obnoxious by that, right? Like you used to be?"

"Right," he said.

They made their way down the wooden steps leading to the beach. The beach was covered in seaweed, and the foamy waters stank of strong salt and something like sulfur.

"Ew, this isn't exactly going to be the walk on the beach that I was hoping for," he said.

"Me either, but at least it's with you." She clasped his fingers in hers. "Even if it stinks."

Angry shouts erupted from the tavern. Abraham's head whipped around. A commotion had started in the rickety tavern. He and Sticks raced back up four flights of broken-up stairs. He cleared the final eight steps in an incredible leap and landed on the seaside porch. The Henchmen and myrmidons had collided in a wrathful tide of angry bodies.

# 57

INSIDE THE TAVERN, ALL THE LOCAL FISHERMAN HAD SCATTERED. THE quavering floor of the tavern became a battle royale, with the men with skin against the men with fins.

Horace had the myrmidon who had flirted with Iris hoisted over his head and pinned to the ceiling.

Tark punched a fish man in the face. Cudgel had a chair shattered on his back.

Bearclaw wrestled across the floor with two myrmidons at once.

Sticks ran down the length of the bar and kicked a myrmidon in the face.

A wine bottle sailed over Abraham's ducking head. "We need to break it up," he said as he prowled into the tavern. No weapons were drawn. It was skin and brawn locked up against muscles and scales. Fists collided with teeth. Sharp talons dug into flesh.

Horace let out an eardrum-shattering yelp. He dropped the myrmidon and backed into the wall. Black quills were stuck in his face, as if he'd been attacked by a porcupine. His sausage fingers started to pluck them out.

Iris rushed up to Horace and shouted, "Leave them alone!" She swung her metal goblet into an attacking myrmidon's chin. He hopped away from her.

Abraham battled into the fray with his fists flying. He landed an uppercut in a myrmidon's gut, which doubled the fish man over. From out of nowhere, a table crashed down on top of his back and drove him to his knees. He scurried out from underneath it and saw Flexor. The tallest myrmidon's talons had extended on all fingers, jutting out over a foot long. He clacked his sharp little piranha teeth together. Abraham started to draw.

"No blades, Captain!" Bearclaw said. He straddled a fish man and punched him in the face. "Let these little guppies fight with their fingernails if they want to." He grabbed the man by his seaweed collar, yanked him up, and headbutted him.

Abraham locked his sword back inside its sheath. He had no idea how good he was at hand-to-hand fighting, but he was about to find out. He rose and faced off against Flexor, lifting his fists. "All right, creature from the smelly lagoon, come on over, and I'll make clam chowder out of you."

Flexor spread his arms out and grinned. His arms looked impossibly long with the super-long fingernails. He slowly walked forward, saying, "I will peel you out of that armor and serve you to my sharks for dinner." He lunged in and swiped.

Abraham ducked, stepped into Flexor, wrapped the man in a bear hug, and slammed him down on the floor. The myrmidon tried to claw his way out of his grip. He rabbit punched the myrmidon in the back of the head.

The myrmidon thrashed on the floor and screamed with a high-pitched sound. "Reeeeeeeeeeee! Reeeeeeeeee! Reeeeeeeeeee!"

"Gah!" Abraham rolled off Flexor's back and stuck his fingers in his ears. "Geez, what is that?" He kicked Flexor.

The lanky myrmidon leader scrambled to his feet as the

earsplitting screeching continued to gush from his lips. He waved his arm, and the myrmidons, one and all, slipped out of the tavern and over the porch rails and dashed down toward the sea. Flexor and his woman were the last to go. They vanished over the railing and disappeared. The screeching stopped.

The Henchmen slowly made their way back to their feet, shaking their heads.

"By the Elders, I didn't know that they could do that," Horace said. He was sitting on a barstool, letting Iris pluck the quills out of his face. "Dirty fighters. Cowardly. All of them."

Abraham and Sticks turned a table over and put it back on its legs. Then he pulled up a chair and rolled his jaw, trying to shake the ringing from his ears.

He sat down. "What happened?"

"Horace started it," Vern said. "He saw Iris getting cozy with that smooth-talking myrmidon and charged over there like a maddened bull."

"I did not!" Horace said.

"You did too," Iris said with a smile. She plucked a needle out from under his eye.

Horace's voice softened. "All I did was march over to have a word. That's when another one of those fish-eyed fools tripped me."

"Then Dominga slung her goblet at the fish-face hooked on Iris's arm," Vern added as he rubbed his swollen jaw. "Ol' Fish Eyes's scales turned red. That's when Horace drug his arse up off the floor and plowed into him."

"You didn't miss a beat, did you?" Abraham said to Vern.

Vern shrugged. "It was going to be a brawl. Everyone knew it the moment that they walked in, except you."

The Henchmen helped the waitresses set up the toppled chairs and tables. Prospero and Apollo lay on the floor, knocked out or passed out, snoring. Cudgel and Tark dragged them across the floor and leaned them in a corner. Within minutes, the deteriorating tavern was back under normal operation. The fishermen who had scattered returned. The place looked as if nothing had happened, aside from some scrapes, bruises, and the dark black heads that dotted Horace's puffy face.

Iris rubbed salve into Horace's meaty jaws. "You didn't have to go to such extremes for me."

"Well... I do."

She smiled warmly.

The Henchmen carried on for a couple more hours until Cudgel blurted out, "I've been pilfered!"

Cudgel's purse wasn't the only one missing. So was Bearclaw's, Vern's, Prospero's, Apollo's and Dominga's. Even Abraham's was missing.

"I think we've been duped," Sticks said.

The young Red Tunic, Twila, burst through the tavern doors. Drenched in sweat, her panicked stare searched the room until she found Ruger. "The horses! The wagon! They're gone!"

# 58

On foot, the Henchmen took off after the thieves who had stolen their horses and wagons. It took coercion, but the tavern keeper and the waitresses had finally spilled their guts. As it turned out, they were in cahoots with the myrmidons, and not just them, either. They were part of a larger local network of brigands that operated on the shores of Titanuus's Crotch, called the Shell. The brawl was just a part of the bigger play. The Henchmen had been duped by thugs and thieves.

Abraham ground his teeth as they walked. Losing their gear was one thing. It was another to lose Jake's backpack. That was the only thing keeping him attached to home. Now, it was gone, and with that gone, he feared losing the lone connection that was a reminder of his greater purpose.

Vern walked up beside him and asked, "So, we can still speak freely?"

"Yes."

"Well done, Captain. We are off to the same lousy start as always." Vern shook his head and marched on.

According to the taverner, the Shell's hideout wasn't a secret. It was a small stone fort in the rocks that overlooked the sea line. It had been built centuries before, during the Coastal Wars, where Hancha and Tiotan fought for the territory. Seeing the land was barren and futile, both kingdoms abandoned the quest and left it to rot.

They walked all night, following the wagon-wheel tracks and hoofprints. They could do without the wagon, but the horses were another matter. They needed them, not to mention their rations. After a few hours of walking, Dominga and Tark, who'd been scouting ahead, returned.

Dominga shone with sweat in the moonlight. She said, "We've spotted the Shell."

---

The Shell was bigger than Ruger's stronghold, but not by much. It was nothing more than a rectangular fort with a three-story-high outer wall with battlements. A jetty of huge rocks made a natural dock that ran up to the portcullis entrance to the fort. Several small craft and barges were docked against the strand of land. No flags or banners flapped in the wind above the fort walls. The lonely-looking place was dim and quiet.

With the others, Abraham spied the fort from their position on the beach. The portcullis door was open. Several rogues sauntered in and out. Many of them stood along the dock and smoked.

"Huh," Gabe said.

"They don't appear to be worried about any pursuers," Sticks said. "Either the Shell has guts, or they are really stupid."

Horace grunted. "Look at their location. Tucked in those rocks, they could hold off an entire army for weeks if they needed to."

"Well, we aren't an army, and we don't have weeks," Abraham said. "But we have to get our gear back. The question is, how do we do that?"

"We kill 'em," Horace said.

"Yes, we kill them," Cudgel added.

"If they weren't smart enough to steal our blades, I agree, we kill them," Vern added.

"Aye, and they are thieves. They deserve death as punishment," Bearclaw stated.

"Well, we aren't here to start a war with the Shell," Abraham said.

"It's not uncommon for the rogues to sell goods back to the ones they were stolen from," Dominga offered.

All eyes turned to her.

"What? I know about these things. The same things happen in Kingsland. I used to be the eyes for a guild house before I got caught up doing this."

"Listen, darlin', we can't buy back something that was stolen from us with money we don't have," Vern said, "though I like the way you are thinking."

Abraham rubbed the scruff building on his face. "This sucks. But I think, talking to them, we'll fare better than fighting them. If Dominga's right and they have open doors for desperate customers, perhaps we can strike a deal with them."

"Let's just kill them," Apollo suggested. Prospero nodded and yawned. "Their ilk has it coming."

"We don't even know how many they have in there. And if we charge in there, they'll tuck their head back inside their shell." He stood. "I'm going in... alone."

"What about us, Captain?" Horace said.

"Just wait outside. If I don't come back out within a few hours, well, feel free to come looking for me. My guess is that in the worst case, I'll return with my tail tucked between my legs."

Iris looked at his behind. "But you don't have a tail. Does he have a tail, Sticks?"

"No, that's not what he means. It's an expression," Sticks said. "But he does have a tail on the front end."

Iris giggled.

"I would like to come with you," Sticks said. "You shouldn't go in there alone. I have some experience with people like this."

Abraham gave it some thought. "Fine. Just us. The rest of you, keep a hundred yards back. And keep your swords in place. I don't want to agitate them. Let's see what Flexor, or whoever is in charge, has to say. I mean it."

"We'll wait, but not forever, Captain," Horace said.

"Good." He looked at Sticks. "Come on."

Together, they made the trek to the Shell's fort. A handful of guards in plain clothing stood between the battlements, pointing crossbows at them. A handful of myrmidons and regular men met them outside the portcullis. Abraham was surprised to see Flexor's woman approach from the inside.

In her bubbling accent, the striking myrmidon looked him up and down and said, "Interesting. You may enter, but you must surrender your weapons."

Abraham unbuckled his sword belt and tossed it to the ground. "As you wish."

Sticks mimicked him.

"I am Kawnee," the lady myrmidon said. She picked up their weapons belts and slung them over her shoulder. "Follow me." She led them inside the fort.

The iron portcullis lowered, making loud squeaks and rattles. It came to a rest on the threshold, sealing them all inside.

# 59

INSIDE THE FORT WAS A WOODEN BUILDING THAT RAN FROM THE front to the back. The bottom of the structure was an open-faced barn, with two levels of apartments above it. The apartments had a walkway and railing on the outside. Windows and doors were behind the railing, as on a motel. Surly men and women, in common garb, were spread out on the walkways, casting heavy stares at Ruger and Sticks. All of them were human.

The other side of the fort's courtyard was made up of storehouses residing beneath the parapets. Some had open bays, while others had closed doors. The air smelled of manure and hay. Kawnee led them straight down the middle. On the wall opposite the portcullis, another smaller portcullis waited. A pair of guards, holding spears, blocked the double-door entrance. They were brutes wearing leather armor, with heavy eyebrows, wide faces, and thick lips.

Kawnee waved her hand.

The lazy-eyed brutes stepped aside.

Ruger and Sticks followed Kawnee through the open gate into

a smaller fort hidden behind the larger one. Unlike the outer fort, this fort was more of a grand hall with a pitched roof held up by stone archways. Six stone cauldrons of fire burned along the wall and corners. The smoke seeped up through small holes in the corner of the ceilings. The heavy doors closed behind them.

Six rogues, man and myrmidon, were posted on the right and left, armed with swords. At the end of the room were three empty wooden thronelike chairs sitting side by side, ascending from smallest to largest up a dais. Flexor sat tall in the chair in the middle, hands on his knees. But he barely caught Abraham's attention. Instead, the man sitting in the top chair caught his eyes. The man appeared to be in his forties, with short blond hair and a receding hairline. The round-faced man's penetrating eyes were as blue as the sky. He wore a black leather vest with a scarlet red long-sleeved shirt underneath. The buttons on the high-collared shirt were pearl white. The man leaned back with the bottom of one foot propped up in the seat of his chair. He didn't appear to be armed.

In a rich and welcoming voice, the blond man asked, "Who have you brought to me, Kawnee?"

Kawnee bowed her chin and said, "Lord Hawk, these travelers have made an inquiry about some of their belongings that they have lost."

"Interesting. What is that you carry, Kawnee?" Lord Hawk asked. He tilted his head. "Bring it to me."

Kawnee approached the wooden throne and laid Ruger's and Sticks's weapons at Lord Hawk's feet.

"Hand me that sword and take your seat," Lord Hawk said.

Ruger and Sticks exchanged a nervous glance. Lord Hawk slid Black Bane out of the sheath. The blackened steel glimmered in the dim light.

Lord Hawk's piercing eyes slowly ran over the blade from top to bottom. He twisted the blade over and again. His eyes slid over and met Abraham's. "This sword is unique. I like it. Who are you that brings me a gift like this?"

"Gift? Uh, no, my sword is not a gift. It's mine and mine alone," Abraham responded.

"Who are you?" Lord Hawk said in a more menacing tone.

"I am Ruger. This is Sticks."

"I didn't ask who she was. Nevertheless, it is good to meet the both of you. Now, tell me in your own words what brings you to the Shell?"

"Lord Hawk, your men stole a wagonload of our supplies, our purses, and over a dozen horses from us. I want them back."

Lord Hawk sat up suddenly in his chair. He turned to Flexor the myrmidon and asked, "Is this true? Did you rob these weary travelers of their goods?"

Flexor shrugged and said, "They lost them in a wager."

"That's a lie!" Sticks blurted out.

"Whoa, lady, you don't come into my fortress and make accusations," Lord Hawk said. He rested Black Bane on his shoulder. "That could be fatal. And before your tongues slip again, let me remind you that I am the judge and the jury around here." He narrowed his bright eyes at Sticks. "Now, let's back up a moment. You lost a bet with Flexor and his men. Perhaps you were drunk and careless. Believe me, I've lived in this part of the world a long time and met many that have made similar mistakes. It's nothing to be ashamed of. So you wish to buy back your gear? Right?"

Sticks's hands balled up into fists. Her mouth opened wide.

Abraham clamped his hands around her mouth, held her tight, and said, "Something like that, Lord Hawk."

"Ah. A man of reason. A very fit warrior of a man, at that." Lord Hawk sheathed the sword, tossed it onto the ground, and stood. "Tell me, Ruger, what did you have in mind?" he asked, patting a strange object on his right hip. "Make me a deal."

Abraham's eyes dropped. Lord Hawk carried a pistol on his hip.

# 60

To say that Abraham was a little freaked out was an understatement. He lifted his eyes and found Lord Hawk's stare on his. He made a straight face and let go of Sticks. She stepped away from him.

*Sonuvagun. Keep it together.*

He'd gotten only a glimpse of the pistol and gun belt. It wasn't an ideal rig, but rather like one would see in the Old West. Lord Hawk wore a black leather belt, and the pistol, which appeared to be a six-shooter, was holstered in leather.

"Well, Ruger," Lord Hawk said as he stepped down from the dais, his hand remaining on the pistol's grip, "are you going to make an offer for your gear or not?"

"I think it would be a lot easier if you would tell me what you want, and we can negotiate from there."

Lord Hawk nodded. He looked back at Flexor and Kawnee and said, "You see, this is a good businessman. He doesn't come into the Shell and insult us. He wants to make a straight deal." He turned back to Ruger and Sticks. "I like that." He scratched the side of his clean-shaven face. "I'll sell you the wagon, horses, and all of the contents, for one thousand shards of gold."

"I don't have one thousand shards. Let me have your purse," he told Sticks.

With a deepening frown, she handed him her cloth purse.

He dumped the contents into his hand and counted. *It's not real. Have some fun.* "I can offer you five gold shards, fifteen silver, and thirteen copper. But I'll pay the rest back when we return from Alderaan."

"Where is Alderaan?" Lord Hawk said.

"Never mind. Do we have a deal, Lord Hawk?" Abraham said.

Lord Hawk leaned forward on one knee, and from several feet away, he said, "I think you are making light with me by offering a pittance." He rested his hand on the handle of his gun. "I made you a serious offer. You offer me a baron's tithe, and now, I'm insulted."

"I gave you the best offer that I'm able to offer. After all, you stole all of our gear. I think my offer is very generous, considering."

"Ruger, I'm going to counter your offer with another. Two thousand gold shards."

"I don't have that. You know it."

"Well, I guess we can't make a deal then. Goodbye, Ruger and Twigs." He moved back toward his chair.

Abraham moved to retrieve his weapon. The rogues, swords in hand, blocked his path.

"What do you think you are doing?" Lord Hawk said.

"Taking our weapons," he replied.

"No, those aren't your weapons. They are mine. It's the price that you pay for getting out of here alive." Lord Hawk sat down. He flicked his wrist at them. "Begone now."

He and Sticks turned away and walked toward the closed doors.

Under her breath, she said, “Great plan, Captain.”

They stood before the doors waiting for them to be opened. It didn’t happen. Abraham looked over his shoulder. Lord Hawk, Flexor, Kawnee, and the rest of the rogues all showed knowing smiles. Ruger smiled back. Out of the corner of his mouth he said to Sticks, “Why do I feel like we are about to be fed to the wolves?”

“Because you marched us right into their den,” she replied.

“Is something wrong?” Lord Hawk said.

Rubbing the back of his neck, he said, “Uh, yes. The doors aren’t opening.”

“That’s because you have to knock,” Lord Hawk said in a suspiciously friendly manner. “Go ahead. Knock three times. Knock hard because my sentries are very hard of hearing.”

Abraham rapped his knuckles against the thick wooden doors. Nothing happened. “This is getting worse and worse, isn’t it?” he whispered.

Sticks nodded.

He turned around and shrugged. “It didn’t work.”

“Oh, that’s because you forgot to say the magic words,” Lord Hawk said. He smiled like a crocodile. “Open… Says… Me.”

Abraham’s eyes grew as big as saucers. “What?” Before he could move a muscle, the rogues in the corners flicked a handful of pellets at his feet.

The pellets burst open and spewed out a choking inky purple cloud.

Abraham and Sticks broke out in a fit of coughing. The strength in his iron-strong limbs faded, and he hit the ground headfirst.

# 61

## The Past

"ISN'T THIS GREAT?" ABRAHAM ASKED JENNY AND JAKE.

They were flying inside a twin-engine Cessna. He was a big guy, and the cockpit was cramped, but a big smile covered his face. He loved to fly.

"What does the altimeter say, Jake?" he asked.

Jake sat in the copilot seat next to him. The light-haired kid wore an Optimus Prime T-shirt. He pointed at the plane's instrument panel and said, "Twenty-two thousand feet. Whoa, that's really high, isn't it?" He looked out his window. "Man, that's so cool. Those clouds look like a bed of cotton you could walk on."

The plane seated eight people, but the only other two on board were Abraham's wife, Jenny, and his best friend, Buddy Parker. They both sat in the next row of seats. Abraham popped a bubble-gum bubble. "Are you two doing all right back there? It's awfully quiet."

"It's just bumpy," Jenny said. The pretty woman wore a white sundress that showed off her tan figure. Her eyes were big. "But I'm getting used to it."

"You will," Abraham said. "And don't worry, this bird is as sound as they come. Hey, Buddy, say something."

"I'll say something. I can't believe that I'm dumb enough to ride in a plane that you are flying. That's what I'm saying." Buddy held his stomach. "How long is this flight going to be, anyway?"

"It's only two and a half hours. We'll land in Charleston before you know it. Just sit back and enjoy the flight. Besides, we have plenty of parachutes."

"Shut up." Buddy was hugging a small pillow. "I should have flown commercial."

"Ah, this is better. No hassles for you at the airport. Now, sit back and prepare for an inflight movie," he said.

"What movie?" Buddy asked.

Jake perked up. "We get to watch a movie?"

"That's right. We're gonna watch Buddy's favorite: *Major League*, starring Charlie Sheen."

Buddy grinned. "Will you shut up and just land this thing? Man, I can't believe I have to jet from Florida back to Pittsburgh for an autograph session."

"And my dad's birthday party."

"Yeah, that too."

"Where did you say it was?" Buddy asked.

"Hinton. Well, Dad's driving in from Hinton to meet us in Charleston. He doesn't know about this birthday present, so I can't wait to see his eyes when we show it to him." Abraham was thrilled to death to buy his dad a plane. His father, Captain Frank Jenkins, was a highly decorated war hero in Vietnam, who flew F-4 Phantoms. He became an instructor after he retired and taught

Abraham to fly as soon as he was able. "Man, he's going to be thrilled."

"Let's just hope that he doesn't think that you overdid it, honey," Jenny said. "You know he doesn't like it when you spend money on him."

"That's why I'm going to tell him that it was your idea."

"Oh no, you won't!" She reached up and tickled Abraham.

He jumped in his seat. "Okay, okay, I won't. Just don't tickle me while I'm flying. I'll pee myself!"

Jake giggled. "You said *pee*."

"So, what's the plan, again?" Buddy asked. He leaned back in his chair and closed his eyes. "We land in Charleston, then what?"

"Well, we land, see Dad, give him his present, then I'm pretty sure that he'll want to fly his new toy. He takes us to Pittsburgh for the autograph session. We'll fly up, back, spend the night in Hinton for the party, and take a commercial flight back to Florida just in time to resume training camp."

"Man, being famous gets crazy," Buddy said.

"It's going to get crazier after we win the pennant. You can count on it," Abraham said.

"The Pirates are going to win the World Series," Jake said. "I can feel it!"

"That's just what I'll need. Abraham and Buddy with even bigger egos," Jenny said.

Abraham and Buddy chuckled. "You know it," Buddy said. "I'm gonna beat my best batting average and crack out over fifty home runs. It's going to be sweet."

"You know it," Abraham said. He looked over at his wiry, tawny-headed son. "So, do you think Grandpa Frank is going to like his present?"

"He'll love it! If he doesn't, I'll take it," Jake said.

"You know, I was about your age when Grandpa started taking me flying. He made sure that I got my pilot's license, too." He dropped his headphones down on his neck. "He used to say, 'You never know when you'll need to fly a plane.' So do you want to learn to fly?"

"You bet I do?" Jake said.

"Well, climb over here into the captain's seat."

"Really?"

"Hon, I don't think that's a very good idea," Jenny said.

"Oh, it will be all right."

"No, it won't be," Buddy objected. "You are the pilot, and you're going to get this metal bird on the ground. Sorry Jake, but ol' Buddy would rather play it safe."

"Aw, shucks." Jake slumped down in his seat.

Abraham hit him in the leg. "No pouting. Besides, those two buzzkills won't always be flying with us."

"Hey!" Jenny punched Abraham in the arm. "You better not."

"Ow, that's my pitching arm." He giggled. "Don't damage the moneymaker, baby."

"Yeah, damage the baby maker instead." Buddy tossed his head back and laughed. "Now that would be funny."

Jen cozied up to Abraham. Her soft lips kissed his cheek. She smelled great.

"What was that for?" he asked.

She took his free hand in both of her warm ones. She placed his hand on her belly and said, "Speaking of babies..."

# 62

Abraham's head jerked up from the floor. He was in the same room. Lord Hawk, Flexor, and Kawnee were sitting in their chairs. He sat up and rubbed his eyes. He'd been dreaming about the past, the accident. It was a day he'd lived over and over again. It set his blood on fire.

Gathering his thoughts, he said, "Where's Sticks?"

Lord Hawk pointed to his left. Sticks was chained up to the wall between the burning cauldrons of fire. Her head was sunk against her chest. "She's resting. It takes some people longer than others to recover from the smoke of slumber. So how are you feeling, Ruger?"

"What do you want?" Abraham replied.

"Do you know what is more valuable than gold?"

*A really good pizza. Ice-cold beer. It depends.* "Good health."

"Ha! Well, I suppose there is some truth to that." Lord Hawk shifted in his seat. "Information. Yes, information is one of the most valuable assets that a man can acquire. Especially if it is information about a certain king."

Ruger stood up and swayed. The slumber smoke had dulled

his senses. Blood flowed into his fingertips, which began to burn. "I suppose. What are you getting at?"

"Well, those horses that you gave to us... Some of them are branded with King Hector's mark. I find that very interesting."

Abraham shrugged. "So we bought some of the king's horses. It happens." He didn't have any idea whether it happened or not. But it could have.

"True." Lord Hawk got out of his chair and walked over to Sticks. He pulled her shirt down at the neck, revealing the King's Brand on her chest. "She is branded like a horse or like a Henchman."

Sticks's head rolled from one side to the other. Her eyelids started to open as she moaned.

Lord Hawk crossed the room and stopped in front of Abraham's sword belt. He lifted it up with his toe and pulled the sword free. He cast a sideways glance at Abraham and said, "Slade the Blade. I never imagined that I would meet you in person."

"I never thought I'd meet you either."

Lord Hawk eyeballed the sword and said, "This must be the infamous Black Bane. The craftsmanship is no doubt high quality, but as a whole, I find it unremarkable. I can say the same about you."

Flexor let out a bubbly chuckle. The rest of the rogues joined in.

"I have a weapon far greater at my disposal, which is more than a match for any sword." Lord Hawk pulled out his gun. The six-shooter had a blue finish and a walnut grip. He spun it on his finger. "This is a weapon greater than any sword ever forged." He tossed Black Bane onto the ground and holstered the gun after a spin on his finger. "But enough about weapons. You, Ruger Slade, are very popular outside of Kingsland. I believe there is a bounty on your head. At least two that I know of—one in Hancha and the other in East Bolg, I believe. It seems that your group gets around and does a lot of damage. I believe that King Elron in Hancha has offered ten thousand pieces of gold for your head and another five hundred per Henchman. That's quite a sum. He wasn't very happy about his aqueduct system that you destroyed."

Abraham didn't remember any such adventure and said, "It wasn't us. King Elron had plenty of other enemies."

"You know, you make a good point. But he blames Hector. Besides, it's not like people have a *picture* of you to go by or anything."

*That's an interesting choice of words. Picture.* When Lord Hawk spoke the "Open says me" phrase, it crossed up Abraham's thoughts. He couldn't help but wonder if Lord Hawk was someone like him. The way he talked and flipped the gun around like a cowboy couldn't have been learned in this world. *Or could it?*

"I don't recall ever being in Hancha," Abraham said. "I could have been mixed up with someone else."

"True. So, Ruger Slade, tell me what is going on and what you are doing. I know that you serve the king."

"Then you know that I can't tell you what I am doing. Not that I'm hiding anything."

"I was afraid that you would say that." Quick as a striking snake, Lord Hawk drew his gun, pointed it at Sticks, squeezed the trigger, and fired.

The bullet blasted into the stone wall right by Sticks's face. She flinched hard and let out a yelp. The loud *bang* echoed in the chamber. Smoke rolled out of the gun barrel.

"If I have to ask you what you are doing again, I'm going to send the next magic stone right through the center of her skull." That was the first time Lord Hawk said anything without even smiling. "Well?"

Abraham didn't doubt the man's intentions. He wasn't going to risk Sticks's life even though the Henchmen would rather die than reveal their service to the king. He eyed the gun. *I wonder how many bullets he has?* His father, Frank, was an avid hunter, and even though Abraham had never had a great love for it, he'd fired his share of guns. He even had a pistol that he kept inside his truck for his own protection. He wished he had it now.

"A campaign ventured into the Spine months ago," Abraham said. "It never came back. We're looking for survivors."

Sticks sighed.

"Fascinating. And what in the world would the king be sending his men into the Spine to find?" Lord Hawk asked.

Abraham's eyes slid over to Sticks. She gave him a subtle nod.

"If I tell you, will you let us go?" he asked.

"You aren't in a position to negotiate." He scratched an eyebrow with the tip of his gun. "But I'll consider it because I like you, Ruger. You're not the stiff neck I presumed. You're more... real."

"We are looking for the fenix."

Led by Lord Hawk, all the rogues in the room let out a gusty laugh.

Lord Hawk finally composed himself and said, "That's the stupidest thing I've ever heard."

"Nevertheless, it's true," Abraham replied.

Lord Hawk pointed his gun casually at Abraham and said, "I've got to tell you, this has been highly entertaining. You've really surprised me, Ruger. You really have. The insults just keep coming. Get back against the wall with your friend, Twigs."

"It's not a lie." He let out more of the truth. "The king's viceroy sent two campaigns into the Spine to find the fenix egg. The queen is sick. The egg is the only thing that can heal her."

"Oh, that is rich." Lord Hawk rolled his eyes. "And the leader of the Sect, Viceroy Leodor, I believe, told you that? My, Kingsland is in even greater flux than I anticipated. Why, it's no wonder that those campaigns failed. No manner of man can withstand the might of the spawn of the Elders. It's too bad for the queen, though. I heard she is very kind."

An awkward silence fell as all eyes in the room watched Lord Hawk pace, clearly mulling something over. Abraham noticed Sticks's nimble fingers working at her shackles.

Lord Hawk tapped his dimpled chin with his middle finger. In a hushed tone, he said, "The fastest sword in the world. Hmm... that makes me curious." He spun on a heel and faced Abraham. "I've heard that you can draw your sword faster than a man can bat an eye. I'll tell you what. I'm going to give you a chance to save yourself and your lady friend." He kicked the sword belt over to Abraham's feet. "Put it on."

Abraham complied, but his sword was still lying on the floor.

Lord Hawk picked it up and tossed it to him. "Sheathe it."

"Okay," he said and did.

Standing thirty feet apart, Lord Hawk holstered his gun. "I'm going to draw and shoot. You can try to block it with your sword. If you dodge, my bullet might not kill you, but it will kill your friend. What do you say?"

"You want me to stop a bullet with my sword? That's impossible."

"True, but it's the only chance that I'm giving you. If you block it, I'll set you free." Lord Hawk stood with his hand inches from his gun.

Abraham's fingers were inches away from his sword. He shielded Sticks with his body. There was no turning back now. He knew it.

Flexor and Kawnee sat on the edges of their seats. The rest of the rogues crept closer to the scene.

"We'll go on the count of three," Lord Hawk said. He fixed his eyes on Ruger. "Kawnee, count."

"One," the myrmidon woman said.

Abraham's hand moved closer to his handle. He kept his eyes

fixed on Lord Hawk. He'd seen plenty of fastballs in his lifetime, but nothing like a speeding bullet. *Ruger, if you are in there, I'm going to need your help on this.* New sweat ran down his temple. His heart raced.

"Two."

Lord Hawk's expression never twitched.

"Three—"

*Bang!*

# 63

THE SPLIT-SECOND MOMENT MOVED LIKE AN OUT-OF-BODY experience. Lord Hawk's hand grabbed the handle. He pulled his gun. At the same time, Abraham felt his sword sliding out of his sheath like a flicker of a snake's tongue.

Lord Hawk's aim straightened.

Abraham's sword twisted upward.

The bullet exploded out of the barrel.

He saw the bullet ripping through the air just as he brought the sword fully around.

Lead smacked into metal with a loud *crack-ting*.

*I blocked it!*

Lord Hawk's jaw dropped. His shoulders sagged. The barrel of his weapon dipped. In a long, drawn-out word, he said, "Impossible!"

Ruger had blocked the bullet. Black Bane quavered in his grip. The runes etched on the metal of the blade glowed the fiery orange of a furnace fire. An unanticipated surge of energy coursed right through him. He set his dark eyes on Lord Hawk. "You're going to pay."

With widening eyes, Lord Hawk pointed his weapon at Abraham and said, "Stop him! Stop him!" He squeezed the trigger.

Abraham positioned his sword blade right where Lord Hawk was aiming. The bullet skipped away from the loud steel with another loud *ting*. Then he blocked the next two shots. Lord Hawk kept squeezing the trigger. *Click. Click. Click.*

"You're empty, fool!" Abraham poised to strike.

---

Sticks twisted free of her shackles. She slipped two small thumb knives out of her sleeves and jammed the knives into the jugulars of the rogues standing guard beside her. A third rogue wearing a silver hoop in his nose chopped at her head. She ducked, dove for her bandolier, snatched it up, slipped it over her shoulder, and rolled flawlessly to one knee. She freed a dagger from her bandolier and stabbed the same attacker in the gut.

Kawnee jumped on her back. Sticks tossed the fish woman over her shoulder. Flexor appeared in the corner of her eye and slugged her in the side of the head. Her legs buckled. She saw stars and drew more blades. She squared off with Flexor. His black fingernails extended over a full foot in length.

She rolled her neck. "Let's do this, fish man."

Flexor chuckled.

---

A pair of rogues collapsed on Abraham just as Lord Hawk scuttled out of the way. Black Bane flashed in a right-handed strike. A mustached rogue's head fell from his shoulders. Abraham blocked a lethal strike, twisted Bane downward, and sank it into his attacker's heavy shoulder. The rogue let out a painful moan. Blood spat out of his mouth, and he collapsed on the floor.

Abraham didn't see Lord Hawk. "Where are you, coward?"

---

Sticks parried Flexor's fingernails with her daggers pumping through the air. Quick as a cat, the myrmidon stabbed with one hand and swiped at her with the other. His length was amazing. In between strikes, she flicked a dagger at his face, but he ducked the missile. She drew another.

Flexor showed his sharp little teeth to her. "Are you ready to die now?"

She wiped her sleeve across her mouth. Kawnee was back on her feet and circling her from behind. They not only had her in numbers, but also had a greater advantage in length. She flipped one dagger high into the air. Flexor's eyes drifted after it. Sticks lunged like a striking cobra. Flexor's quill-like claws slashed across her face, but the damage was done. She plunged her dagger deep into his heart.

"Gack!" Flexor gulped for air. "Gack!"

Kawnee rushed to his side. She caught him as he fell. "No, Flexor, no."

"Sticks!" Abraham said. He had Lord Hawk by the collar and was dragging him out from behind the wooden throne. Everyone else in the room was dead. "Are you all right?"

Her face was bleeding, but she said, "Yeh."

---

"Miscreants! You are not going to escape one way or the other. I have dozens of men outside that door," Lord Hawk shouted.

Abraham ripped the gun out of Lord Hawk's hand and cracked the man in the head with it. He eyed the gun. *Smith & Wesson. I'll be. An old police revolver, maybe. Thirty-eight special.* He tucked it into his belt.

"Ow!" Lord Hawk screeched as his head started to bleed.

Abraham didn't see any more bullets on the man. He patted the man down. "Do you have any more bullets?"

"No. Wait," Lord Hawk said. "How do you know about that?"

"I am Ruger Slade. I know things." He needed to feel out Lord Hawk. There was more to him than met the eye. "Is there another way out of here?"

"No. Brothers! Brothers! Enter!" Lord Hawk screamed. "You are finished now. Mystical sword or not, you won't overcome all of them."

The double doors burst open.

"Hahaha! You're doom—" Lord Hawk lost his voice. "You aren't my men. Who in Titanuus's Crotch are you?"

Horace, Bearclaw, Vern, Apollo, and Cudgel burst inside, coated in fresh blood from head to toe. Gore dripped from their weapons.

"Captain!" Horace said. "Are you well?"

"Well enough," Abraham said.

"My men, my men," Lord Hawk said as he craned his neck toward the door. His two brute guards lay in pools of their own blood. "What have you done?"

"We killed them all," Bearclaw said.

"All of them?" Lord Hawk said as the wind went out of his sails. "But there were dozens of them."

Vern slung the blood from his long sword and said, "*Were* dozens. Now, they are food for the scavengers."

Lord Hawk buried his face in his hands and sobbed. "They are all dead. All my men are dead."

"No, Lord Hawk, I still live," Kawnee said.

Lord Hawk lifted his face. "Yes, Kawnee, you know what to do."

Kawnee raised her arm and tossed pellets toward the floor.

"Get out!" Abraham said.

The chamber filled with inky black smoke. Abraham and the Henchmen blindly made their way out. When the smoke cleared, Lord Hawk and Kawnee were gone. So was the gun.

# 64

Lord Hawk and Kawnee might have gotten away, but the Henchmen got their gear back. The Shell's fort looked more like a slaughterhouse than a battlefield. Dozens of rogues lay dead on the ground, on the parapet walk, and slumped over the railing of the apartments. None of them survived, that Abraham could see.

Near the middle of the courtyard, Iris was patching a wound in Prospero's thigh. A crossbow bolt protruded from it.

"This will hurt," she said.

"I know," the scruffy-bearded Prospero replied in his gravelly tone.

Iris ripped it out.

Prospero grimaced as his eyes watered.

Iris pinched the wound, and blood seeped through her fingers. She began dressing it with salve from a small jar and clean bandages. "You need to ride in the wagon for a while. My salve takes time to do its work."

"I think if you'd kiss it, it would make it much better." Prospero grinned.

"Close your eyes and keep dreaming," Iris said.

Abraham helped Prospero up to his feet. The older warrior hobbled over to the wagon, and with Abraham's help, he climbed in.

Abraham turned around to find Horace on his heels. He leaned back and asked, "Do we have everything?"

"All of the horses are accounted for, Captain. The company is still searching for Lord Hawk," Horace replied.

"Good. But let's not get preoccupied with it. After seeing this massacre, I don't think he'll show his face again anytime soon." He rummaged through the wagon and found Jake's backpack. His hand tightened on the straps. *Thank the Lord. If I lost this, I might lose myself.* He slung it over his shoulder. "Horace, let's walk."

"Aye."

Bearclaw, Vern, Apollo, Tark, and Cudgel were moving the dead inside the apartments. Vern had a sneer on his face when Abraham caught his eyes. The swordsman's flaxen waves of hair were mixed with blood. Abraham stared back until Vern looked away. Looking to the others, he said, "Tell me, how did you take so many? The rogues had the advantage."

"We tore through them like a wrecking machine. And we told you, we fight better drunk than sober. This wasn't the first time we've taken a fort like this," Horace said. He dug the bloody tip of his spear into the ground, coating it with dirt. "And it was a tactic that you created. Well, the old *old* you, that is."

"I hate to ask, but fill me in."

"Iris is our mystic. Better for healing than hurting, but she can make lightning in the sky so long as she is near water," Horace explained as they walked toward the storehouses below the parapets. "The eyes of the crossbowmen behind the parapets fastened on it. Tark and Dominga scaled the walls, gutted two of them, stole their crossbows, and shot the others. It was a well-executed assassination."

"I see."

Horace spat tobacco juice. "In the meantime, alone I approached the gate and started making a fuss. Hence, the two rogues guarding the portcullis were focused on me. They were laughing at me. Called me fat. That gave Tark and Dominga enough time to scout the fort's interior while the rest of the Henchmen started scaling the fort's wall. While they did that, Iris moved the lightning through the sky and above me. With all eyes on it, the Henchmen attacked.

"Tark and Dominga took the brutes down that guarded your entrance first. We didn't want whoever was inside to know that we were coming. The company worked their way down from top to bottom. Half of them were dead before they knew what hit them." Horace spat. "The rogues had steel but no armor. And not a one of them was a skilled swordsman. They didn't have a chance against the likes of us. We did as we always did—we butchered them. They're thieves. They had it coming."

Abraham entered the storehouse entrance. It consisted of a bunch of wooden shelves with barrels and bags of supplies. The storehouses were interconnected by one opening that led to each other.

"If you see anything we need, take it," he said absentmindedly.

He reflected on everything that had occurred. He'd underestimated the abilities of his own men. He should have known better by now. The Henchmen were seasoned fighters, one and all. He just wished he had more memories of their adventures. Then, there was the encounter with Lord Hawk. The man had a gun that looked like a beat cop's revolver that they didn't carry anymore. It turned his wheels, that and something else. He'd deflected bullets with his sword—a sword that glowed and sent an adrenaline rush right through him. *Holy crap, who am I?*

Sticks flagged them down from inside the walls of the last storage bay. "I found something." She led them inside the last storage room. A steel door, inches thick, was centered between huge stones that made up a separate wall. Dents had been made from the inside, bulging the door out.

"I think it's a dungeon," she said.

Horace fanned the air in front of his nose. "It stinks in here. Rotten."

"Did you hear anything?" Abraham asked as he ran his hand over the strange bumps on the door.

Sticks shook her head. She twirled a key ring on her finger and said, "No, but I found this."

"Open it."

# 65

"Don't you want to knock first?" Sticks said.

Abraham shrugged and rapped his knuckles on the door. It made a hollow echoing sound.

Horace awkwardly put his ear to the door. "I don't hear anything. But I'll be ready." He stepped back and lowered his spear. "If something jumps, I'll get it."

Sticks put the key inside the lock and twisted.

Abraham pulled his sword. A rung was on the door, so he grabbed it and started walking the door backward. He grimaced as he gave it a fierce tug. The door seal started to give. The metal door scraped along the metal frame.

"I don't think it's been used in a while," he said.

"Maybe there is treasure in it," Horace suggested. "It would be a good spot."

The door broke the threshold. A mighty stink came out.

"Eww!" Abraham covered his nose. His eyes watered.

"Close the door. Close the door. It smells like dead carcasses in there," Horace said with a souring face. "Ack! Ack!"

With a dagger in hand, Sticks peered inside. The cell was pitch black. The light from the lanterns hanging on the storeroom walls offered little illumination inside the cell. Sticking her head inside, she said, "I don't think the Shell stored anything valuable here. Something died. I don't care to find out what it is."

"Agreed," Abraham said. Flies buzzed out of the dungeon room. "Come on, let's close it. We need to move on. I don't want to disturb the dead's slumber in their tomb. Whatever dead they may be."

"Aye, Captain. Let's not bring any more bad fortune upon ourselves," Horace said.

Sticks stepped aside.

Abraham put his shoulder into the door and pushed it closed. The door groaned on the crust-covered hinges. The door stopped inches from being closed. He pushed against it. It wouldn't budge.

"Let me help you, Captain," Horace said. He leaned his spear against the wall and put his shoulder on the door. "Old doors often become askew on the frame if they haven't been opened in a long time." The burly man put his weight into it. "Hurk!"

The door didn't move.

"Wait!" Sticks said. "I just heard something move."

"What?" Abraham replied. His boots and Horace's boots slid over the ground. The door was opening by the power of some unknown force. He put his back into it. "Sticks, what do you see?"

Sticks walked backward, her eyes up and mouth agape.

Abraham and Horace jumped away from the door.

A towering shambling figure covered in long strands of gray hair stepped out from underneath the doorway. It looked like an old and malnourished bigfoot.

"Holy Harry and the Hendersons!" Abraham said.

Horace grabbed his spear and said, "It's a troglin!" He charged forward, thrusting his spear at the monster's side. The troglin snatched the head of the spear in its huge paw. It held the spear fast. It and Horace engaged in a tug of war.

Abraham closed in, carrying his sword in the wrath guard position. "Get back in your cage, beast!"

"Nooo," the troglin said in a very deep and weary voice. "I mean you no harm."

"Sure, he doesn't." Horace dug his heels into the ground and pulled his spear with all his might. "Turn your back, and he'll rip your head off and eat it like a melon." The troglin released the spear. Horace stumbled backward and crashed into the wall.

The troglin's head touched the eight-foot-high ceiling. It bent its neck over. It had large eyes and a long apelike face. Moaning, it dropped to a knee, took in a deep breath and said, "Ah, the air smells sweet again." Its eyes slid over to Abraham. "I can't stop you from slaying me. I'm too old and weak to fight. It took all I had in me to fight that bald big belly off. But, whoever you are, I give you my thanks for freeing me so I don't die in my own stink."

"Let's do it then, Captain. Brain him with Black Bane before he eats all of us," Horace said.

"I don't think he's going to eat us," Abraham said. *Oh my. A talking bigfoot. Now I know this world isn't real.* "Are you?"

"I am very hungry, and the fat one looks delicious, but no. I would not attack my liberator. I'm grateful," the troglin said.

"And smelly," Sticks said. She appeared smaller than a child beside the beast of a man.

"I'm sorry. I imagine I do reek, but I've become accustomed to it. Lord Hawk fed me then forgot about me." The weariness in his deep but pleasant voice strengthened. "If I find him, I'm going to squeeze his head until it pops between my fingers. The dirty little liar."

"Well, he's gone, and all of his men are dead."

Bearclaw, Vern, Tark, and Cudgel rushed into the room.

"We heard a scream," Cudgel said. He set his eyes on the troglin. "Gah!"

# 66

AFTER AN HOUR OF STRONG DEBATING, ABRAHAM GOT EVERYONE settled down. By a large majority vote, the Henchmen wanted to kill the troglin. For the time being, they chained up the troglin and led him outside, under the stars, where he gazed with appreciative wonder.

With everyone gathered in the courtyard, Abraham said, "I've heard all your opinions, but this isn't a democracy. The troglin lives. Find some food and feed him."

"They eat people," Dominga said.

Sitting in the middle of the company, the troglin said, "That's not entirely true. Have we eaten people? Yes, but we thrive on all creatures in the animal kingdom. The same as you. We just don't cook it."

"If the Captain says feed him, then feed him," Horace said, looking at the two male Red Tunics. "Go!"

The Red Tunics scrambled into the stables underneath the apartments. The livestock had started to roam free. Pigs, chickens, and a pair of mules wandered aimlessly, and some came through the portcullis, now open.

With a torch in hand, Bearclaw said, "We are set to burn the fort from the inside out. All of the dead lie inside, prepared for a consuming burial."

"Just make sure all of the livestock is out," Abraham said.

The Red Tunics returned with a pair of chickens in their hands. The birds dangled lifelessly, their necks snapped. The troglin's tired eyes locked on the chickens, and he licked his lips. The Red Tunics shuffled toward and dropped the chickens at his feet. The troglin's chains rattled as he scooped one bird up and stuffed it all in his mouth.

"Ew, feathers and all," Dominga said.

As the troglin crunched down his dinner, Abraham turned to Bearclaw and said, "Torch it. Torch it all." He realized that he needed to exercise more faith in his men. All of them had proved capable, and they hadn't let him down yet. He hated to burn down a perfectly good building, but it was the right thing to do. The Shell was a bunch of petty thieves who preyed on the weak, extorted them, and hid inside their fort. This time, they'd crossed the wrong people and paid for it dearly.

The morning sun rose over the ocean. The new day had come. The burning wooden structures crackled and popped. Beams collapsed inside the flames. Black smoke billowed up and was carried out over the sea. On the other side of the portcullis, Prospero and Apollo covered all the ships in oil and burned them. If Lord Hawk returned, he'd have very little left to come back to.

Abraham looked out toward the jagged mountainous peaks of the Spine as Sticks stood with him. He yawned. "Say goodbye to a good night's sleep. I've got a feeling it's going to be a long journey. I hope everybody enjoyed unwinding last night! It sure beat the heck out of a good night's rest!"

Sticks rubbed his back. "Someone gets cranky when he doesn't get his sleep, doesn't he?"

"It's not the sleep. It's not knowing what's going to happen next. We haven't even kissed the toe of the mountain, and we're already weary. Now we have to navigate those hills." He shook his head. "At least we have our gear back."

The troglin gulped down the bones of his last chicken and said, "Pardon me, eh, Captain, is it?"

"Yes?"

Holding his hands out in a gentle manner, the sasquatchlike creature said, "First off, thank you for the chickens. They were a delicious appetizer." He licked his fingers and burped out a feather. "Excuse me. And, again, I'm grateful that you set me free. I'm happy to repay the debt, but not without a proper introduction. My name is Solomon. Solomon Paige."

"Uh, nice to meet you, Solomon," Abraham said. With inquisitive eyes he asked, "Do all troglins speak like you?"

"Troglins speak, but not like me," Solomon admitted. "I'm a bit of an outcast. Not because of my speech but some of my other mannerisms. It's a very lengthy story, and I'd probably die of old age before I managed to tell it all." He raked his fingers through his long gray hairs, which were thinning on the top. A few of his animal-like fingernails were missing. One shoulder stooped lower than the other. The muscles underneath his fur had probably bulged with the firmness of a young gorilla's at one time, but now, the hardened sinew sagged. He still must have been seven hundred pounds of man. He wet a thumb and smoothed over his bushy eyebrows. "Forgive me for eavesdropping, but I overheard that you are venturing into the Spine. Are you aware that my king dwells in crags and caves of those magnificent hills?"

"We know," Horace growled. "Everyone knows about the troglin that come down out of the mountains and raid villages. The women are carried off, the children eaten, and the men with arms ripped out of their sockets."

The Henchmen gathered around, their hard eyes locking on Solomon. Fingers tapped on their weapons.

Solomon scanned the group. "No doubt, there is truth to the stories that you have heard."

"Heard?" Horace tamped the butt of his spear on the ground. "I've seen it with my own eyes! Wild beastmen creeping down from the mountain and slaughtering everything in sight. I've seen the devastation with my own eyes! Captain, he was probably one of them! I say we kill him."

"I've made my decision," Abraham said.

He was fascinated with Solomon. The hairy old brute spoke better than he did. And something modern about his mannerisms perked his interests too.

"I'm not judging someone without proof."

"Of course not," Vern said. "You'd rather we lowered our guard first so it's easier to kill us."

"Shut up, Vern," Abraham said.

Solomon made a peaceful gesture with his hands and said, "I'm not debating the actions of my kindred. They are very territorial people. If you invade that territory, they will react. But they are content in the Spine's gaps. I'll tell you this, if you cross their path without some sort of guidance, you will have a fight on your hands." He looked up at Abraham. "May I ask what possesses you to traverse the Spine of Titanuus?"

Abraham threw him a softball question. "Ever hear of the fenix?"

Solomon's soft eyes grew. "Yes. I even know where it lives."

# 67

Led by a troglin wearing shackles and chains, the Henchmen traveled up into the Spine. No one talked to Abraham, not even Sticks. Horace, with the help of Vern, had them all convinced that the troglin would lead them straight into his den. Abraham didn't rule out the possibility, but they needed some sort of guide. Solomon would be as good as any. Plus, Abraham liked the troglin. He spoke more like the people he was used to being around.

*I'm either stupid, crazy, or brilliant. Maybe all three. I don't know. But when I truly wake up, I'll have a lot to talk about. Maybe I'll write a book.*

They rode all day, not stopping, through narrow paths without incident. That gave Abraham time to reflect on the dream he'd had when Lord Hawk knocked him out with the slumber smoke. If there was a blessing to be found in Titanuus, it would be that it kept his mind off the past. The loss of his wife and son made his heart ache every day. He could never stop thinking about the accident, could never escape from it. He relived the horror over and over. He didn't want to relive it again but felt ashamed for trying to forget it. He needed an escape.

The painkillers had given him a needed escape. They not only relieved the pain but also took the burden off his mind. He'd lived like a zombie for years, walking in numbness to the outside word, refusing to cope with his problem. But the time came when he had to pay his dues. That time came all too soon. The bills stacked up. The collectors came. He was miserable. He'd been on top of the world and crashed down out of the sky. And he hadn't even hit rock bottom yet.

*I shouldn't like this world. But I kinda do. Forgive me, Jenny. Forgive me, Jake. I miss you.*

The company came to a stop on a plateau halfway up the base of the mountain as they moved away from the sea. It was a patch of grass and shrubbery, with wild blue-purple berries in the branches.

Solomon pointed at the bushes and said, "The birds can eat them, but you can't." He sat down and hung his head. "By the Elders, my back hurts."

Abraham's dismounted his horse, which was lathered in sweat. He was too. "I thought it would get colder in the mountains."

"Why would it do that?" Solomon said. "You are closer to the sun."

"Yeh." The setting sun started to dip beneath the sea. "Huh, looks like the sun is going for a swim."

"They say the sun lights the waters from underneath," Solomon said. As the others started to make camp, he asked, "Abraham, I have a question I'd like to ask while the others are not around."

He eyed the troglin suspiciously and said, "All right. What is it?"

Solomon eyed his backpack that hung from the saddle. "How did you acquire that pack?"

His eyes narrowed. "I found it in a tunnel, the north end of the Old Kingdom. Why?"

"That design is very unique. Is that a pirate sewn into the pack?"

"I don't know, maybe. It sort of looks like a buccaneer or a pirate."

Abraham felt a tingle run up his spine. The two of them were having a mental chess match with one another. Or so it seemed. Whatever was going on, Solomon was very intelligent. Abraham could see it in his eyes.

"Have you ever seen a pirate before?" he asked.

"In a manner of speaking? Um..." Solomon rose up and looked over Abraham.

Abraham looked over his shoulder. The Henchmen were keeping their distance, setting up tents, including his own. "I don't think they are going to bother us. Were you getting at something?"

Solomon lowered his voice and said, "When I stepped out of the dungeon, you said, 'Holy Harry and the Hendersons.' What does that mean?"

Abraham's heart skipped, but he played it cool. "I don't know. It's just something I picked up. Why?"

"I'm going to say a few words. I'm curious if they might seem familiar. Television. Movies. Pittsburgh."

Goose bumps rose on Abraham's arms. "You're from Earth, aren't you?"

"Pittsburgh, to be exact."

"Holy moly. Tell me more." Abraham cast a backward glance. No one was looking. "So this is real? I'm not dreaming."

"Well, I don't know about that. Sometimes I think that I'm dreaming or trapped in a nightmare," Solomon said. "Back home, I was a vegetarian, and now, I'm trapped, or transformed, into this carnivorous body. I abhorred meat, and now"—he patted his stomach—"I can't get enough of it. I still appall myself, but when I'm hungry, I'm dangerously hungry."

"I can't believe this. So, you're from Pittsburgh?"

"Born and raised. I taught nutrition classes at Duquesne University. I was a well-educated hippie and driving a red VW bus. I thought I knew it all." Solomon shook his head and cast his stare toward the sky. "So, I'm driving down to West Virginia University for a series of nutrition seminars. I'm in my love bus, toking reefer, and jamming to the Beatles, when I cross through a sun ring of light in the Fort Pitt tunnel. I was pretty sure that I was tripping when my bus went from pavement onto dirt. The engine died, and I'm wandering aimlessly through a tunnel. That's when I crossed paths with, well"—he ran his hand over his body in a showy motion—"this horrid version of Chewbacca.

"At that point, I was pretty certain that I was tripping. Being a nutritionist, I had a thing for 'shrooming back then. Needless to say, I shouldn't have been behind the wheel because sometimes when I was, it felt like I was flying. Anyway, this old and shabby troglin body pounced." He held up two fingers and firmly said, "It wrestled me down and consumed me."

"It ate you?"

"I can't explain it, but it consumed me, entirely, in a very weird out-of-body experience. The next thing I know, I am it, and me is gone." He flapped an arm, shaking his hairy, dangling triceps. "Now I'm this. Is that what happened to you?"

"Something like that. So what year was it when you left?" Abraham asked.

"Nineteen ninety. You?"

"Two thousand and eighteen."

Solomon paled. "Oh my."

# 68

THE HENCHMAN TRAVERSED THE RUGGED MOUNTAIN TERRAIN FOR two more days. Per Solomon's advice, they abandoned the wagon. It was sound advice, for the farther they traveled, the narrower the passages in the rocks became. The Spines' foreboding landscape was full of surprises. The wild mountain goats were bigger than horses, the dragonflies the size of crows. Pumas with blood-red coats lurked in the rocks. Strange valleys were nestled in the hills, which could contain entire civilizations. Hot breezes would come and go. The air was dry and stagnant at times, but in some spots, it became so humid that sweat soaked their clothing like rain. All in all, the treacherous trek was borderline miserable.

Abraham shifted in his saddle and used a cotton jerkin like a towel to wipe his face. He rode with Sticks at his side. She was the only one making conversation with him. Apparently, he'd gotten too cozy with Solomon. In privacy, he'd shared his history with Solomon. They seemed to hit it off—maybe too much. The others were grumbling, so they decided to keep their distance. Earning the trust of his men had been hard enough. Now, he was asking them to put their trust in a man-eating troglin.

"Everyone is giving me the cold shoulder, even you?" he asked Sticks. "Care to open up about what you are feeling?"

"You're the Captain," she said. Her two ponytails were down, and the ends of her brown hair were damp. "You decide. We follow."

"I might make the final decision, but I still like to entertain advice from my men. No one is saying a word." He looked back. Bearclaw and Vern rode five horse lengths behind them with sour looks on their faces. "Even Vern is keeping his mouth shut. Not even a jab."

"You're letting a monster lead. Not you. Besides, it's a fatal mission anyway. Everyone knows it. We won't be coming back."

Abraham gave her a stern look and said, "We aren't going to lose. I don't know how we are going to win, but we aren't going to phone it in."

"Phone it in?" she said.

"It's an expression from my world. It means give up before we've even started."

"I see. Well, at least I might get to see a fenix before I die. That should be something."

Abraham smiled. "See, that's a positive way of looking at it. Keep your little chin up."

Sticks made an odd expression and tipped her head back.

"That's better."

Tark and Dominga returned from the front. They'd been scouting ahead with Solomon. Their brows were knitted together.

"What's going on?" Abraham asked. "Where's Solomon?"

"He's waiting ahead at an impasse," Tark said. The lean, athletic bearded black fighter dripped with sweat. He wiped his brows with a forearm. "He said he'd wait for the others to catch up. It's treacherous."

"Let's go, then," Abraham said.

The Henchmen rode another mile until they caught up with

the troglin. Solomon waited in front of a fiery chasm that had split a small forest of leafless, vine-covered trees. The chasm blocked the path with a stream of lava flowing through it. It was very wide, too wide for the horses to jump or cross.

"Crap," Abraham said.

Horace dismounted and marched over to the fiery gap. "Well done, troglin. I can only hope this is the river where the fenix lives."

Solomon shook his head. "No. This passage was free and clear before. Believe me, I've traveled these peaks for years. This is what happens as a result of the Spine contracting. It's always in travail. The fires below seep out when the rock cracks as Titanuus's body bows."

Abraham believed Solomon. The vegetarian turned troglin had spent years in the Spine, trying to find a portal back home. He'd first arrived in the Spine in his VW bus. It was here that the troglin consumed him.

He lifted his eyes. Thick corded vines hung in the surrounding trees' dead branches. Apparently, a thriving forest had been there at one time, but the vein of lava destroyed it.

"Solomon, is there another way around?"

The troglin lifted a long arm toward the rugged cliffs overlooking them. "It will be a dangerous climb, either up or down." He reached out and grabbed one of the vines that hung in the trees that dangled over the fiery gorge. "It's possible to use these vines."

The blackened trees were leaning over the gap from both sides. Some of them had fallen over and rested against each other.

Abraham waved the two male Red Tunics over. "Are you good climbers?"

Both the young men nodded.

"Take your hatchets, climb over using the vines, and chop down more of those surrounding trees. We'll do the same from this side and make a bridge for the ones that don't climb so well." He glanced at Horace.

"I can swing in the vines," Horace said, "carrying two people at the same time."

"Let's play it safe. And maybe we can get the horses across."

The two Red Tunics tucked their hatchets into their belts and hustled over to the chasm. The pair of wiry men, slight in build, jumped up and grabbed hold of the vines. The vines made for a natural ropelike bridge that dangled over the burning chasm. Using the gnarled knots in the vines like steps, they started crawling over the twenty-foot-wide chasm.

Abraham dabbed his face with his shirt and said, "This will work out."

A fiery wormlike creature burst up out of the molten lava. It had a head like a snake and little legs like a centipede. As it rose out of the lava, the Red Tunics screamed. One of them chopped at the monster with his hatchet. The fire worm opened its mouth, struck, and swallowed the fighting man whole. A second fire worm popped up out of the lava and closed quickly on the other trembling Red Tunic clinging to the vines. It gobbled the man up.

The fire worms plunged back into the liquid and vanished beneath the surface.

The Henchmen lined the edge of the chasm with their crossbows and spears pointed at the molten surface. They eyeballed the churning stream of death. The dark outlines of the fire worms could be seen swimming away below the surge. They were gone.

Abraham's heart raced. "That was fast." He glanced over at Twila, the last Red Tunic, who was shaking like a leaf. "Looks like you're the last."

# 69

USING THEIR HATCHETS, THE HENCHMEN BUILT A BRIDGE AND managed to safely cross the chasm of lava. No more fire worms appeared. The horses wouldn't cross with riders, but with effort, they finally traversed the bridge.

Loaded down with heavy packs, the horses climbed through the clouds hugging the mountain peaks. The lathered-up horses whinnied and nickered often on the trek. The company led the nervous horses up the winding mountain paths on foot.

"Your hairy friend knew about those fire worms," Horace said, leading his horse by the reins. He was huffing and puffing up the hillside, using his spear like a walking stick. "I wonder what he has in store for us next."

"He's not leading us to a trap, if that is what you are getting at," Abraham said. He and Horace were alone, as far as he could tell. He couldn't see twenty feet ahead or behind because of the fog. "We're going to go forward, not backward. Besides, we don't have anywhere else to go."

Horace's horse nickered and snorted.

"We should have left the beasts behind. This mountain spooks them," Horace said.

"You should have said something earlier."

"I hate leaving good horses behind." Horace's eyes slid up to where Solomon led at the front. "I bet if we left them, his kindred would eat them. They'd have a feast and laugh at us right now." Horace twisted his bull neck around and scanned the rocky ledges above. "I bet there are troglin all around us. Waiting to pounce on his signal."

"You've made it abundantly clear that you don't like him. I get it. But you need to move on, Horace, unless you have a better idea on how to find a fenix."

"Sorry, Captain. This is unfamiliar territory. It makes my stomach queasy." When Horace's horse nickered, he petted its head. "Easy, beast. Easy."

"We all feel the same."

Abraham moved along, carrying sixty pounds of gear on his shoulders for fear of the horses bolting away with it. They were jumpy, too jumpy to ride. His legs burned, and his lower back was on fire. They'd been walking for two days. The mountain was a hot and humid mess, like the dark recesses of a jungle. A breeze came but quickly went.

"Man, I'd do anything for a Dilly Bar right now."

"Pardon, Captain?" Horace said.

"It's a dessert in my world, an ice-cold cream coated in chocolate. You'd definitely like it."

"Sounds tasty."

"You have no idea."

The group walked until dark, taking turns on watch but staying close together. Solomon didn't sleep, that Abraham could tell. He still hadn't said another word to him. The next morning, the Henchmen geared up. The horses finally settled, so they loaded them up again and headed up the twisting paths, which ran along cliffs and into the clouded mountain peaks. Finally, hours into the long ride, they emerged from the clouds and came face-to-face with more mountains.

"Sweet Christmas, this place doesn't end," Abraham said.

The trek led them up another thousand feet until they could see the clouds like mist below them. They journeyed onward, climbing another peak until they all caught up with each other at the top of that hill.

Abraham and the company stood by Solomon and looked downward into the mouth of a crater that stretched as far as the eye could see. Parts of it were filled with black tar pits at the bottom. Birds' nests were nestled in the cliffs. Rocky formations like stalagmites seemed to grow out of the ground in both rounded and jagged formations. A sulfuric stink lingered in the stagnant air.

"This is the place that you seek," Solomon said as a chill north wind came down from the peaks, stirring gray hairs on his stooped frame. "The troglin call it the Elder's Birthing. They say the fenix is the guardian of the hive that spawned the Elders ages ago. All trespassers not born of Elder blood will surely die."

"It makes for a strange nest for a bird," Abraham commented.

"The fenix is not a bird. It's an abomination, they say," Solomon said.

Horace spat brown juice down into the crater. "Looks like a troglin dwelling to me."

"Agreed," Bearclaw said.

"Well, you can gawk at it all you want, but we're going in," Abraham stated. He scanned the eyes of everyone in the company. "Let's hear the Henchmen's creed."

"Death before failure," Horace muttered.

"What?" Abraham said loudly.

More of the company joined in and quietly muttered, "Death before failure."

He cupped his hand behind his ear. "I can't hear you, Henchmen!"

The Henchman's faces started to light up. On the signal of Horace's fist pumping in the air, united, all of them said, "Death before failure!"

Abraham gave an approving nod. His juices started to flow. "The hell with the odds. Let's go find that egg!"

# FROM THE AUTHOR

***If you want to see this series continue, please leave a review on the King's Henchmen.***

BOOK 1 LINK.

Reviews are a huge help to me! **Post a review, email me the link, and I'll send you for a FREE copy of Book Two, but I can only do this in the US.**

**Email: craig@thedarkslayer.com**

With that said, I really hope you enjoyed this first book. This is just the tip of the iceberg in Abraham/Ruger's strange journey. Book Two will contain even more excitement and reveal more strange places, races, and creatures that you've never seen before.

For those of you that have been with me for the past 10 years, hey, thanks for all of the support! If you are new to my work, welcome to one of my many worlds. I hope you continue to enjoy it. Cause, you know, it would be really cool if you did. Heh-heh. I have over 70 books and several bestselling book series to choose from. Oh, and for those of you that know me, keep an eye out for Easter Eggs from my other series that I've planted, because all of my worlds tie together.

ORDER BOOK 2 THE KING'S ASSASSIN NOW

KING'S ASSASSIN LINK

*Check me out on Bookbub and follow: HalloranOnBookBub

*I'd love it if you would subscribe to my mailing list: www.craighalloran.com

*On Facebook, you can find me at The Darkslayer Report or Craig Halloran.

*Twitter, Twitter, Twitter. I am there, too: www.twitter.com/CraigHalloran

*And of course, you can always email me at craig@thedarkslayer.com

See my book lists below!

## ALSO BY CRAIG HALLORAN

Craig Halloran resides with his family outside his hometown of Charleston, West Virginia. When he isn't entertaining mankind, he is seeking adventure, working out, or watching sports. To learn more about him, go to www.thedarkslayer.com.

**Free Books**

**The Red Citadel and the Sorcerer's Power**

The Darkslayer: Brutal Beginnings

Nath Dragon—Quest for the Thunderstone

**The Henchmen Chronicles**

The King's Henchmen

The King's Assassin

The King's Prisoner

The King's Conjurer

The King's Enemies

The King's Spies

**The Odyssey of Nath Dragon Series (New Series) (Prequel to Chronicles of Dragon)**

Exiled

Enslaved

Deadly

Hunted

Strife

**The Chronicles of Dragon Series 1 (10-book series)**

The Hero, the Sword and the Dragons (Book 1)

Dragon Bones and Tombstones (Book 2)

Terror at the Temple (Book 3)

Clutch of the Cleric (Book 4)

Hunt for the Hero (Book 5)

Siege at the Settlements (Book 6)

Strife in the Sky (Book 7)

Fight and the Fury (Book 8)

War in the Winds (Book 9)

Finale (Book 10)

Boxset 1-5

Boxset 6-10

Collector's Edition 1-10

**Tail of the Dragon, The Chronicles of Dragon, Series 2 (10-book series)**

Tail of the Dragon #1

Claws of the Dragon #2

Battle of the Dragon #3

Eyes of the Dragon #4

Flight of the Dragon #5

Trial of the Dragon #6

Judgement of the Dragon #7

Wrath of the Dragon #8

Power of the Dragon #9

Hour of the Dragon #10

Boxset 1-5

Boxset 6-10

Collector's Edition 1-10

**The Darkslayer Series 1 (6-book series)**

Wrath of the Royals (Book 1)

Blades in the Night (Book 2)

Underling Revenge (Book 3)

Danger and the Druid (Book 4)

Outrage in the Outlands (Book 5)

Chaos at the Castle (Book 6)

Boxset 1-3

Boxset 4-6

Omnibus 1-6

**The Darkslayer: Bish and Bone, Series 2 (10-book series)**

Bish and Bone (Book 1)

Black Blood (Book 2)

Red Death (Book 3)

Lethal Liaisons (Book 4)

Torment and Terror (Book 5)

Brigands and Badlands (Book 6)

War in the Wasteland (Book 7)

Slaughter in the Streets (Book 8)

Hunt of the Beast (Book 9)

The Battle for Bone (Book 10)

Boxset 1-5

Boxset 6-10

Bish and Bone Omnibus (Books 1-10)

**CLASH OF HEROES: Nath Dragon meets The Darkslayer mini series**

Book 1

Book 2

Book 3

**The Gamma Earth Cycle**

Escape from the Dominion

Flight from the Dominion

Prison of the Dominion

**The Supernatural Bounty Hunter Files (10-book series)**

Smoke Rising: Book 1

I Smell Smoke: Book 2

Where There's Smoke: Book 3

Smoke on the Water: Book 4

Smoke and Mirrors: Book 5

Up in Smoke: Book 6

Smoke Signals: Book 7

Holy Smoke: Book 8

Smoke Happens: Book 9

Smoke Out: Book 10

Boxset 1-5

Boxset 6-10

Collector's Edition 1-10

**Zombie Impact Series**

Zombie Day Care: Book 1

Zombie Rehab: Book 2

Zombie Warfare: Book 3

Boxset: Books 1-3

## OTHER WORKS & NOVELLAS

The Red Citadel and the Sorcerer's Power

Lightning Source UK Ltd.
Milton Keynes UK
UKHW020629010522
402233UK00003B/189